W9-CUJ-843

Dedication

This series is dedicated to those *Diné* who still follow the Beauty Way—and while their numbers are fewer each year—they remain the well from which the people draw strength and feed the *Hozo* that binds them together.

Day of the Dead

R. Allen Chappell

Acknowledgments

Again, many sincere thanks to those Navajo friends and classmates who provide "grist for the mill." Their insight into Navajo thought and reservation life helped fuel a lifelong interest in the culture, one I once only observed from the other side of the fence.

Cover painting by Catalina Felkins

Cover graphics and layout by Marraii Design

Author's Note

In the back pages, you will find a small glossary of Navajo words and terms used in this story, the spelling of which may vary somewhat, depending on which expert's opinion is referenced.

Table of Contents

1

The Pact

"Carlos needs a good killing." Tressa was not one to sugarcoat a thing and this was how she put it to Little Abe.

Abraham Garza, fresh up from Mexico and already in love with the woman, didn't even blink. Where he grew up, threatening to kill a person was common enough. Tressa Tarango, however, actually meant to kill Carlos—he was pretty sure of it now—this wasn't the first time she'd mentioned it. Little Abe didn't *even* want to know why. One thing he did know—she wouldn't be telling him if he wasn't to have a hand in it.

"Well, that might make his Uncle Hector unhappy?" Little Abe had no use for Carlos Espinosa, but killing him outright might have more serious consequences than she knew. This wasn't Mexico, after all. Here, they don't just put you in jail, they might just decide to kill *you,* too. Mexico, rough though it is, does not have a death penalty, or at least not an official one.

Tressa narrowed an eye at the dining room door and slashed the air with the edge of her hand. "Hector Espinosa is no better than his nephew." She turned to look Little Abe in the eye and lowered her voice. "Maybe you're right, Abraham. Maybe *Hector* needs killing, too." She said this as though it had been Little Abe's idea to start with. "We should kill them both," she whispered.

"We...?" Abe was now certain she considered him part of it and dared think their relationship was progressing. But it made him just a little uncomfortable, too, *Un poquito nervioso en la cabeza,* as his old grandmother would say—a little bit crazy in the head. There were so many people depending on him. *I am only a busboy for Christ's sake...sometimes not even that...sometimes I am just the dishwasher.*

Tressa Tarango had grown even more attractive with time—it happens—and those so lucky may consider themselves among the chosen few. Abraham thought her the most beautiful woman he'd ever seen. Still, he hadn't signed on for killing; it was just the trap he'd left Sinaloa to avoid.

This job was supposed to be a foothold in a new life—that's how Little Abe looked at it. That's what his father told him. Something better than filling an early grave down in Sinaloa... "Eventually, it could lead to something big," his Papá said.

Espinosa's *Cantina y Restaurante* was easy work to Abe's way of thinking, and the money was good, too. He knew people back home who would kill for an opportunity such as this. No *Señor*! Tressa, or no Tressa, this talk of killing would require some thought. It might be all right to do away with Carlos, but Hector Espinosa was his father's childhood friend and down in Sinaloa that still meant something. It was only by that grace his *papá* was able to wrangle such a favor for him. Señor Espinosa even put up the money for a *coyotero* to lead him north. Granted, he was required to deliver a certain suitcase—a suitcase worth considerably more than Little Abe himself— and he was well aware, should anything go wrong it would be him left *holding the bag*, in a manner of speaking.

"Don't screw this up, *Mijo*," was his father's last blessing. "This can work into something really big for you up there." And that's when he said it: "Here in Sinaloa you will most likely just fill an early grave." The old man paused, scratching at his chin with a ragged fingernail as he considered his son for what might be the last time. Little Abe was his only hope and it brought a tear to think this boy was all that stood between him and an uncertain old age. True, he didn't need much, a couple of *milpas* for a little corn and beans, maybe a few chickens. No more than that. The elder Abraham, now forced to look back over a lifetime in so dangerous a business, was amazed at how little he had to show for it. Little Abe was indeed his final play.

When old Abraham Garza handed his son the battered suitcase he chose each word as though his life depended on it. "Should you do anything to anger those people up there, Abraham—no matter, if it is *your* fault, or *their* fault, or even *nobody's* fault—it will be your old papá's head on the chopping block." There was a tremor in the old man's voice and he pulled a long face for the boy. "I am only hanging on by my toenails with these people as it is, Abraham." He frowned, shaking his head and then, lowering his voice to a deadly whisper, leaned closer to the boy. "One word from '*El Escuche*' Espinosa…and you will have no more Papá—no one to look out for you and love you as I have." He said this with such finality as to leave no doubt whatsoever in his son's mind.

Tressa watched as Little Abe thought his way through the implications of her latest proposal and thought she saw a flicker of hesitation, fleeting and dark as a bat out of hell, but a warning, nonetheless. *It is only right he should be cautious,* she reasoned. *This is not after all, a small undertaking.* She knew to consider it less might indicate a lack of intelligence on the boy's part. Without Little Abe, her task would be daunting, if not impossible. Evil and conniving people were all around her, watching her every move. No, clearly, this simple young man from Sinaloa was a godsend.

"So, you think we got to kill 'em both? Maybe killing only Carlos could be enough?" No one liked Carlos Espinosa anyway.

She sighed, "No, I don't think so, *Hombrecito*." Then smiling, she shook her head in such a way he might realize how foolish the question was.

It was obvious to Little Abe; planning the Espinosas' death bothered Tressa no more than wringing the neck of a yard chicken for the dinner table. Abraham sighed. The woman was right, of course; Hector, left alive, wouldn't rest until he brought them both to ground and it probably wouldn't take him very long either.

If there was one thing Tressa Tarango learned from her late husband it was that a hurtful act must never go unpunished. "If you let something like this pass, you will always be at that person's mercy." This was how Luca Tarango thought. He was a man who lived by few rules, but this, and one other, he held inviolate. "On the other hand," he would remind her, "should you be shown a kindness, there is an obligation to repay that favor as well, else you will forever be in *that* person's debt. Both good and evil deserve reward and repayment in the spirit they were offered." Luca Tarango was a hard man and knew what it took to survive among rough people. Over the years she had come to realize there was an undeniable wisdom in his thinking. Tressa hadn't forgotten these things, she was only biding her time...waiting for *the right moment,* and now the time of reckoning had come. Debts accrue interest, especially those owed to a man such as Luca Tarango.

Little Abe turned back to his sink of dirty dishes and a little bead of cold sweat ran down his back as he thought of his old father in Sinaloa. *The old man was probably right, it wouldn't matter whose fault it was.* Something bad would happen eventually. He knew now he was in it for real.

Tressa smiled as she watched him take an empty tray to the dining room and congratulated herself; *he was exactly the person she needed.*

As the door swung open, Tressa could hear laughter and polite applause as Carlos Espinosa's guitar music ended. He had been a lawyer, and a drunk, back in Mexico; her husband's lawyer, and later, *her* lover. Here, he was just a drunk who worked odd jobs for his uncle, and played a little guitar music for the customers.

When first they met in his seedy little office behind *Mercado Central*, she was hesitant, thought meeting with the young lawyer a mistake. Yet despite his shabby surroundings, Carlos was undeniably charming and spoke in so elegant a manner Tressa could not help being encouraged and was compelled to explain her situation.

The attorney listened politely to the halting, sometimes tearful, account of her husband's plight, smiling encouragement from time to time, as he scribbled away at a little pad. When she finished Carlos began speaking, and so eloquently she was left with little doubt of his abilities. Coming around the desk he patted her shoulder as he described several similar cases, and all with happy endings. Going over his notes, the lawyer allowed as how her husband's charges were not so serious that a man of his talents couldn't bring the matter to a speedy and agreeable conclusion. Of course, a certain amount of money would be required, upfront, to grease a few palms along the way, which he declared, would be offset by keeping his own fee to a minimum, a mere trifle, relatively speaking. Tressa, comforted by such generosity, was now totally convinced this handsome young counselor was the solution.

When eventually Carlos learned Tressa had money put back, and a nice little *casita* to boot. the man became even more solicitous. He sensed opportunity here, something well beyond stringing her husband along in what he already knew to be an impossible legal entanglement.

Only days later, the young attorney—retainer safely in pocket—approached Tressa with a far more troubling outlook, explaining with downcast eyes that her husband's case had become more complicated. There were, apparently, other charges pending— more serious charges that might not be so easily resolved.

The wife and the lawyer met with the unfortunate Luca at the prison; there, Carlos went so far as to advise the man he might be better off to plead guilty, gain favor with the prosecution, who in turn might speak on his behalf.

"I think we can make a deal," the lawyer assured him. "We cannot win this thing outright, Luca. But if you throw yourself on the mercy of the court the judge may go easy on you and most likely consider a lighter sentence."

Luca didn't like the idea, but he was not an educated man—who was he to say how these things worked? His wife seemed satisfied this Carlos Espinosa knew what he was talking about; this was all he had to go on.

The lawyer's sights were now zeroed in on his client's young wife, and with the added inducement of a dowry of sorts, she was seen to be even more desirable than he'd first imagined. Carlos plied his wiles of persuasion and in very little time Tressa Tarango was completely won over to his new plan.

Faced with the cold bare facts of the business it was not hard for Tressa to envision a better life with Carlos Espinosa. She was not getting any younger she thought *and looks do not last forever.*

"Up north," Carlos assured her, "we can build a future together, one without fear of reprisal." Tressa, convinced now that waiting for Luca could only leave her an embittered old woman, became more and more certain this handsome and fine talking lawyer was her best option.

As it later turned out, the judge did *not* look kindly on Luca Tarango, and his sentence, when it came, was even more severe than anyone could have anticipated.

Nothing seemed to work as Carlos said it would, and Luca was now faced with twenty years in the most notorious of Mexican prisons. The day following the verdict, Luca received a brief note from his wife saying he should not worry; his lawyer would appeal. Then without warning, Tressa's visits to the prison abruptly ended. Weeks passed and still Luca heard nothing. Finally, there did come word from relatives that his wife had sold their house, and along with his lawyer, fled north to the *Estados Unidos*.

Eventually, Luca received a brief letter saying only that Tressa was sorry to inform him their relationship was at an end. In a short postscript she mentioned enclosing ten dollars as a peace offering, implying it was all she had left in the world. The money, if there had been any, apparently did not survive the prison mail inspection. Luca was stunned, He folded the worn envelope, but not before noting the logo of a Mexican restaurant in Colorado, many miles to the north and well across the border with the United States. Gazing past prison walls, Luca saw things he didn't want to see and was forced to steel himself against what he knew must lie ahead. The news, coming as it did on the heels of so interminable a sentence, left him no recourse but to engineer his own escape, the doing of which nearly impoverished his entire family. Once Luca set his mind to a thing it was without thought of cost or consequence. None were inclined to cross a person of his reputation. Luca's goal was now a very different sort of justice and no one dared dispute the wisdom of it.

Eventually, Tressa heard from an uncle; her husband had found his way out of prison and was determined to *rescue* her. Underlying these words, however, she detected something more ominous, causing a hint of fear to shadow whatever solace might have been intended. It had never entered her mind her husband might be clever enough to find her, and so far away, too.

Only weeks later a last note reached Tressa, this one to inform her of Luca's death on the Navajo Indian reservation. This time there was no suggestion of compassion—her own uncle inferring there was no one else to blame. Tressa, at first incensed at the veiled accusation, eventually came to realize she had indeed treated her husband poorly, and from the very start, too. Clearly, she was the cause of Luca's downfall. She was the one who begged, then hounded him to leave their humble life in the village, move to the city with its strange ways and eventually fall into a very different sort of life. A life she made certain would provide her those things she'd long coveted. No matter what else the man may have been, or done, Luca always tried to put her interests ahead of his own.

~~~~~~~~

After Carlos Espinosa went through Tressa's money, he almost immediately lost interest. Washing his hands of any further responsibility for the woman, he thereafter paid her little attention of any kind. There was no performing together in his Uncle's *cantina*—him singing and playing the *guitarra,* while she danced the traditional *bailes* of her people—a picture once so glibly painted. There would be no comfortable home, or fine car. There was in fact, no home or car at all. There were only miserable little rooms behind the bar where she and a few other employees were forced to live under the thumb of Hector Espinosa. Carlos, who had a small apartment in town, still took every cent she earned, leaving Tressa to the discretion of his Uncle Hector, a coarse and presuming man, who took his pleasures where he found them and refused to hear any complaints against his nephew. He declared Carlos to be important to his business, said he was grooming his nephew for bigger things, and couldn't be bothered with her little problems. She would just have to adjust, he told her.

Little Abe pushed his way through the swinging door balancing a full tray of dirty dishes that rattled and clinked as he shook his head. "Well, it looks like that *pendejo* has worked his oily magic on those two *gringas* at the bar. They are buying him drinks right and left. I'm surprised he hasn't fallen off his stool."

He said this hoping Tressa would fret, and fume, and possibly see *him* in a kinder light.

Tressa only looked away as though she hadn't heard.

"*Ingrato.*" Abe spit the word as though it had stuck in his throat, watching from the corner of an eye to see how she would take this latest affront, determined now she should take note of so grievous an insult. Pushing her too far, however, might be a mistake. She wasn't a fool and could be unpredictable to say the least. Still, he couldn't help adding, "*Las dos chicas son gorditas y muy feas también. Pero...no le hacen nada a Carlos.*" Little Abe was doing his best to improve his English and only fell into his rural dialect when upset or at a loss for a particular word. His father had spent good money on English tutors, knowing full well his son might one day have need of the skill up north. Under the further tutelage of Tressa Tarango, the young man was showing remarkable progress.

The young women at the bar *were* unattractive no matter which language he chose, and Carlos Espinosa really *didn't* seem to care. Little Abe would not have given either of those girls a second glance, even if he was just a busboy...sometimes only the dishwasher.

Tressa frowned, *Aye, Dios mio...has the man not disrespected me enough?* She shot a steely glance at the swinging door and had to force herself not to rush for a peek through the little window. *I am beyond that now,* she told herself. Then gritting her teeth, seething inside, she imagined what Luca Tarango would have done to this pitiful excuse for a man—if only he had been given the chance. Her husband would not have blamed *her* for any of this. No, not at all, in her own mind Luca would have blamed the split-tongued Carlos Espinosa. How could a poor girl from the country be expected to deal with such a man? Yes, Carlos would already have suffered a fate worse than death at the hands of Luca Tarango—of that she was certain—and probably, his Uncle Hector would have come to a similar end. Now, however, it was upon her to take revenge on these tormentors.

She owed Luca, there was that as well, and each day the debt weighed more heavily on her soul. She would soon remedy that.

Little Abe grew cautious as he saw the woman struggle through mental turmoil so desperate one eye twitched to a mere slit, and for a moment he thought he had perhaps gone too far. But as quickly as it came, the anguish seemed to slip away, replaced by an even more disturbing air of calm resolution. Tressa smiled as though to herself, and motioned him back to the dining room.

El Dia de los Muertos was almost upon them, and God willing, it would bring with it a final atonement. Down in Mexico it was a day of celebration and veneration of the dead, allowing the living to make amends for past indiscretions or wrongs. People disguised themselves *as* the dead—painting their faces and dressing in costumes to allow the living to pass, unnoticed, among the spirits of the deceased.

Then too, Tressa thought, *there are still those Indios on the reservation to be dealt with. They, too, will learn the cost of their recklessness.* She had no idea what evil her husband had worked on those people, but whatever it was it would not deter her quest for personal atonement. Her recent letter to Investigator Yazzie might just provide the information needed to find her husband's killer. It was this Charlie Yazzie who sent her official notice of Luca's death. His letter was brief, not saying how or by whose hand or even why Luca died, only that he was dead, and his last thoughts were of her. The message twisted a knife in her belly and she put it away until she had the strength to deal with it, along with her other poor choices.

Everything hinged on a certain progression of events, and dealing with Carlos and his Uncle must come first. She was well aware their major source of income was not from the restaurant and bar—those were only a front for the real business. Carlos knew a lot, and in the beginning, foolishly talked of these things, thinking to bind her more closely to him. It was something he now regretted.

She and Little Abe would need money, and though it would come at great risk, she could see no other way. Her future plans would be expensive to implement, but certainly no more than Carlos owed her. They might not hit the mother-lode, but there would be something.

Hector Espinosa was not called "The Ear" for nothing. His informants were everywhere, and there was little he didn't know about his employees. By the same token, however, there were things the help knew about him, dangerous things and the reason he kept his people close. Nothing would come easy for Little Abe and her, and the smallest mistake could lead to a most unpleasant end.

It was nearly ten o'clock when Tressa hung her apron on the nail in the supply closet, patted her hair, and inspected her blouse in the cracked mirror over the sink. The dinner rush was over and Abe could handle what little food the bar patrons might order. Now it was time for the real customers to begin filtering in.

It was said in Mexico that only five or six regulars were required to make a go of a bar business. Five or six loyal drinkers appearing each day, that would be enough to keep the lights on and the rent paid. Everything else was…how did they put it in this country…gravy. Hector Espinosa's bar had at least a dozen such customers, and not all of them came just to drink. The real business had to do with *La Familia's* enterprises in Sinaloa. That was the center of everything. Little Abe was quite familiar with that end of the business and learning more every day. His

father's connections in Sinaloa were proving their
worth.

2

Déjà vu

"So, George Custer and Harley Ponyboy are out surveying a new site, are they?" Charlie Yazzie knew very well they were, but the conversation had lagged and he thought he would kick-start it before getting into the real reason for his visit—ease into it so to speak—so as not to lend undue urgency to the thing.

Thomas Begay turned to the Legal Services Investigator, now apparently lost in thought, and answered, "Uh… yes, I offered to go along and help but George said it was a simple job and the two of them could handle it all right." Thomas looked slightly askance at his friend, watching for some indication he might be joking. He'd already told him this very thing, and only the day before. He knew Charlie Yazzie well enough to know he had some ulterior motive. Rather than risk making a fool of one or the other of them Thomas decided to play along, see where he was headed with the thing. He pursed his lips, nodded and further admitted, "I have plenty to do around here anyway, what with the old man not doing so well, and the kids in school." Thomas said this last part barely above a whisper, looking across the room to make sure the old Singer was still napping in his recliner. The last thing he needed was to arouse the ire of his father-in-law. He watched a moment, smiling, as he remembered an old Navajo proverb: *"It is hard to wake a person who is only pretending to be asleep."*

Lucy Tallwoman, working at her loom, sounded matter-of-fact, "Well, I hope those two haven't gotten into a bottle up there." Thomas's wife sat at her weaving and just across the room from the others. She kept to her work. She was on a schedule with this piece but didn't want to miss out on anything interesting either—which was why she put the loom in the living room in the first place.

Sue Yazzie poured another round of coffee and sat the pot back on the tray. "Oh, I don't think they'd be drinking up there." She really had no idea what the Professor and Harley Ponyboy might be doing, but preferred to think they had not fallen off the wagon; both had been clean for a good long while.

Charlie Yazzie smiled at his wife. "Let's hope you're right." He grinned over at Thomas who looked ready to voice an opinion…then seemed to decide against it.

Thomas, too, hoped the pair were all right, but was well versed in the pitfalls they faced. Any other time, Thomas Begay would have felt slighted to be left out of such an expedition, but as he mentioned, he had enough to do right there at home. George and Harley would have to take care of themselves this time.

Lucy was obviously happy her husband hadn't been invited along with them. George's failed reconciliation with his sometimes-romantic interest, Aida Winters, had to hurt, and Harley's previous try at romance hadn't turned out much better. Lucy clearly suspected their woman problems might cause one or the other of them to take a backward step; if one did, she figured the other might well follow, including Thomas if he were to be with them.

Old Paul T'Sosi snored softly in his sleep—if he was asleep. His daughter again looked his way and listened. Her father had not been well for some time, and as his eightieth birthday approached, he seemed despondent. As the days passed into autumn she became even more worried by his continued air of malaise.

Paul's state of mind was now such, the family had to keep an eye on him to prevent him wandering off. Even the children could see he was having trouble finding his way home from time to time. Still, the old man occasionally took the sheep out but now one of the youngsters went along, shadowing his every move. The fall weather had not brought his usual rise in spirits—she had come to expect it and was disappointed. Lucy studied her father a moment longer and then, slowly shaking her head, returned to her shuttle. *We will have a Sing for him...that's what we will do...* They could afford it, and it was the only thing left she thought might help. The old Singer had an abiding mistrust of hospitals and white doctors.

Giving a Sing for a *Hataalii* was no easy matter; it would be complicated, and just the right man would have to be found if the idea was to be acceptable to Paul T'Sosi. Lucy Tallwoman thought she knew just the person. She would talk to Sue about it. While Charlie's wife was not overly traditional, when it came to these things she had a good sense of who her people were.

The Legal Services Investigator, at last, thought this might be the time, to bring up his more pressing announcement. "I just wanted to mention while we're all together; I had a call from Officer Red Clay yesterday morning. Billy told me Agent Smith at the FBI called him...said they would like a short meeting with Thomas and I tomorrow morning. Billy wouldn't say what it was about, acted like he didn't know, so I wasn't going to mention it...at least until I knew more...but now I have a pretty good idea what's up."

Thomas glanced at the investigator. He wasn't expecting this and didn't like the sound of it.

Charlie threw his wife a sidelong glance before going on. "Normally, I wouldn't say anything, but the fact is I *am* just a little concerned." He paused, a moment as he searched for just the right way to put it. Looking through the window, past Lucy Tallwoman's loom, shadows were falling across the gullies and arroyos. *Sundown's coming earlier...fall has slipped up on me.* He shrugged and forced himself back to the business at hand. "It appears Robert Ashki got out of prison a few days ago. I don't necessarily expect anything bad to come of it. Still, I thought a little heads-up wouldn't hurt.

Thomas Begay snorted and leaned forward in his chair, "I thought that no good Ashki got ten years for corruption...obstruction of justice...and as I recall, tampering with federal witnesses. How can he be out already?"

"Yes, well, it seems former Councilman Ashki still has a few friends in high places...what few didn't wind up in jail along with him." Charlie seemed less confident in his previous downplaying of the news. "I suppose we'd better be sure John Nez, knows about the release. Ashki has been known to carry a grudge and you, Thomas, along with your Uncle John and I, could be high on his list." Charlie paused and frowned. "I'm pretty sure this is what Agent Smith wants to talk to us about." Unlike past FBI men, Senior Agent Fred Smith seemed to make preventive measures a priority in his work, at least more so than previous Bureau heads. But then, Fred had been raised in that country and was more aware how things actually worked at reservation level.

Charlie glanced over at Thomas, holding up a finger to indicate there was more. "There's one other thing I may as well let you in on...not related to the Ashki situation...and probably even less of an issue, but just so you know…" Charlie studied the sleeping form of old Paul T'Sosi and lowered his voice even more. "Several days ago, I had a letter from Tressa Tarango. I'd sent her a letter just after her husband's death…mostly just telling her he was deceased, and asking where she wanted his personal effects sent."

Thomas Begay sucked in his breath. "Luca Tarango? The *Mojado*? He's been dead several years. I thought we'd heard the last of him…and her, too." Thomas couldn't help thinking it strange this announcement should come so close on the heels of the other, and wondered if Charlie had some reason to tie the two together. He couldn't imagine it but refused to put anything past Robert Ashki.

Sue Yazzie and Lucy Tallwoman locked eyes for an instant. Sue lifted an eyebrow at her friend and shrugged, as if to assure her this was the first she'd heard of any letter from the serial killer's wife.

Charlie, as though channeling Thomas's thoughts, again made the point the two cases were separated by several years and had no obvious connection. He was pleased to see no one appeared overly concerned at this last news. It was obvious the two reports were likely more of a weird coincidence than anything else.

Later, as the two women were busy preparing food for an early dinner, Thomas Begay called into the kitchen saying he and Charlie were going to take a little walk to meet the kids at the bus stop.

Lucy Tallwoman looked out the kitchen window and watched as the two men ambled down the dirt track together. "Thomas hasn't met that school bus once this year."

Sue didn't look up from what she was doing. "I wondered about that." She was beginning to think there might be more to all this than her husband was letting on.

Lucy couldn't forget Robert Ashki's central involvement in the plot to abduct Thomas's daughter, and although it had been several years back it brought a shiver. Federal Prosecutors hadn't made that particular charge stick, but not from want of trying.

There was a chill in the air. *Winter is coming,* Thomas thought, as they waited for the school bus. Across the asphalt strip to the east, the tip of the great Shiprock floated in a blue haze from the coal-fired power plant on the San Juan. A sudden cold gust brought a swirl of dust and caused both men to be glad of their wool-lined Levi's jackets.

Neither Thomas nor Charlie Yazzie had said a word during their walk to the bus stop. Thomas thinking his friend might be making more of the Ashki affair than was warranted. When finally Charlie did speak, however, Thomas detected an underlying note of urgency—a tone Charlie was not ordinarily prone to use.

"If I know the former Councilman he's not happy with your uncle taking his seat on the Council. Ashki's the sort who might want a little payback."

Charlie was definitely having misgivings about the return of Robert Ashki.

"Really? You think the bastard would make a move against us after all this time?"

Charlie turned to face his friend with a lifted eyebrow. "I remember the look he gave us in the courtroom. It probably wouldn't hurt to keep an eye out for any of his shenanigans."

Thomas nodded, thinking. *"Shenanigans" is an odd word, coming from a Diné, even from one who went off to college.* He first thought it might be a Navajo word he had misheard, but Professor Custer used the term on occasion, that was probably where Charlie got it. *It did almost sound Navajo,* he thought, rolling it around on the back of his tongue. He tried to think of a similar sounding *Diné* word but couldn't come up with one.

Charlie Yazzie, guessing the cause of his friend's confusion was amused and looked away.

"I'll call up to the chapter house at Navajo Mountain and leave a message for Uncle Johnny to get ahold of me. They still don't have any phone service out to his place." Thomas couldn't help smiling, "I doubt they ever will have either…and that suits Uncle John just fine."

Charlie nodded. "I guess you better tell him about the Mojado's widow while you're are at it. I can't imagine she's savvy enough to find out who killed her husband…but, you never know." He looked past Thomas, toward Navajo Mountain. "John Nez may now have *several* enemies."

"Oh, I expect he has more than several," Thomas grinned. "John is fond of saying, 'Show me a man who has no enemies and I will show you a man who hasn't done a whole hell of a lot."

Charlie chuckled, "I guess that's about right. My grandfather used to say, 'Back in the old days men were judged by the fierceness of their enemies." Still smiling he ventured, "Maybe that's why your Uncle John Nez is so highly thought of."

Thomas smiled also, but in the way a man smiles when he's been handed something significant to think about.

The school bus appeared only minutes late and Thomas, already pacing back and forth, was obviously relieved to see his children come down the steps.

~~~~~~~

The next morning they found Tribal Officer, Billy Red Clay waiting patiently in front of Farmington's Federal Building.

Thomas grinned at the policeman. "Good to see you here so early Nephew. I wish sometimes I lived as close into town as you." The two men shook hands; Thomas *was* pleased to see his clan nephew and slapped him on the shoulder.

Charlie Yazzie also shook hands with the policeman, but wasn't smiling when he looked Billy in the eye and asked, "Any more idea what's going on this morning?" He was nearly certain the young officer knew more than he had revealed in his phone call.

"No, not really. You probably know as much as I do." Secretly, Billy was thinking, *I'm the damn Liaison Officer between Tribal and the Federal Bureau of Investigation. I really should know more than I do.* He turned back to his uncle and changed the subject. "How's everything out in the country this morning, Uncle? Is Old Man T'Sosi still not feeling well? My mom heard he'd been sick. She told me to be sure and ask about him next time I saw you."

Thomas just shook his head, "He's not doing so good, Billy, and he won't go to a doctor, neither. He says he *is* a doctor."

Billy Red Clay rubbed his few chin whiskers, as though that small attention might encourage them to offer a better account of themselves. He frowned finally and said. "Well, you tell him my mom sent her best wishes. We all hope he gets better quick."

Thomas nodded before glancing over at Charlie with a helplessness he couldn't hide. He, too, hoped Paul would get better, but was beginning to have serious doubts.

Upstairs, Charlie Yazzie, raised an eyebrow when the receptionist said Agent Smith would be a few minutes late. As far as he knew, Fred Smith was seldom late for anything. The woman looked the three over and waved them to the adjacent conference room. "He'll be along shortly; there's a pot of fresh coffee on the sideboard...feel free to help yourself." The woman had a recognizable Oklahoma accent along with a slightly superior air, which is not generally the case with those people, at least not in Charlie Yazzie's experience.

The three moved directly to the coffee and began fixing their cups. Thomas was pleased to note a small pitcher of real cream. He liked cream in his coffee; he'd grown up with canned evaporated milk on the reservation and had only come to real cream late in life. He held the little stainless creamer up for the others to see. "Our tax dollars at work," he smiled and splashed a healthy dollop atop the small mountain of sugar already in the cup, then added steaming coffee to the brim before stirring, careful not to slop any on the polished mahogany sideboard. The other two men stood patiently as Thomas took a long slow slurp and pronounced the brew perfect. The Navajo take their coffee seriously and go out of their way to make the slightest occasion an obligatory time for the drink. Thomas headed to the table, saying under his breath, "You'd a thought, though, they could afford a few doughnuts or something, them getting us out so early and all." Thomas was partial to doughnuts and considered them the ultimate token of hospitality.

The men had hardly seated themselves when the sound of voices came from the outer office. Agent Fred Smith bustled through the door carrying a cardboard box that had the picture of a doughnut on it; the word "Spudnuts" was emblazoned on the side.

Thomas's face broke into a grin, and even Charlie Yazzie couldn't help smiling.

"Sorry I'm late guys: there was quite a line at the doughnut shop this morning." Nonetheless, the FBI man sounded pleased with himself.

Charlie nodded at the box. "That was awfully nice of you Fred." He personally knew people who drove all the way in from Shiprock some mornings, just to line up at the Spudnut counter. It was a Farmington institution for both whites and Indians alike.

Agent Smith sat the box on the table and then shook hands all around, saying each man's name in turn. He had grown up with the *Diné*, and even worked in his grandfather's trading post when he was in school. The FBI man knew how to get along with the Navajo, inquiring after various family members, and then when questioned, offered a few words about how his own brood was getting along. As the others delved into the doughnut box, Fred went for his coffee, which he took black, then found a seat at the head of the table.

Thomas pushed the Spudnut box toward the FBI man while pursing his lips in approval of the three still warm doughnuts on his napkin.

As they began, Fred wiped a few flakes of glaze from his lips before saying. "First off, I'd like you boys to know how much I appreciate you coming in. I'll try not to take up too much of your time this morning. I'm sure we all have other things to do." The agent looked around the table before getting down to business. "We have sort of a situation, I guess you could call it." He hesitated before going on. "You may have heard that Robert Ashki was released from prison a few days ago. You know him better than I do; I was still working out of Albuquerque at the time of his trial." He pulled a small notebook from his pocket and leafed through it before looking up. "The assistant warden where Ashki was incarcerated called to say one of their informants reported the man making threats against certain people here on the reservation and, according to him, the threats were ongoing during the time Ashki was an inmate. It's prison policy to pass along such information should they feel it warranted. In this case they obviously thought it was."

Here the FBI Agent appeared thoughtful for a moment. "I took it upon myself to pull our own file on the ex-Councilman and there *are* things there that seem to lend weight to the seriousness of the warden's report." Fred adjusted his glasses and looked at Charlie, and then at Thomas Begay. "There's more to it than I can let you in on at the moment, but suffice it to say, I have some concerns you should be made aware of." He indicated the

Tribal policeman. "In the last day or so, Billy Red Clay here has come into possession of further information, some of which—I grant you—could be rumor. I specifically asked Billy not to mention any of this beforehand, but this is why he's here this morning." Fred eyed the young Liaison Officer who in turn looked at Charlie and then away. "I'll let him fill you in on that part of this morning's business."

Billy produced a notebook, not unlike that of the agent's, but in his case he had only to flip open the first page to read from his few notes, which he did while occasionally glancing up at Charlie. "One of our own informants says he recently overheard Robert Ashki claim he was going to 'get even' with both Thomas Begay and Charlie Yazzie. The message was left recorded on our answering machine early yesterday morning. The caller said he was a concerned citizen." Billy frowned despite himself, "We could see who he was by the caller I. D."

Thomas chuckled. "That doesn't say much for your informant's 'smarts' does it, Nephew?"

Billy Red Clay turned color. "The man's been pretty reliable in the past, and he did do a short stretch in the same cell block with Ashki. Only got out a few months ago. I know for a fact there was no love lost between the two."

The four men discussed the various aspects of the information, the three Navajo finally concluding that "getting even" covered a lot of ground.

Thomas smiled. "That could mean anything from throwing eggs at our house, to doing someone bodily harm. I'm not really worried about it myself, but I will let my uncle John Nez, up at Navajo Mountain, know what's going on. He lives near Robert Ashki's camp up there, and he'd be the one most likely to run into him, but I doubt he will be worried by it either."

Charlie wasn't so sure. "I think we may be missing the point here. A little advance warning might not be a bad thing. We should all be aware by now of what Ashki's capable of."

Agent Smith nodded agreement. "After reading the Ashki trial transcripts, I'm inclined to agree with Charlie." He looked at all three *Diné* when he said, "I would appreciate hearing any further information that might come your way down the line." He turned even more serious when he said, "I know how things get around on the reservation and would hope you might let me know first before taking any action on your own." This last thought seemed to conclude what he had to say and looking at his watch, Agent Smith called the meeting to a close. But as they were on their way out he touched Charlie on the arm and pointed to his office.

The Legal Services Investigator caught Thomas's eye, indicating he and Billy should go on without him. He saw Billy frown as he followed Thomas out.

In his office the FBI man, glancing toward the reception area, shut the door behind them, and once in his chair reached across and turned off the intercom. He raised his eyebrows at Charlie as he did so. The precaution gave the investigator pause, putting him slightly on his guard.

Charlie took a seat across the desk, where he waited for the Senior Agent to take the lead.

"There's something else I would like to discuss with you, Charlie, on a more personal level. Something off the record, but possibly even more important than what we discussed earlier."

Fred's manner changed imperceptibly as he leaned across the desk and lowered his voice. "Charlie, for the last month or so the Bureau has been involved in a joint effort with the DEA. Drug Enforcement is spearheading a multi-agency push targeting the Sinaloa trafficking cartel." He paused, rolling his pencil across one finger and under the next. "Their agency has turned up information which may have implications for the reservation. Given the increased drug problems we've been experiencing, both on, and off Indian land, I'm sure this doesn't surprise you. For whatever reason, DEA seems to think *you* may be able to help.

Charlie pulled his chair closer to the desk, but didn't say anything.

"In fact," the agent went on, "the Drug Enforcement folks have enquired as to any information we might have regarding *your* involvement in a past murder case on the reservation. They seemed most interested in anything to do with a

Tressa Tarango, wife of one Luca Tarango, the suspect in a string of killings on Indian land. I've taken the trouble to go over the files here. From what I can gather from my predecessor's rather sketchy notes—the previous Senior Agent, Eldon Mayfield, considered you to be directly involved in the death of Luca Tarango. He also had reason to believe you might later have corresponded with his widow?" Fred raised both hands in such a way Charlie knew he expected an answer.

"Fred, it's common knowledge what my part was in the apprehension and death of Luca Tarango." That day was probably the closest Charlie had come to dying, and even now he had a hard time dealing with the memory of it. "As far as my correspondence with his widow goes, it consisted of a single letter notifying her of her husband's death, less than two short paragraphs as I recall." Charlie put his hands flat on the table. "Eldon and I never got along well. You know that yourself, Fred."

The agent nodded to the truth in that and went on, "I also took the trouble to contact Tribal Police, thinking their account of the incident might offer some additional information. Eldon Mayfield wasn't the most thorough person when it came to filing reports. I've been aware of that for some time." The FBI man frowned and shook his head. "Tribal somehow couldn't locate their case file, saying it may have been misplaced and they would get back to me. I'll have Billy Red Clay look into that." Fred rocked back in his chair. "Here's the bottom line: We may need your help on this one, Charlie."

Now, the FBI needs my help, after all the times they asked me to butt out of an investigation. Charlie saw the humor in this, and looking across at the FBI Agent saw Fred knew exactly what he was thinking.

Smith smiled. "I know…I know…"

"Well, the funny thing is, Fred, I did have a letter from Tressa Tarango just a few days ago. That's after two years not hearing a thing from her."

Smith looked down at his notes. "That's interesting; the County Coroner had a letter from her, too—also about two weeks ago—she wanted to know where her husband was buried and if their office still had his personal effects." Fred brought his chair back upright and emphasized his next words with a lifted finger. "Drug Enforcement asked the Coroner's office to notify them should anyone enquire about Tarango's remains." Agent Smith had been trying to put all this together in his head, but it wasn't adding up, until now. "Drug Enforcement has their own way of doing things, Charlie. "The DEA said the coroner finally did call, saying Tarango's wife had been in touch, and asked if it would be all right if they released information to her. The suggestion was *not* to write her back at all." Fred shook his head and frowned. "I believe now I know why, too."

"Oh, and why would that be, Fred?"

"The DEA wanted her to *have* to go to *you* Charlie. They think you can do something for them.

They obviously know something we don't, and they're looking for a plant."

"A *plant*?" Charlie was smiling and looking for Fred to smile in return, something signifying the agent was kidding him.

Fred didn't smile. "You *know*, Charlie…a mole…an undercover guy." The FBI man nodded, saying, "That's the first thing these people usually come up with, it's the primary way they do business; it's their stock in trade you might say. You're their guy. Now it's making sense."

Charlie sat there attempting to keep a straight face. The two men looked at one another for nearly a full minute, each waiting for the other to say something.

Charlie was the first to cave. "I'm not their *guy*, Fred. You better dial those boys up right now and tell them that—I'm not their guy! I've got a job. I'm a lawyer and a legal department investigator. I'm the exact opposite of what they want."

Fred didn't say anything for a moment but when he did, he had a set to his jaw. "Okay, Charlie, I'll call them…but I know these people. They're not going to give a damn what *you* think you are. They're very good at picking people who can help them— they're building a case—and they don't give up easy. You'll hear from them all right."

"Where are they?"

"The people I've been talking to? They're in Denver…at least they were at the time we spoke."

"Good, I doubt they'll make a trip all the way down here then."

Fred Smith raised an eyebrow and shrugged.

~~~~~~~

When the Legal Services Investigator went back outside, Billy Red Clay was nowhere in sight. His uncle Thomas, however, lounged against the Tribal logo on Charlie's white Chevy. "My nephew got a call on the radio, said he had to leave, but I have to tell you, he's pretty anxious to hear what happened in there. He didn't like being shown the door—him being the Liaison Officer and all."

"Yes, well, then you can tell him his name didn't come up in the conversation."

Thomas grinned. "Then, I expect he'll like that even less." He waited for Charlie to fill *him* in on what had happened, but when he didn't, Thomas just shrugged it off and turned back toward his truck. He knew he'd get it out of his friend sooner or later.

~~~~~~~

It was almost noon by the time Charlie Yazzie looked up from his desk and considered the hour. The morning stack of work had been reduced, but not by nearly as much as it should. The FBI conference had put a damper on his usually keen work ethic. The idea that a federal agency might have the temerity to approach *him* to go undercover was unsettling. He'd had dealings with the DEA before—minor cases, mostly—involving local people there on the Rez. Drugs were a major problem on the *Diné Bikeyah*, as they were on most Indian reservations, and Legal Services did sometimes get involved one way or another. Drugs were now a close runner-up to the rampant alcohol addiction, still the leading cause of mental and other health disorders, and a major contributing factor to growing criminal activity.

The irritating beep of the intercom interrupted Charlie's already meandering train of thought. He considered not answering and waited out the three-beep series, only to be left with the equally insistent pulsing red light. It was a new system and Charlie was having a hard time getting used to it. He tapped the button, but before he could adjust the volume the new receptionist's voice filled the room. She was a loud talker, as the Navajo say.

"Yes, Gwen?" He hoped it was still Gwen—receptionists seemed to come and go almost on a weekly basis. The office staff had nearly doubled over his years there, but at the same time, employee commitment had (in his opinion) declined. That problem, too, would eventually appear on his plate…another thing to sort out.

"It's never easy at the top" That's the advice his old boss left him when he stepped down and handed over the reins, adding in his usual cryptic manner,

"Especially when you are dealing with a People in transition."

Transition to what? That was the question and was it a transition forward? Charlie watched as the indicator lights jumped back and forth from phone to phone. Gwen—if that was her name—had apparently dropped the connection and wasn't sure exactly which button to push, so she was pushing them all.

"Is that you Mr. Yazzie?" Her voice reminded him, vaguely, of a small donkey's bray.

"Yes Gwen, it's me...what can I do for you?" Charlie partially covered the speaker before she could blast an answer.

"I have a Mr. Begay here, who says he has an appointment, but I don't see it in the book?"

"That's all right Gwen, send him on back...uh, is there anyone with him?"

"Yes, there is, sir, another gentleman is with him. Um... a Mr. Ponyboy, who says he has an appointment too."

Charlie sighed and shook his head, "Send them both back here, Gwen." The investigator closed the file he'd been working on and putting it on top of the others, shoved the stack in a drawer.

As usual, Thomas Begay was first through the door. Grinning at the Legal Services Investigator, he said, "I see we are all now a 'Mister' this morning. Where'd the new girl come from?"

"Secretarial school." Charlie made a face. "Temp Services sent her over last week."

"Well, she doesn't seem very good at recognizing important people when she sees them."

Harley Ponyboy chuckled at this and offered, "She's my cousin from Todalena. She knew who we were, all right." Then Harley remembered why they were there. "Thomas thought it was about lunch time—you know he likes ta be early on Friday." The two stood, waiting to be offered a seat. They could see Charlie was busy.

"How was the dig, Harley?" Charlie ignored the comment about lunch, hoping to avoid that trap, but *was* curious as to what the professor and crew were up to. He missed being involved in the digs.

"It wasn't much. George was just hired ta do a preliminary evaluation for right now. It might turn into something later I guess—if they cut a new service road; if they do that, it will have ta go right through the site. Right now, we are trying to line out the paperwork, "just in case," at least that's what it looks like ta me."

Charlie motioned them to sit down and sighed as he watched the two jostle for the same seat. Harley Ponyboy shouldered his taller companion aside and settled himself in the padded leather chair nearest the desk. He grinned at Thomas Begay and made a rude gesture.

Charlie wiped a hand across his face looking as stern as possible. "What's up guys? I've got a ton of work this morning."

Thomas pointed a finger at Harley. "He got paid and after he filled up his truck, he still thinks he has enough to buy us all lunch. You don't wanna' pass that up."

"It's the fried chicken special over at Café Diné Bikeyah," Harley crowed. Charlie could tell he'd been hanging out with Thomas all morning.

"Isn't George coming?"

"He said he had to get the reports in the mail first, but he might drop by if he finishes in time. That don't look likely ta me. I told him, 'that special won't last long, George.' …You know how he likes his fried chicken."

Charlie knew it was probably useless trying to argue himself out of the early lunch, but determined to make it a quick one. There *was* a good likelihood of running into Billy Red Clay at the café and there were a few questions he had for the policeman. He thought that alone might justify the time spent. He'd been concentrating on setting a good example for the new employees, and being careful not to take long lunches seemed important.

They all three went in Charlie's truck, and pulling into the parking lot at the *Diné Bikeyah*, Thomas, was first to spot his nephew's Tribal Police unit. "Looks like Billy's here."

Billy Red Clay and a new recruit had taken the big table by the back window, but when Charlie's group worked their way back there Billy informed them he had two more people on the way and pointed to the empty, but smaller, booth, in the rear of the room. Thomas, frowning, led the way. He thought his nephew was acting like he had a burr under his blanket about something.

Charlie, too, was thinking the Liaison Officer a little brusque and made a mental note to sound him out later. Billy Red Clay was no longer the carefree patrolman he had once been. The added stress and responsibilities of his new position seemed to be weighing on his usual good humor.

At the table, Thomas took the chair facing the door, citing his oft-repeated admonishment regarding the fate of Wild Bill Hickok who, as he often cautioned, had been shot from behind when putting his back to the door. Thomas once saw it in an old movie starring the now-forgotten Tom Brown and had never been fully able to erase the scene from his mind. When he and Harley were drinkers—usually in the lowest sort of places—he had been particularly aware to take heed of such precautions.

In those volatile times, Harley Ponyboy might have agreed Thomas had something to worry about, and taken a measure of comfort from such safeguards. Today, he only smiled at the notion.

Though the three spent a goodly amount of time studying the menu, in the end it was agreed the "Special" was what they had come for. The orders were placed with a finality that denied any subsequent change—a thing frowned on by the cook, who might in turn, retaliate in various ways.

Thomas, with his unimpeded view of the door, was first to notice the two men in suits, hesitating just inside. The pair searched the rapidly filling restaurant until one of them spotted who they were looking for—at the big table in the back.

As their waitress brought a tray of salads and water, Thomas took advantage of the distraction by nudging Charlie, to whisper, "Now there's a couple of ducks out of water," indicating the two with his chin as they passed beyond their table.

Charlie barely looked up as he reached for his salad. "Uh-huh..." He had hoped to get through the lunch as quickly as possible and without the usual drama brought on by strangers, which were generally few and far between.

Harley caught Thomas's inference and followed the well-dressed pair from under the brim of his hat, "Look like out of town *law* ta me." Both he and Thomas were loaded with experience when it came to recognizing lawmen no matter the agency or how they were dressed.

Charlie, dabbing at his Thousand Island dressing, finally glanced in the direction the two were looking and thought it possible the pair were indeed lawmen of some sort. "Well, Billy is the Liaison Officer for Tribal. They could be FBI."

"No, they're not FBI," Thomas murmured, and then pulled his hat lower. "Those boys are Feds all right, but I don't think FBI...they're...something else."

"Maybe there's some sort of audit going on…or maybe Tribal's undergoing a training session—the Feds do that for them occasionally." Charlie was unimpressed and still concentrating on his salad, but when the waitress returned with their food he took a quick peek past her and a good hard look at the window table. He still didn't comment but his expression changed slightly, and Thomas Begay caught it.

The chicken was done perfectly; everyone agreed it had earned its "Special" designation and should again be taken advantage of the next time it came around. George Custer would be sorry he missed it.

As the three finished lunch, Charlie, anxious to get back to the office, excused himself by mentioning he was trying to set a good example at the office. The other two exchanged a quick glance; both remembered him saying he wanted to speak to Billy Red Clay about something. The new recruit Billy came in with, left, and Thomas's nephew was now deep in conversation with the men in suits.

Thomas thought maybe Charlie had forgotten and said, "Didn't you have something you wanted to ask Billy?"

Charlie looked over at Red Clay's table and thought about it but quickly turned away. "He looks pretty busy right now…I'd best catch him later."

In the restaurant parking lot, Harley, still licking his lips over lunch, patted his stomach, "The Doc's gonna' be sorry he missed that special fried chicken. It don't come around very often."

Charlie acted as though he hadn't heard, still looking back at the cafe giving the impression the investigator was thinking of returning...but he didn't.

Back in his office Charlie was uneasy and the more he thought about it, the more uneasy he became. Although he knew it was silly, he wondered if the men in the suits might actually be DEA, and if they were, what were they talking to Billy Red Clay about? Paranoia? He knew better, but still... *The best thing to do is put it out of my mind.* The entire thing was pretty far-fetched to his way of thinking. Realistically, he doubted he would ever hear from anyone at Drug Enforcement—despite what Fred Smith might think.

As Charlie pulled up the drive to his house that afternoon, he didn't see Sue's pickup and it took him a moment to remember it was her grocery-shopping day. His wife was in Farmington and probably wouldn't be home until later despite having the kids along. It was the blue sedan, in her parking place, that was unexpected. He didn't recognize the car, but he did recognize the two men sitting inside—the same two men in suits from the restaurant. Charlie pulled in alongside, noticing the Colorado plates and the disguised two-way antenna. Thomas was right they weren't FBI. He shut off the engine and got out. The car's driver met him halfway to the front of the truck.

"Mr. Yazzie." He didn't bother making it a question. He was a big man in a cheap suit, and appeared a bit uncomfortable. "Officer Red Clay pointed you out at lunch today. We'd hoped to have a word with you when you'd finished your meal...but when I looked up you were gone." His smile faded. "I left a message for you at your office, but you must have missed it. I didn't hear back." He looked at the investigator and seemed to expect a reply before going on.

"New receptionist...I didn't get the message." Charlie looked the man straight in the eye. "But I wish I had now, I might have saved you the trip out here."

"Oh, it's not that far, Mr. Yazzie, and we didn't have anything else to do anyway." He was smiling again when he put out his hand. "I'm Agent Freeman...Bob Freeman, Department of Drug Enforcement. My partner and I are out of the Denver office." He pointed to the car. "That's my partner there in the car. He's waiting for a callback on the radio."

Charlie nodded, and pushed his tongue against the inside of his cheek to keep from saying anything. *You always want to let these people do the talking.* Or so he'd heard.

"I was wondering if I might have a word with you, if you have just a minute." The agent waited a few seconds before going on. "We could come back tomorrow Mr. Yazzie, if you're pressed for time right now. Whatever's more convenient for you."

Charlie took a deep breath, "I assume from that, you're going to be around for a while?"

"Just as long as it takes, Mr. Yazzie. I'm not on a schedule… I can be here as long as it takes."

Takes for what? Charlie was wondering as he glanced over at the man in the car; the other agent was talking into a handset, filling in a form at the same time. He seemed to sense Charlie looking at him and gave the investigator a quick nod.

Charlie acknowledged the man with a lift of his chin and supposed he might just as well get this over with. "I was about to feed the horses. You can tag along if you like." He turned without waiting for a reply and headed for the corral. Both horses were standing at the fence, curious about the strangers probably, and hoping they wouldn't interfere with dinner. When Charlie forked a bale off the stack it tumbled and rolled almost to the agent's feet. "Sorry, I should have warned you…these are heavy bales."

The agent nodded, hooked the two strands of baling twine with one big hand, and with little apparent effort carried it over to the horses. It obviously wasn't his first time to feed horses. Charlie, right behind him, took out a pocketknife and cut the strings. There were two feeders hanging off the fence and the agent stood back as Charlie filled the first one; both men watched the mare lay her ears back at the gelding and take over the feed.

"She's a little bossy, isn't she?" The agent eyed the broken bale, watching as Charlie filled the other feeder. "That's good-looking hay you've got there, about a forty/sixty mix, I'd say."

"I suppose that's about right if you take out for the weeds." Charlie smiled. The man seemed to know something about horses, and hay, too. Bob was a smooth operator, all right. The old people had a name for it, but Charlie couldn't bring it to mind.

"Nice little place you've got here, Charlie. You don't mind if I call you 'Charlie', do you?" He didn't wait for an answer. "What I'm here for, Charlie, is to see if you might be willing to help us out on a little problem we have coming out of Sinaloa, Mexico, and by 'we' I mean your people and mine."

Bob Freeman was the sort of man you wanted to like, but the investigator knew that could be a slippery slope, especially in view of what he now suspected they were really after.

"We're told you know Tressa Tarango."

Charlie looked down the line of peach trees along the fence. He'd planted them two years before, and thought he'd put them just out of reach of the horses, now he could see he hadn't. A few trees had mangled branches on the corral side. Bringing his attention back to the agent, he said, "You were told wrong, Bob, I've never seen the woman...let alone know her."

"Well, it seems she knows you Charlie. That's what's important to us right now."

"What makes you think I can help you, Agent?"

Freeman chewed on this a bit before answering. "It's complicated Charlie, and a lot of it's classified. It would require a certain, leap of faith on both sides, if you know what I mean."

"No, I guess I *don't* know what you mean, Bob." Charlie started the water and both men concentrated on watching the tank fill. "I'd have to know a hell of a lot more about it to even begin thinking how I could help."

This didn't seem to bother agent Freeman. "I can understand that. We didn't just pick you out of the phone book, Charlie. We've taken the trouble to learn something about you, and we think you're the man for the job. Possibly the only man for the job."

Charlie shut off the water and turned to the agent just as Sue's pickup turned off the highway and up the drive. "Drop by my office in the morning. I have Saturday off, but I have to go in for a couple of hours. Let's make it early...say about seven o'clock?" The agent glanced down the drive, gave a little half-salute and nodded.

Charlie watched as the blue sedan maneuvered back down the lane giving Sue plenty of room to get by. He saw his wife's head turn as the car passed, and wondered who he could tell her it was.

~~~~~~~

Charlie Yazzie liked to sleep in on Saturday mornings but had very little sleep of any kind the night before. He reached for the steaming travel-cup as he started the truck, and was nearly down to the dregs by the time he hit the outskirts of Shiprock. There was almost no one on the streets. The sun was still not quite up; the little town looked cold and grey and would, until the sun edged above the big water tank on the hill. Charlie was glad now that Sue hadn't settled for an apartment, or even trailer house in town, just so they could be close to their jobs. The little settlement of Waterflow had been the right choice, a bit of a drive, but worth it. She hadn't worked since before the babies came, but had been threatening to go back when they started school. He didn't want to think about that right now; he could worry about that when the time came.

When the Legal Services Investigator pulled into the parking lot, the blue Ford sedan was already in front of the building. He saw only one person in the vehicle, the driver, who appeared to be busy fiddling with the radio.

Bob Freeman had come alone and when he rolled down the window, Charlie called over to him, "Your partner sleeping in this morning?"

Bob seemed in a more serious frame of mind than he had the evening before but smiled as he got out of the car, then stretched and yawned. "No, I had to put him on the early flight to Albuquerque this morning. Something came up." The agent looked like he'd had no more sleep than Charlie.

When the men settled themselves in Charlie's office, the first thing Agent Freeman said was, "I hope you've had time to think about our little talk last evening?"

Charlie didn't change expression. "There really wasn't that much to think about, Bob. Maybe you can give me a clue as to what you're really after." Charlie didn't mean to sound rude, but was fully aware it might come across that way.

The DEA agent nodded. "I understand where you're coming from, Charlie. I spent a good bit of time on the telephone last night explaining that very thing to my boss. He finally agreed to lifting a few restrictions and thought we could let you know more about what we need from you...should you decide to go with it, of course. Your position here at Legal Services had something to do with it—along with your past involvement with the Robert Ashki prosecution. Not to mention a good report from the FBI and Officer Red Clay's input, as well."

Charlie had pretty much figured this was about Tressa Tarango, but still couldn't link Robert Ashki to Luca Tarango's ex-wife. His curiosity was up now, however. "I can't, for the life of me, see what connection the Tarango woman might have with Ashki...or with me for that matter?"

Agent Freeman took a deep breath. "Both of those people have only recently come across our radar. Tressa Tarango has been a 'person of interest' for only a short while, mostly due to her friendship with Abraham Garza Jr. He's the son of a former cartel member in Sinaloa by the same name. We've been tracking "Abraham the Elder," as he's known down there, for several years now. He no longer holds the influence in the organization he once did. Oh, he still knows most of what goes on but he's lost the ear of the powers that be. He's been relegated to the sidelines, almost ignored I guess, and he resents it. So we're focusing on the father by way of the son." The agent paused, took a breath, and continued. "As far as this Robert Ashki goes, he only entered the picture a few days ago; when Fred Smith over at FBI made us aware he was out of prison and thought the man might have it in for you and a few of your friends. As it turns out, Ashki apparently does have an agenda, something we've had to factor in before asking your help. We still don't know his whole story…but we're working on it." The agent stopped to see how Charlie was taking all this, then indicated the investigator now had the floor.

"How do you know so much about Tressa Tarango in so short a time?" Charlie was honestly interested in the mechanics of the agency and was fairly certain the agent had further information regarding Robert Ashki he wasn't willing to divulge.

"We have someone inside, Charlie; he's been embedded I suppose you could say, for quite a while, even before Tressa Tarango was a factor."

"You mean a plant, right there in the restaurant where she works?"

"Well, we don't refer to them as plants but yes, I guess you could say so. You'll understand why we don't say more about him at this point, his job is risky enough as it is."

Charlie nodded. "I hope you don't want me to give up my job and work in a restaurant." Charlie was only half-joking, but the agent saw the humor in it and took it as a sign he was making headway with the Navajo. He was beginning to think the man had more going for him than some thought. He didn't bother to dissuade him of the thought that their informant worked in the restaurant.

It was only after another thirty minutes of animated discussion that Charlie began to feel more comfortable with the agent. Finally he came right out and asked, "What sort of timeline are we talking about, Bob…for my part…*if* I should come on board I mean?" Charlie had no intention of "coming on board," at this point but was beginning to find the proposal interesting and couldn't help a certain curiosity in hearing more about it.

Freeman grew more cautious. "Our investigation has ramped up considerably in the last forty-eight hours. We now think our prime target, the younger Abraham Garza, or Little Abe as he's known, may have been roped into a dangerous plot by this Tarango woman. It complicates things and, quite frankly, it's the reason your help has become so important. We can't stand by and let this guy get by us, Charlie. Not with nearly two years work invested.

And I might mention, several of our people's lives on the line, here, in the states and in Mexico.

Agent Bob Freeman had not played his last card. This Charlie Yazzie might, if nothing else be swayed by dedication to duty. The drug problem was real enough, and from what he'd heard of the man, he was convinced the investigator would help. He was, in fact, fairly certain he had the investigator coming his way.

~~~~~~

After the agent left the office, the Legal Services Investigator watched as early arrivals filed into the building. He'd trained most of them and couldn't help wondering what he might be getting himself into; there was after all, his family to think about. Though Freeman had mentioned he would probably never be in any real danger, Charlie knew that might be a weak promise at best; realistically, the consequences might be far more real than the agent let on. In the end, Charlie Yazzie left the meeting with more information than he could get his head around, and was still having a hard time processing it as he left the office. The DEA man, as a final incentive, had made mention of the burgeoning drug problem right there on the reservation; a problem Charlie was well aware of and already knew a good deal about. Over the last few years just about everyone in law enforcement had come to recognize the trafficking affecting their part of the country originated in Sinaloa State. Charlie had seen its debilitating effect on families in every part and social layer of the *Diné Bikeyah*.

Charlie pulled out of the parking lot with the thought in mind he should swing by Billy Red Clay's office over at Tribal. Billy had mentioned he was working this Saturday morning, as well, and Charlie had the feeling the young officer might know more than he'd originally been willing to say. The more he thought about this the more it bothered him. He'd known Thomas's nephew since he was a kid and had been a big supporter of the young policeman since he joined the force.

When the Dispatch Duty Officer notified Billy Red Clay of his visitor, he had the woman buzz him right in then sat back in his chair with an air of expectancy. He was confident Drug Enforcement would already have talked to Charlie, and was more than a little interested in how that went. When he spoke to the two DEA Agents the day before they were, in his estimation, quite thorough; their recent background checks with the FBI had turned up only favorable reports on Charlie Yazzie despite the few conflicting notations made by the previous Senior Agent. For Billy's part, they were mostly interested in Tribal's personal experience with the investigator—his credibility, and how he dealt with other agencies on the reservation. But they wouldn't say why nor would they divulge their purpose in the inquiry. FBI Agent Fred Smith had already made him aware this would be the case, even before he set the meeting up, but that didn't make their reluctance to share information any easier for the policeman to swallow. In Billy's estimation, transparency among the various law enforcement agencies on the reservation was becoming a hard commodity to come by.

The office door was open and as Charlie walked in the thought crossed his mind that Billy's "office" might well have been a supply closet before Tribal Police repurposed it for the fledgling officer's workspace. There were several people at Tribal who thought the Liaison Officer too young and inexperienced for such a position. Professional jealousy was, as in agencies everywhere, not unknown at Tribal.

Billy motioned for Charlie to take the only other chair in the room nodding his head in such a way Charlie thought it a sign the officer was aware of the reason for his visit. His guess was rewarded when Billy launched the conversation with, "It's pretty much a one-way discussion with those boys, isn't it?"

Charlie smiled and rubbed his forehead—he was feeling a headache coming on and he didn't often get headaches. "I don't suppose you know anything that might be even a little helpful here, do you, Billy?"

"Not me. I'm pretty much out of the loop on this one. Fred Smith said I shouldn't ask, either. Those boys mainly just wanted my personal take on you.

You know, Charlie, your character and all. I also gave you an A plus in deportment, and another one in your dedication to duty. They seemed satisfied enough with that when they left. No one's looking into any malfeasance on your part, Charlie." Billy made the big word sound as though it was a regular part of his vocabulary. He grinned at his one-time mentor. "I don't suppose *you'd* care to let *me* in on what's going on, would you?"

"Can't." Charlie didn't change expression as he said this, just waited to see how his young friend would react.

Billy expected this before he asked and nodded, knowing better than to press him. Charlie didn't tolerate coercion well, not in any form. The policeman had known and respected the investigator, since he'd joined the force. Both his Uncle Thomas, and his first boss, the late Lieutenant Samuel Shorthair, had the highest regard for the Legal Services Investigator, and their view of the man continued to color Billy's perception.

"I hear Tribal can't find the file on the Luca Tarango murders?" Charlie hadn't really meant to bring this up, but decided it was time he and Billy got a few things straight between them. In that regard he wanted Billy to at least know something of what went on in his meeting with FBI the day before. "Fred said you were looking into the matter of the file and he seemed pretty confident you'd come up with it." He looked at Billy, and then away as he could see this was not the case.

Billy, shaking his head, sighed audibly letting his frustration show. "Charlie, we've ransacked this entire building, that file is simply gone. Disappeared. Some of my own reports on the case were in that folder. The last time it was officially checked out was nearly two years ago. That was long after the case was closed. It might have gone missing most any time after that."

"You're saying someone took it?"

"Looks like it. We're still searching, but by now I don't have a whole helluva lot of hope we're going to find it. As you can imagine, the Captain's not happy. We've had files misplaced before—they eventually turned up—but that's not the case this time.

Charlie interrupted, "Your files are kept in a secured area, right?"

"Secured as far as outsiders go, yes, but nearly everyone here has access. Of course, nothing is allowed to leave the building. That's what I'm doing down here this morning, going through personnel files. I don't know what I'm looking for, just hoped something would jump out at me I guess. So far I've got nothing." Billy sat back in his chair. "I'm not saying a file couldn't be switched, which would be the smart way for someone to go about it, I suppose, but apparently someone, somehow, just took this one without regard to consequences. I even thought it might have been taken with the intent to copy it and then return it. I have even considered the possibility it might still be here somewhere. None of it makes any sense to me."

On his way home Charlie ran the thing around in his mind a time or two, but it only became more confusing the longer he mulled it over, *Why would anyone want that file in the first place?* Most of it was originally released to other agencies and some of it was already public knowledge. As he thought back over the events leading up to the death of Luca Tarango he realized there was one thing that hadn't been made public, something few knew, even now: who had actually killed the man. That part of the proceedings had been sealed by court order. That might explain it.

3

The Trap

Tressa Tarango opened the kitchen door just a crack and looked to see if the old *vaquero* had taken his usual seat at the end of the bar.

Sancho Mariano had a small place in the hills just outside town, and drove his ancient pickup to the *cantina* on a regular basis. He would nurse a beer and commiserate with the young Mexican waitress. She was from that area in Sonora he remembered and he considered her, as one would family, because of it. Sometimes, when business was slow, the young woman would spend a few idle moments talking with him, engendering forgotten feelings of his youth.

Tressa liked the old man and later took pains to befriend him. She thought her situation might someday become so desperate as to require outside help, and possibly even refuge should it come to that. Over time she let slip how things were there at Espinosa's, and how sad her situation had become. The old man was so sympathetic and understanding that she couldn't help divulging what brought her to be in such a mess, and other things, too, things probably best kept to herself.

Old Sancho, for his part, seemed genuinely concerned, and after a while Tressa began confiding more and more in the man, who now seemed almost like a father. She went so far as to tell him she planned to leave the Espinosa's, and take her husband's bones back to Mexico for a proper burial in the red dirt of their village. This information seemed to affect old Sancho in some strange manner and he finally admitted he hoped his own remains could be taken back to his old home place in Sonora. He had already made arrangements for it, in fact, and informed his son of those wishes.

Sancho Mariano was not at his usual seat that night, but in his place a tall Mexican hunched over a drink—watching her in the mirror. The discovery made her shiver. There was something vaguely familiar about him but nothing she could quite put a finger on. A long, puckered scar ran down one cheek and his eyelid on that side drooped slightly, injuries she thought most likely the consequence of a knife fight. She came from a country where such scars were not unusual—knives being the most common cause. Tressa Tarango had a good bit of experience in sizing up the sort of men found in bars, men she was now expected to be nice to, even persuading them to buy her the occasional drink or two. This man was not that usual sort. There was something far more sinister, dangerously so, she thought. Tressa hesitated before exchanging glances with the bartender, whose job it was to vet such clientele; a duty the man seemed somehow reluctant to perform this night. The big man behind the bar only shrugged back at her and stayed polishing the glass he was working on. He did, however, move a little farther down the bar to occasionally wipe down the polished surface in front of the stranger, which caused that one to frown and lift his glass each time to avoid the bar rag. It was clear from the sharp-toed boots, and *bracero* style hat that the man was not long out of Mexico.

The barman, not so much concerned for Tressa's welfare, as he was to know this newcomer's game, finally concluded the man would bear watching and studied him more carefully; he noticed the man had hardly touched his drink in over twenty minutes. Only the week before there had been someone else lingering over a drink, looking the place over. It was decided *he* was from a *familia* in their same business; possibly one entrenched nearby and perhaps there to check out the traffic, discover some vulnerability in their operation that might be exploited. There *was* another family, originally from Chihuahua but more recently of Sonora state, which now controlled the bulk of such business in several of the neighboring towns. The Espinosas were ever on their guard to protect their interests, always on the watch for interlopers, and suspicious of any outside interest in their own newly-established territory. Truth be told, they themselves were the interlopers, and that gave them all the more reason to be cautious.

It didn't take the barman long to decide this latest person might be one of the competition's local spies, but if he was he was new and poorly trained for such work. The stranger was tall—knifelike in the manner of a switchblade that might suddenly come un-sprung. In any case, there could be no doubt he was trouble. The barman moved back to his position near the cash register and pressed the hidden button to alert the back office. He would rather be a bother to his cousin, the bouncer, than have *El Escuche* think ill of him should this customer prove to be other than what he pretended. His cousin *had* been somewhat touchy of late and wouldn't like having his dinner interrupted. But that couldn't be helped. That other person, from the week before and nearly certain to be a spy, had wound up in a dumpster at the other edge of town. The morning news reported him lucky to have survived so severe a beating. The man would not say a single word to police as to what brought him to such a poor pass. *No,* the barkeep thought, *it is better to take a scolding should I be wrong, than suffer my own trip across town to a dumpster.*

No more than a minute passed before Tressa, now sitting at a small out of the way table nervously folding napkins and wrapping silverware, saw the bouncer sidle into the room wiping his mouth with the back of his hand, and with a nod from the barkeep, he moved quietly to the side of the outsider. The enforcer leaned close to the stranger and whispered something in his ear. The man slowly turned on his stool to look the bouncer up and down before coming to his feet. He was the taller of the two and clearly capable. Without even speaking, however, he allowed the big man to take him by one arm and direct him outside. The barkeep smiled as he watched the pair leave. This impostor would rue the day he thought himself man enough to spy on their organization. However, as time wore on and still his cousin didn't appear, he became more worried, and after a while longer grew suspicious. He frowned at the door and hoped his cousin hadn't killed the man outright; that was strictly forbidden and might cause more trouble than good. The stranger did not return, but neither did the bouncer. Ten, then twenty minutes passed and the barkeep, not a small man, and certainly one accustomed to seeing to such things himself when necessary, went at last to find what had become of his *primo*.

There was no one outside and the barman, now thinking a bit of caution to be the better part of valor, peered through the darkness lit only by dusty neon signs. He could see no sign of any trouble. Wiping his hands on his apron he moved to the back of the building, staying in a circle of light shining from atop the one lone utility pole. He was alert for any sort of movement and careful not to stray off onto the dark edges of the property. The bartender was inherently more cautious than his cousin whose job this was.

After watching a few minutes he still saw nothing he thought suspicious, but felt increasingly aware of being watched and a chill went to his very bones. Finally with a dismissive shake of his head, he went back inside to his warm, safe place behind the bar only shrugging his shoulders at Tressa as he passed. He turned once, frowned, and looked back at the door. He figured to wait a while longer before reporting the incident. His cousin was a little strange, even as a boy, and was known to take his time about a chore, but in the end most always made a good job of it. Perhaps he had dragged the stranger out to the far edge of the field bordering the river—maybe he had left him out there in the brush. If he had killed the man, surely he had enough sense to throw the body in the river where it would drift downstream and not be associated with their place of business.

It was some time before the bouncer came staggering in the back way, badly beaten, and with a knot the size of a small *tomatillo* on the side of his head. He had regained consciousness, he said, in the field behind the bar and then dragged himself nearly to the kitchen before regaining his feet. He came holding both hands to his middle, covering what later proved to be a shallow stab wound to the stomach. He begged Little Abe not to let word of it reach *El Escuche*. And when the barman was informed of his cousin's condition, he, too, thought they should keep the incident to themselves. It was decided the injuries were not serious enough to require reporting and in truth, thought the man might find himself even worse off should the *patron* think him incapable of handling his duties. He was actually rather a genial sort when not at his trade, and was generally well liked. No one wanted to see such a person come under the unpredictable judgment of *El Escuche*.

It was near closing time before things settled down; the bouncer's wounds being dressed by Little Abe, whose past experience in Sinaloa allowed him to take a workmanlike stab at it. As Tressa helped Abraham clean up the mess, she thought the young man strangely complacent as he recounted the result of the beating the bouncer had suffered. The man himself still wouldn't speak of it—but no matter—the fear in his eyes told them all they needed to know.

Little Abe could feel a darkness shutting in on him. It was starting. Just like in Sinaloa.

~~~~~~~

Tressa helped Abe close down the kitchen, her mind occupied with the ominous events of the evening, she felt for the first time an almost palpable fear and became even more determined to escape her chancy existence, the sooner the better too. Still she did not intend leaving without her just due. She was determined to extract some sort of financial compensation for the Espinosa's many injustices and if things went as planned, Carlos and his Uncle might pay the ultimate price. Later, worn out and with her mind still in turmoil, she made her way to the shabby room at the rear of the building. Passing the partially open door of Hector Espinosa's office, she saw the old man arranging stacks of bills on his desk, ticking off figures on a sheet of paper, obviously pleased with the results.

She thought how easy it would be to slip in and hit him in the head…but no, *this is not the night for it, Saturday night will bring more money.* A small but popular *mariachi* band had been engaged for the next evening—they would draw a good crowd—even though Carlos Espinosa would, as usual, be the featured performer. It would be loud and noisy. *Yes, Saturday night would be best…we can wait a little longer,* she thought.

It was some hours after midnight when a scratching at the window woke her, and Tressa, thinking it was Little Abe, decided to ignore him, confident the twist latch was secured. Perhaps there was no one there at all. She tried putting the noises down to anxiety…or paranoia, but when the sound came yet again, louder this time, she knew there was definitely someone there. She waited, hoping against hope it could be Little Abe and that he might eventually give up and go away. When the sound was heard a third time she had no choice but to leave her bed mostly for fear someone might hear and grow curious. The last thing she needed was some sort of incident when so close to freeing herself of these people. She put on her threadbare robe and clutching the wretched thing together at the throat, felt her way to the window just as the scratching came yet again. A voice, barely above a whisper, reached her and she quickly stood to one side, not daring to look out.

"You and I have things to talk about, *Señora*. I have information for you." The voice was deep and like velvet. She knew instantly who it was though she had never heard the voice in her life.

The next morning, at the small table where the help took their simple breakfast, Tressa looked about to make sure they were truly alone, then leaned across the table to Little Abe as he sat buttering a piece of toast. Since coming north he had become fond of toast and now preferred it in lieu of his usual *tortillas con mantequilla.* He thought the toast made him appear more sophisticated in the eyes of the help—most of whom thought him only putting on airs, laughing at him, but only behind his back. He was, after all, from Sinaloa and those people had a reputation.

Tressa kept her voice low as she beckoned him closer. "Last night a man came to my window, Abraham."

"A man?" Abraham drew back in his chair puffing out his chest in indignation, and then gesturing with his toast, he demanded, "What man? What *man* would come to a woman's window in the middle of the night?" Actually, he could think of several who might do such a thing but feigned outrage nonetheless. He was well aware he had no real hold on this woman and felt it behooved him to appear jealous in order to strengthen whatever tenuous bond they might have forged.

"It was that man from last night, the tall *Mexicano* who did such a beating on Miguel." She sat back and watched this register. Abraham dropped his toast and put a hand to his chin in surprise.

"Really, Tressa? Really?" Now Abe was the one leaning forward. "What did he want?" He said this expecting the worst, and was almost relieved to hear it was only information the man brought her. "What did he say?" and then, as he listened to the answer, immediately regretted asking.

"He didn't say much but told me when the time was right he would be in touch."

Abraham now imagined Tressa was lying, keeping something from him. He narrowed an eye at her but said little else lest he undo what few feelings she might still harbor for him.

4

The Sing

Henry Bill showed up at Lucy Tallwoman's house early the next day after receiving her message. She'd had to call his niece, who lived near enough to the highway to have a phone. Henry's camp was a good distance away—down 491 past Naschitti, then well back into Coyote Canyon on the crossover road to Crownpoint. His niece had to drive him better than a hundred miles to his appointment; all the while doubting he'd actually been chosen to perform so complicated a ceremony as the *Blessing Way*."

Henry was old, himself, nearly as old as Paul T'Sosi, and while he was not as well-known as some *Hataaliis*, he *had* once studied under Paul's Uncle, the inimitable Elmore Shining Horse; this alone caused Lucy to think he might be able to do the healing ceremony just as her father remembered it. Both she and Thomas were acquainted with the "*Blessing Way*" and knew it was sometimes thought to be helpful in cases of mental confusion. Her father's recent malaise of spirit and obviously wandering mind had the entire family worried. He had twice now wandered off, only to be brought back by neighbors. Paul T'Sosi, however, could not, by any form of coercion, be persuaded to visit the new clinic with its white doctors and formidable diagnostic machinery. "Everything in the place is white...it's like walking into a snowstorm." *As though a machine could divine ills of the mind...or spirit.* The old Singer rebuked them each time the clinic was mentioned.

The *Blessing Way* would be a good bit more expensive than the clinic, no matter who performed the ceremony, and that cost would fall directly upon Lucy and Thomas, the last of Paul's known family. Even Thomas's children would be called upon to help supply animals from their small flocks. The old man was the only grandfather they knew, and they would be expected to help, and at the same time be proud to do their part. There were no other relatives to share this cost or work. Not that she and Thomas couldn't afford it; her weavings were growing ever more popular. Distant collectors bought them through the local trader, acting as her agent. He'd sold her mother's work even before hers, and Lucy suspected her own success was due, in part, to her mother's reputation. A few of the more knowledgeable collectors now competed for Lucy's weaving. Some of the larger pieces were being purchased sight unseen even before leaving the loom. She occasionally thought of those pieces. At least one, she knew, was hanging on the wall of a New York penthouse. A patron once sent the trader a picture cut from a home decorating magazine of that early piece and it did not make Lucy Tallwoman happy to see it there. That was part of *her* on that wall—no matter the *ch'iónit't,* woven in to allow her spirit's release— a tiny bit of *her* always remained, and now it was locked up in a New York tower.

~~~~~~~

Old Paul T'Sosi had many friends who would attend a Blessing Way; word would spread like magic to the far reaches of the reservation. The *Blessing Way* was a popular ceremony—one that might improve the *hozo* of anyone attending.

The old Singer was surprised to see Henry Bill show up at the door of his hogan. He could see by his daughter's face what the venerable *Hataalii* was there for, yet manners alone decreed the man be made welcome. While appearing reticent at first, Paul, was secretly pleased to see his old friend regardless of purpose. The two old *Singers* quickly fell into talk of their early days as understudies to Paul's famous uncle. Elmore Shining Horse made his reputation in a time when a Singer was greatly venerated among the people.

Ignoring Henry's niece, and Paul's own daughter, the old men refused to go to the house, settling themselves instead in the more familiar surroundings of Paul's hogan, a structure both felt more conducive to talk of holy things and any *Diyin diné'e* who might be attracted by their singing. When the women left, the pair proceeded to while away the afternoon with talk of the old days and barely touched on Paul's declining health or what was to be done about it.

Henry's niece was content to follow Lucy to the house to help plan the proposed ceremony, including, of course, her uncle's remuneration for so lengthy a cure. A Blessing Way often took nine days depending on what version might be performed. The niece felt her uncle should earn at least enough that she, too, might be paid a little something for helping out. She'd discussed the matter with her uncle on their way in that morning and had a figure in mind she considered reasonable.

"This ceremony will take a lot out of my uncle," she said. "People don't realize how hard it is to get everything just right." The niece intended to make the most of the opportunity. "He's not in the best of health, himself, you know."

"Well, maybe if he cures my father, we could do a trade—hold a curing for him in return...maybe then each of us could break even on the thing." Lucy knew this wasn't what the niece wanted to hear and only threw it out as a bargaining chip to nip in the bud any unreasonable demands. The Navajo are shrewd traders and enjoy the negotiations in such transactions. small though the profits might be.

As it turned out, the prescribed cost *was* reasonable, more so than Lucy would have thought. The feeding of so many people, on the other hand, still required a good deal of additional expense, not to mention considerable work on the part of the hosts. The major food items would consist of lamb and goat from their own flocks; that was what people preferred and expected, the niece agreed. The two women had nearly finished going over the logistics of the lengthy production when faint singing was heard from the *hogan*. The pair smiled at one another knowing things must be progressing as they hoped.

When, finally, the two old men came to the house it was with the news they had come to a decision.

"A full *Blessing Way* will not be needed after all," Henry Bill said. "So, no invitations need be sent, or expensive preparations readied." The two old men were in agreement; it would be best to first try an abbreviated form of the ceremony, perhaps taking only a day—two at the most. Henry Bill intended to concentrate on Paul's particular symptoms and not include everything under the sun.

Lucy knew such shorter chants were becoming more the norm these days, but questioned Henry Bill as to the effect, or lack of it, should they go with the lesser ceremony. The niece, for her part, was skeptical anticipating a much smaller return from the now shortened curing ritual. A request for a full *Blessing Way* did not come around every day and her disappointment in losing this one was obvious. The girl's uncle, however, seemed somehow pleased with the conclusion, and there was no arguing with that.

"Oh, I have talked for a long time to your father," Henry Bill explained, "and we have come to the idea that a shorter cure might work just fine." The two old men nodded in unison. "It's not like he's crazy you know." Henry Bill said this, looking first in Lucy's direction and then verifying it with her father who again nodded, attesting to the truth of the statement. "Paul only needs a little 'adjustment' to his *hozo*. We have studied on it and both of us, being well acquainted with the symptoms, have figured out what might be causing his. We are now together on the way it should be handled." This seemed to conclude his diagnosis and prescription for a cure. He then looked to Paul T'Sosi that he might express his view of the matter.

Paul didn't hesitate, "I agree with my old friend here as to what needs to be done. I, too, think a day or so would be plenty." Obviously, the old Singer was satisfied with the way things had gone, and in fact, already appeared to feel better just knowing the problem was out in the open and addressed in a fashion he could understand. That, in itself, seemed to bring some modicum of relief. Paul paused a moment before going on and directed his next thought to his daughter. "You know I don't want to be a burden to anyone, but it is plain to me you people are not going to be satisfied until I have undergone some sort of treatment, for whatever it is you think is wrong with me. We will try this first and see if there is any improvement. Henry Bill, here, knows what he is doing and will try his damnedest to fix me up." This about summed it up for Paul, and looking toward the kitchen he asked, "Is the coffeepot on?"

~~~~~~

Thomas Begay spent the better part of his day at the Yazzie place in an effort to straighten out some work Charlie had done on the driveway the previous afternoon. Sue called that morning in a dither, asking if he couldn't drop by and run the tractor over the drive again—at least make it passible—before her husband got home and made it any worse.

For days Sue had complained to anyone who would listen that the drive was like a washboard. It was about to shake her teeth loose, she said.

Charlie, apparently tired of hearing it, had stomped out in a huff declaring his intention to fix it once and for all. It was almost too dark to see when he came in and he didn't mention how the job turned out.

Thomas shook his head as he drove up the lane, and saw, at once; the back-blade on the tractor had been angled too sharply, gouging out huge ruts in the graveled track. This would take a while, he thought. He would have to change implements first. This was a job for a box-blade with teeth set as far down as they would go. It would not be a quick operation. Thomas understood this kind of work and unlike Charlie, didn't get in a hurry.

The next few hours were spent putting the road in some semblance of order, and when Thomas finally did quit and turn off the tractor, he was satisfied the surface was at least as good as when Charlie began "smoothing it out a little," as he put it. There were now none of those bone-jarring riffles said to be the original offenders.

As it neared late afternoon Charlie Yazzie turned up the drive and saw Thomas putting the tractor away. He couldn't help noticing the additional progress made on the road.

Thomas met the Tribal unit as it pulled into the yard, and even before the window was half-down, he began to explain. He knew what his friend would be thinking. "I didn't have anything else to do today and thought I'd run by and see if I could borrow your tractor." He indicated the driveway with a push of his chin. "I saw where you'd worked on the road last night, so thought I'd might just as well make a pass or two on it before you got home…maybe save you a little time."

Charlie looked back down the road and nodded, *I must have done better than I thought*. "It didn't take very much did it? I figured it was pretty good when I quit last night."

"Oh, no, I only had to touch it up here and there. Didn't take long at all." Thomas was a poker player and knew how to keep a straight face.

"Well, you know you're welcome to borrow that tractor anytime, you or Harley either one. You boys have pitched in on it, one way or the other, since we got the thing."

Thomas nodded back before saying; "I might pick it up the next day or so. I just wanted to drop by and make sure you wouldn't be needing it." Thomas and Harley didn't have any actual money invested in the tractor but did occasionally do some maintenance on the diesel, and when they did borrow the tractor they always made sure to do some little job around the Yazzie place as well.

Charlie got out of his truck and after eyeing the road again, expressed satisfaction with how it turned out. The two then, naturally enough, gravitated to the horse pen where Charlie pulled down a fresh bale of hay and Thomas put the hose in the tank before turning on the water. As the horses jostled for position at the feeders, the men leaned on the top rail and eyed the two equines. It is something people who live with livestock do. There was even something in the Bible about it, Charlie thought, something about "...it is the master's eye that fatteneth the cattle." He thought that was it. For many years he didn't really understand what it meant.

"Sue tells me you folks are having a curing chant for the old man. So, I'm guessing he's still not any better?"

"No, maybe a little worse, in fact. Lucy just thought she had to do something. It'll be the weekend after next unless something changes. I told her to hold off inviting people till we know for certain." Thomas chuckled, "That old Singer, Henry Bill, from over around Crownpoint will be in charge. I've heard he can be a little gnarly, if you know what I mean? But I expect he'll get plenty of direction from Paul, so maybe it will work out okay." He raised an eyebrow. "If it goes off, there'll be plenty of people there, that's for sure. My uncle Johnny up to Navajo Mountain may be coming down for it."

Charlie smiled. "I'm sure. Sue is already planning what food to bring."

Thomas scuffed the toe of his boot in the dirt. "My nephew tells me you've been talking to some DEA Agents...still not anything you can say about that, huh?"

"You know I can't say anything about privileged information, right?" Charlie shook his head at the ground. "You and Harley don't seem to understand what 'privileged information' is, and your nephew, Billy Red Clay, shouldn't have mentioned anything about it, either." Charlie said these things as one friend to another, and no offense was meant, or taken.

Thomas smiled and shrugged. "Oh, you know how it is out here, Charlie...Billy being clan and all... I just thought you might want to update me a little, that's all."

Charlie sighed and pushed away from the corral, "Did you let John Nez know about Robert Ashki being out...and that I'd heard from Luca Tarango's wife?

"I told him, all right. He'd already heard about Robert Ashki being back, and just like I thought, he didn't seem to give a damn. You know how Uncle John is...he don't worry a whole hell of a lot about anything." Thomas grinned. "I guess it runs in the Salt Clan. He said he'd talk to Ashki the first time he saw him around...if he ever does." Thomas, who had been concentrating on the horses, directed Charlie's gaze to the mare and shook his head. "She *is* a little pissy, isn't she?" Then shrugging his shoulders as though his back might be bothering him, he returned to the talk at hand. "As far as the Mojado's wife goes, John acted like that wasn't worth thinking about either. That's just how he is, Charlie; he deals with stuff when it happens and don't spend time worrying about it till he has to. He probably picked up that way of thinking over in 'Nam."

Charlie looked toward the house as though expecting Sue to be peeking out the window at them, and she was, from behind the curtain. "Well, you were involved in both cases and if something does come up—I mean anything that might pose a problem for you, or the family—I will let you in on it. You can count on that. I don't know much for certain about any of it just yet, but I'll try to keep you posted if I hear."

"Fair enough then." Thomas turned off the water. "We'll be looking forward to seeing you people up at our place...weekend after next...don't forget now." Thomas pointed at the tractor shed "I adjusted that blade a little, something must have gotten out of whack."

Charlie turned and looked at the rear end of the tractor. "It did seem like it was a little hard to control...maybe I should have used that box-blade with the rippers on it."

Thomas shuddered at the thought of his friend directing the rippers, but only nodded that Charlie might be right.

~~~~~~

Charlie Yazzie was a morning person; everyone he knew was a morning person. Not many *Diné* he'd been around stayed up late at night unless they were young and bent on partying. The Yazzie family was generally in bed by nine, he himself generally up at the crack of dawn, with Sue and the kids not far behind. So, he was surprised when he went to put the coffee on the next morning. Looking out the kitchen window he saw DEA Agent Bob Freeman peeking back at him from behind the windshield of the blue "sneaker" unit.

Charlie, bleary-eyed, peered back at the man for a moment before fully registering who he was. *What th...* He stood still, holding the coffee pot under the faucet as water poured over the rim. He shook his head as he poured off a good bit and motioned for the agent to get out and come in. He sat the pot back on the stove and went to open the door. Bob Freeman bounded up the steps seeming fully awake, only his slept-in clothes gave him away; he'd obviously been out there a while.

Charlie, deadpan, waved him through the door as he took down another cup. Following the agent to the table, he indicated a chair with its back to the hallway that led to the bedrooms.

Bob sat himself down and grinning sheepishly up at the investigator, said, "Sorry about the hour Charlie. It seems your Dispatch Office isn't manned all night."

"No, and there's never anyone there on Saturday or Sunday either, Bob." Charlie was attempting a smile as he said this but couldn't quite pull it off, not in any recognizable form. "All our weekend business goes through Tribal's dispatcher. There's seldom anything urgent enough for us to be called out on, though it has happened from time to time."

The coffee began perking behind him and Charlie turned back to the stove and brought down the heat. "I hope this is something really important, Bob. My wife and kids will be up shortly and I'd rather not have to explain you to her."

"I understand that, Charlie, and believe me I won't be making a habit of this. It's just that something's come up and I think you should be aware of it."

Charlie got up and closed the door leading to the bedrooms, then swung past the stove for the coffee. At the table he poured both cups full and started to push the sugar bowl over when the agent waved a finger no. It was the rare Indian who didn't sweeten his coffee and Charlie thought this just another little difference between he and Bob. Charlie fixed his own cup, stirred it, and sat contemplating the man, before smiling, "This better be good, Bob."

"I wish it were good, but the fact is…it's not. Our informant in the Sinaloa operation was badly beaten and stabbed last night up in Colorado."

"Your informant was beaten? I thought you said it wouldn't be dangerous?"

"I said *your* part wouldn't be dangerous, Charlie. You wouldn't be an informant, which can be tricky under the best of circumstances. As I said, this guy isn't an agent, he's an offender; one who racked up federal charges in a previous case—still pending by the way—but serious enough he thought he might be better off turning state's evidence. He wants out now, saying he'd rather face the old charges and go to jail. He'd thought he might be safer in an American prison but has now been convinced otherwise. We're afraid if this guy talks our entire operation could be compromised. A week or so ago one of our local surveillance people was found in a dumpster. He'd taken it upon himself to do a little *inside* reconnaissance...young guy, looking to score points on his own...you know that never ends well. It looks like he's going to be all right eventually, but probably won't ever walk without a limp. Both guys were working for us, but they were independent operatives—neither one aware of the other. Our entire operation might be blown if the informant caves to the Espinosas. That could leave us with no one inside the organization, at least not on this side of the border. It would be like starting over up here."

"Your surveillance guy wound up in a dumpster?" Charlie's interest in working with the agent was fading. "I wouldn't be a surveillance guy, right?" Charlie touched the tip of his tongue to his upper lip and considered, "This might be a good time to tell me exactly what I would be, Bob."

"Don't worry about that. We'll take care of you no matter what. Like I've said before, while your part will be delicate, it shouldn't be dangerous." The agent played with his spoon, twiddling it back and forth between two fingers. "We first need to find who beat and stabbed our guy and then find our informant, who'll most likely have to be set up in a witness protection program. Assuming, of course, he can be found. It's beginning to look like the man may have disappeared entirely...either on the run...or, and I hate to say this, already dead."

"Whoa...that's pretty heavy talk, Bob. I can see what you're up against—what I don't see is how I can be of any help; not from what you've told me so far." Charlie was thinking this was less of an opportunity than he first imagined, and he might be better off opting out while he could.

"We think you *can* help, Charlie. The man who roughed up our informant may be Robert Ashki. Fred Smith, with the FBI, called to advise us the man was out of prison and making some pretty serious threats against you and several others. The description fits and when we checked with the prison warden we found Ashki spent the last few years hanging out with some pretty bad boys. The warden said Ashki became a tough cookie himself—other inmates thought he was crazy and many were actually afraid of him. And that's a pretty desperate crowd down there as I'm sure you know."

"Ashki?" Charlie came upright in his chair. "You have to be wrong, Bob. Robert Ashki was well past forty when he went up...a Tribal Councilman...more or less just a businessman—even though it was mostly crooked business. Oh, he was known to coerce and bully people all right. The man was, for damn sure corrupt to the core, but that's about the extent of it. He threatened people on a regular basis but we have no real proof of physical violence. Don't get me wrong, I wouldn't put anything past him, but this seems a little over the top, even for Ashki." Charlie looked the agent in the eye and shook his head, "He's never had any drug ties either, not that anyone here is aware of. The FBI's file on him doesn't mention anything about drugs and neither does Tribal, and believe me, I've read both files from front to back."

"Did those files say he made some serious threats against Thomas Begay and his son...and Thomas's uncle John Nez, too? Being in the joint, even for only a few years, can change a man in some awfully serious ways, Charlie"

"No, the files I read didn't mention those things. I'm not saying they're not true, but I find some of it pretty hard to believe."

"Well, there you have it, my friend. No one's infallible, God knows my own people fall down often enough."

Charlie turned toward the bedroom and inclined his head, listening, as baby noises filtered down the hall. "Uh-oh, someone's waking up."

Bob Freeman had children of his own and immediately came to his feet, stretched, and nodded to the Legal Services Investigator. "I'll give you a call in about an hour. I'm expecting an update then. We'll go from there." The agent reached out a hand and Charlie shook it, despite the apprehension he might be sealing some sort of implied contract. At the door, the agent half-turned and held up a finger, as though touching the brim of an imaginary hat. Charlie immediately thought this, too, might be some sort of salute, or insider signal, and again wondered if he'd fallen under some secret covenant. But for what, he couldn't envision.

"I thought I heard voices?" Sue stood in her robe peering out the kitchen window as she studied an almost invisible haze of dust lying over the new driveway.

Charlie, obviously lost in thought, leaned back against the open front door. When he finally turned back to the kitchen he sounded distant, yet smiled when he said, "I had the radio on. I turned it off when I heard the baby. That's probably what you heard." He had no reason to lie, but then, he'd heard this was the way these things started, first the paranoia, then the lying. This wasn't who he was, but he couldn't help wondering if it was who he might become should he fall in with these people.

5

The Calling

Tressa Tarango could not have imagined the far-reaching consequences of the bouncer's beating, or its effect on the stateside tentacles of the Espinosa organization. Coming on the heels of the previous week's disturbance—the one ending in the dumpster incident—it didn't take Hector, "The Ear" Espinosa very long at all to be made aware of his enforcer's failure to carry out his duty. The punishment was rumored to be immediate and severe enough to strike fear in the hearts of anyone even remotely associated with the man. Even Little Abe felt the heat of Hector's displeasure; not reporting his rendering first-aid to the bouncer was seen as a lack of loyalty and a direct affront to *El Escuche* himself. It was only through the auspices of his old father, and what friends he had left in Sinaloa, that Abraham escaped even more serious repercussions. His chance of promotion to a better position, however, was now just another broken dream.

Carlos Espinosa was assigned to keep an eye on both the busboy and Tressa; the two of them being lumped together as cohorts, troublesome, and an ongoing problem—a problem not likely to go away on its own. In the back office, permanent remedies were already being discussed.

The barkeep, for his part, was taking evasive action. His cousin's lack of ability in handling his recent assignment was a personal embarrassment. *Cabrón! The man made his living beating up people.* The barman had no proof of other incompetence or transgressions, but his cousin *had* been acting a bit strange since his last courier expedition from Mexico. He'd thought little of it until now but was determined to distance himself from his relative, and as quickly, and completely as possible. Something was certainly not right with the man. The bartender was thinking, as a precautionary measure, he should put out word his cousin might be leaking information. To whom, or about what, he couldn't conjure up, not in any believable way, and was thus forced to abandon that particular strategy. He would never know how close he was to the truth but would soon come to the realization it didn't matter.

Little Abe was certain both his and Tressa's days were numbered, and perhaps her plan to kill the Espinosas, *if she'd ever really had a plan*, should be immediately put into action.

The two of them, sitting in Tressa's miserable little room—made even more depressing by the tone of the conversation—sat staring hopelessly at one another, neither able to contribute a comforting thought. Despite his ongoing attraction to her, Abraham's faith in the woman was faltering

"I'm afraid, Tressa." He couldn't put it more bluntly than that. He could see now that an early grave in Sinaloa was no different than an early grave anywhere else. He eyed the bottle of cheap tequila, already half-empty on the table, and gritted his teeth. "If we are going to do 'em, we better do 'em pretty quick."

Knowing Abe had grown up in this sort of violence, Tressa thought he could be right. A little frightened herself now, she felt she might indeed be losing control of an already tenuous situation, and that could mean the end of both of them. She poured Little Abe a hefty shot from the bottle. She'd already had several herself, and didn't quite trust her ability to handle another, not quite yet anyway. She knew tequila required a certain amount of restraint. She was not, ordinarily, much of a drinker and felt she might already be treading on thin ice. With a slight slur, she admonished Abe in a loud voice, "Be a man, *Hombre!*" She slapped the table. "You need to pull yourself together. *Ese! Ahorita!*" She grabbed his arm. "Thish is no time to falls apart on me Abraham. Tomorrow is Saturday. If we can make it till then, we have a chance to fix them good and maybe have a little traveling money thrown in. You know…if they don' kill us before that."

This was not the self-assured talk Little Abe had come to expect from the woman. He did, however, take some measure of heart from the fact she wasn't giving up completely. He calmed himself, to the extent he was able to ask how they should go about it. "We don' got no gun or nothing…"

"No, Abraham, we don' have a gun, but I don' expect you to kill them with your bare hands either— much as I'd like to see their necks wrung like a couple of *pollos*." Here Tressa leapt from her chair, and flapping her arms, danced a little circle, laughing, fluttering her fingers in the air, and making choking noises, as she jerked her head from side to side.

This was very disconcerting for Abe. Thinking the woman's mind might have snapped he unconsciously drew back from her…*there had been a lot of pressure…* and this is when Little Abe took into account the bottle of tequila, already half-gone when he came in. This epiphany lessened his anxiety to some extent. Tressa was just a little *borracha*. He was feeling the effect of the liquor himself, but for him, the tequila was tempering his fear; replacing it with a growing sense of confidence. Maybe things weren't so bad after all. It was quite obvious now that everything might eventually fall to him…and he was ready. He intended to show this woman how a man handled himself in such a situation, though that man might, himself, be teetering on the brink of disaster.

~~~~~~

Turning the hall corner, Carlos Espinosa had seen the tail of Little Abe's white apron disappearing into Tressa's room. He'd thought all morning the little wetback was acting suspiciously, exchanging guarded glances and worried looks with Tressa. Carlos congratulated himself on his assessment of the situation. Easing up to the door he put an ear close against the peeling paint and held his breath as he listened. His lips twisted in a grim little smile at their conversation. *These two little louses are biting off a big chew—one they will soon choke on if I have any say.*

An hour later, going about his business out front, Carlos still had not reported the plot. It came as a thief of good intentions. *It might not be such a bad thing should his uncle no longer be boss.* If Uncle Hector fell, *he,* Carlos, would be next in line to take over the operation. Surely the big man in Sinaloa would think him the logical choice to take his uncle's place, especially when he delivered up these two murderous little traitors. The trick would be to let his uncle be eliminated first *then,* Carlos could eliminate those two scheming nobodies before *he* should become a victim in their vicious plot. It would require some quick and serious thinking on his part, but given the opportunity, this was the sort of thing he was good at. No one ever seemed to recognize his true capabilities; everyone constantly underestimated him, but that was about to change.

R. Allen Chappell

~~~~~~~

Saturday morning Tressa Tarango's head was pounding like a drum. Little Abe poured her another jolt of coffee—strong black Mexican coffee—with just a hint of cinnamon to quicken the heart. Eventually, she realized the noise was not all in her head—the mariachi band was practicing out back in the shade of the *ramada*. Though it hadn't been easy, Abe had finally taken her bottle away the previous evening and tried desperately to bring the woman to her senses. She did seem better now, but still not her old self by any measure.

From time to time, Abe noticed from the corner of an eye the smug face of Carlos Espinosa, peering at them through the little round window in the kitchen door. The man didn't bother coming into the kitchen to deride or insult them and that in itself was a cautionary sign. Abe was getting a bad feeling from all this. He wished Tressa would at least recover enough to let him know what was to be done. His confidence of the previous evening had evaporated with the alcohol, leaving him once again frightened and feeling dependent. His head was hurting, and he desperately needed some sign she was ready to resume some semblance of leadership.

Tressa, finally able to focus on his face, murmured in a low and ragged voice, "Did Carlos already take Hector's breakfast tray to him, Abe?"

It had long been the nephew's duty to oversee the preparation of his uncle's meals, the man trusted no one else to do it. "Who knows," he would tell Carlos, "what evil might lurk in the minds of these ungrateful peasants?" Usually, the food was delivered to the office with Carlos's own hands, the coffee, laced with the old man's favorite liqueur. Carlos shared the meals with his uncle, as further indication of his willingness to assure the food had not been tampered with.

Abe, glad to hear a sensible question at last, was quick to reply, "Yes, he took the tray a little while ago."

"And did he put a few of those special little *arbol* peppers on the side? You know, the ones from Hector's private jar in the back of the refrigerator?"

"Yes, I believe I saw them." In his mind's eye Abe could almost see the little red peppers jiggling along on the tray.

"Good." She said, almost instantly feeling better, and thought, *everything seems to be the same as usual—nothing seems to have changed.* She gave Abe a little half-smile and said, "It's going to be all right Abraham." And then to herself, *tonight is the night.*

All day long Carlos Espinosa hovered outside the kitchen, taking covert little peeks through the window and smiling to himself.

"You don't think he suspects anything do you Abe?"

"I don' see how he could, Tressa...unless he's a witch, or able to read minds. Old Man Espinosa probably just told him to keep an eye on us, that is all it is."

Promptly at eight o'clock Carlos checked on his two charges before preparing to take his place with the band which would begin around nine, a little later if the crowd was not yet big enough or people were still eating.

It was after midnight when the *mariachis* quit playing, were paid, and packed up their instruments. They would pick up their sound equipment and the oversize marimba the next morning. By two a.m. the last of the customers had dwindled to two or three past-their-limit drunks who were escorted out and the doors locked behind them.

Little Abe was taking his last load of glasses back to the kitchen when he saw Carlos at a back table sorting money into bags, one from the restaurant, one from the bar, and the last containing the cover charge among other things—only a little of which he paid to the band when he finally settled up. It was the establishment's biggest night ever. The old man would be pleased Carlos thought, giving Abraham a sly grin as he passed with the money bags in one arm and his and his uncle's late-night dinner tray held above his head.

Little Abe pretended not to notice but back in the kitchen he told Tressa about the money and said,

"You were right to wait till now, Tressa. There is a lot of money tonight."

She looked nervous but smiled, "I toll' you so Abe. Tonight's our night. Here's how we're gonna do it..."

6

Underworld

It wasn't *even* an hour before the DEA Agent called Charlie back. The Legal Services Investigator hardly got "Hello" out of his mouth before the agent began talking.

"I'll try to make this quick…we have a lot going on right now." He forged ahead without waiting for Charlie to reply. "First off, you were right about Robert Ashki—it wasn't him who roughed up our guy in Colorado." The Agent stopped to take a breath and Charlie jumped in before he could continue.

"When did this change, Bob? You seemed pretty sure it was him an hour ago?"

"Well, now, I'm sure it's not. Robert Ashki's been dead for two days—car wreck. It seems he borrowed a clan-brother's pickup and was on his way to Albuquerque when he went off the road just out of Cuba." The agent paused a moment to let this sink in.

Charlie took a deep breath and held it, trying to get a grip on what he was hearing. "He's dead? That's all you know, Bob? Why didn't it show up on the wire yesterday? I talked to Fred Smith before I left work on Friday, and *he* didn't say anything about it either."

"He didn't know, Charlie. No one knew it was Robert Ashki; he wasn't carrying any ID. Probably hadn't had time to renew his driver's license after getting out. New Mexico State Patrol assumed from the truck registration that it was this *clan* brother who was driving. They only found out it was Robert Ashki, this morning when they were finally able to get in touch with his brother's wife, who lives up at Navajo Mountain. The guy is pretty hard to get ahold of, I guess. Anyway, the State Patrol is waiting on Forensics. We haven't heard anything back from the Coroner's Office in Albuquerque, either." Bob paused, and Charlie could hear the rustle of papers. "The investigating officer didn't seem to think the truck's damage was all that bad, at least not bad enough to kill the guy, but you know how that goes, sometimes it doesn't take much to kill a man. They estimated he was doing a little more than the speed limit, which is sixty-five on that stretch; the truck was coming down onto the flats when it happened...not much in the way of skid marks either. Apparently Ashki didn't see it coming. That's according to the State Patrolman I talked to, we may know more later on today. I'll keep you posted but I expect the FBI will be all over it by then."

"Well, I'll just be damned," Charlie couldn't believe it. "Who'd a thought Robert Ashki would go out like this."

"Oh, and one other thing, Charlie. Tribal's missing file folder...they found it behind the truck seat. Apparently, it was behind some sort of panel, or more likely it was hidden there. It looked like someone may have searched the truck after the accident, but it was dark and they missed it. I figured you'd want to know." The connection faded but Bob's last statement was clear enough. "I'm guessing there are people relieved to hear Ashki's dead." He paused before going on, "Maybe you'd know someone with a reason to take him out?"

Charlie couldn't deny Ashki's death might make more than one person happy. "There's several people who'd fall into that second category Bob, you'd be surprised how many. There are, for sure, some who will sleep better tonight knowing he's gone." Privately, Charlie was thinking that would be about everyone involved in the Ashki case, including his co-conspirators. "There will be few tears shed over Robert Ashki's death."

"That's about how we had it figured, Charlie." The agent sounded serious when he added, "Having too many suspects almost makes an investigation tougher than having too few."

Charlie waited for the agent to comment further and when he didn't, thought he might as well bring up another question. "So, Bob, does this mean you won't be needing me on this one?" Charlie sounded almost disappointed, even to himself, and he hurried to correct that impression, "What I mean to say is, Bob...it's not a problem...not a problem at all."

On the other end Agent Freeman smiled, it wasn't the first time a reluctant recruit was finally convinced to help them, only to be disappointed when he found he might not be needed after all. It happened more often than one might think, especially with people leading less than exciting lives. Bob Freeman being unaware Charlie was not one of those people, continued, "I'll let you know when I hear something further. I'll see that Fred Smith is briefed as well, but he's probably been notified—the ball has most likely fallen into his court by now." The agent didn't hesitate to clarify his position. "Charlie, I'm not saying we won't still need you at some point." The agent wanted that door left open. "We would, of course, welcome your input on what's going on up there." The agent then closed the conversation with, "By the way Charlie, none of this is restricted information; the State Patrol released most of it to Albuquerque media sources hours ago. It'll be all over the news up there tonight...Ashki being who he was."

Charlie barely hung up the phone, when it rang again. *This might be Sue calling from town*...was

99

what he thought, but it wasn't his wife. It was Thomas Begay, and the investigator could instantly tell from his friend's tone the news wasn't going to be good.

"The old man's come up missing, Charlie, we can't find him…pretty much looked everywhere, and nothing." There was more concern in Thomas's voice than Charlie had heard in a long while; Thomas was not ordinarily one to show his feelings.

"He's not out with the sheep, is he?" It was a silly question and Charlie immediately regretted asking it.

"No, Charlie, the kids have the sheep today. Paul left sometime after they did. We noticed pretty quick when he didn't come in for his morning coffee, but we didn't think it was a big deal until he still hadn't shown up an hour later." The emotion came through as Thomas found it necessary to clear his throat before going on. "I have to admit it's starting to worry me. This isn't the first time he's taken off like this—without letting anyone know where he's going—but never for this length of time. We checked with the neighbors and none of them have seen hide nor hair of him."

Charlie, unable to come up with anything he thought helpful could only offer, "Well at least we can rule out Robert Ashki being in the mix. I just got a call from the DEA in Albuquerque that Ashki's body was found in a wrecked truck south of Cuba.

I'm still waiting to hear what actually happened down there."

Now it was Thomas Begay's turn to be surprised. "Robert Ashki... Dead? When was that? My Uncle Johnny's wife, Marissa, called just last night from their chapter house. When I asked about Ashki, she said, John ran into Robert's brother a day or so ago. The brother told him Robert caught a ride up there a few days ago, and borrowed his truck. He said Robert told him he had to make a trip to Albuquerque to look into some legal business. Something to do with a lawsuit he was pursuing. His brother couldn't seem to remember what it was all about."

"Well, your Uncle John will probably hear about Ashki pretty quick; it's supposed to be all over the state and local news by noon." Charlie couldn't imagine living so far out you had to drive most of an hour, back and forth, just to make a phone call, a transistor radio the only dependable source of news from the outside world.

Thomas didn't say anything for a while and Charlie waited, letting him think it through. Thomas's mind sometimes ground to a halt when trying to think about two things at once.

Finally it occurred to Charlie to ask, "Have you thought about getting Harley Ponyboy over there to see if he can get a lead on what direction Paul may have taken?"

"I thought about it but decided not just yet. Paul may have just walked down to the highway and hitched a ride into town. You know how he is, he don't want to be a bother to no one. He can't drive himself anymore—says his eyes aren't good enough even in the daytime."

"Well, I'll call Sue and let her know he's gone missing. She has the kids in town today for a birthday party. I'll have her keep an eye out for him. Shiprock's not so big he can avoid her for long if he's there—she'll be seeing a lot of people today and I expect someone will know something." He chuckled, "These days it seems like Sue knows just about everyone in town."

Thomas laughed, too, "Between her and Lucy I bet they do know everyone."

Charlie thought a moment before asking, "Have you already called your nephew? Billy might be able to come up with something."

"I did call Billy a while ago, when I couldn't get you on the phone; he said he'd have Officer Sosi watch for him on the highway coming into town. Hastiin has that stretch on his patrol route today and will keep his eyes peeled."

"I'm sure Billy will be poking around, too; he likes Paul. That old man will turn up soon, I'd bet on it."

7

The Fuse

Tressa snapped her fingers in front of Abe's nose. "Are you listening to me, *Burro*?" Her alcoholic indulgence of the night before had left her short-fused, and should Abe's lack of attention be any indicator, with somewhat less authority than she'd previously enjoyed. She was afraid Abe might have been doing some thinking on his own and that was not good...not good at all. Little Abe was better at *doing*, than he was thinking, and though not slow-witted, or without talent, he still was at his best when supervised. "Everything has been arranged, Abraham." Tressa spoke in a low but forceful voice, hoping to make plain her recovered powers. Abraham, hearing the harshness in her words, paid more attention and finally decided Tressa was indeed back.

Little Abe listened carefully now as she outlined what was required of him. He thought it surprisingly little considering the scope of the proposed venture. Apparently, he would not have to do any actual killing now—she would see that Carlos and Hector were taken care of—but *he* would have a critical role in what came after. This suited Little Abe just fine, he was still somewhat leery of doing a killing in a country flaunting the death penalty. Not that he was incapable of such a thing should it become necessary, he was pretty sure he could do it if it came right down to it.

Still, Abe had to admit, even *he* had his limits. He'd heard it said the prisons in this country were downright pleasant when compared to their Mexican counterparts—death penalty excepted. Some of those condemned, might well have been found innocent, had they the advantage of modern investigative techniques. Without them, however, a few poor souls were executed only to be cleared posthumously. It was, from what he'd heard, a particular problem in regard to minorities.

In any case, it was what it was. He had always deemed it part of the risk a person took when he allowed himself to be caught in the first place. He'd tried not to think any further than that. Now, he had a different view of things, as his old father in Sinaloa liked to put it, "It depends whose head is on the block."

Tressa was adamant, "It's all very simple, Abraham, and I have already set the wheels in motion. When Carlos and the old man have their supper tonight those little chilies they are so fond of will be loaded with something that will knock them out. It takes a while, but it should work. They won't give us any trouble."

"Knock them out?" *This was not the plan! The plan was to kill them, prevent retaliation, and satisfy Tressa's lust for revenge.*

"Yes, Abe, we are going to take them with us— make it look like a robbery and kidnapping. Smart. No? There will be nothing left behind to make things more difficult."

"Take them with us?" *No, this was not the plan...it was nowhere near the plan.* This was something entirely different and Little Abe had a good idea where it came from. That man who came to Tressa's window...he was the one who put this in her head.

She looked askance at the young man and lowered one eyelid as she smiled. "You can drive a pickup, can't you Abraham?"

Little Abe drew himself to his full height and put on his most disdainful face. "Well, of course, I can drive a pickup, Tressa. Do you think everyone in Sinaloa still rides around on donkeys?"

Tressa smiled her show of confidence. "Of course not, Abraham, it's just that getting out of here without attracting attention will be very important. The driving rules are a little different from Mexico. It's not like we can bribe our way out of trouble with a little *mordida* here and there." All the while, Tressa was thinking, *No, everything must go exactly right if this new plan is to work, and you, Little Abe, had better be able to carry out your part."*

Little Abe was somewhat taken aback as Tressa endeavored to explain the new plan in detail. *If there were to be no killings, how risky can this be?* Despite his growing doubts Abe thought it a bit early to consider jumping ship, which could prove even more dangerous.

When the two of them crept down the hall to the old man's office, each with a little satchel containing their few belongings, Tressa stood aside as Little Abe grasped the knob and opened the door just a crack. Peering in from this limited vantage he could make out very little in the light of the small desk lamp. One thing he could see quite clearly, however, were the bags of money sitting in the middle of the desk. Giving Tressa a confused look, he beckoned her closer and opened the door a bit wider for her to see. Abe stood looking in bewilderment at the empty office, Tressa, on the other hand, didn't seem entirely surprised. Inching into the room, the pair still could see no sign of Carlos or old Hector Espinosa, but the side door to the office was ajar and standing in the dim opening was the tall Mexican who had visited Tressa in the night. The two of them stood stock-still, leaving only the stranger undaunted. Silently, the man pointed to the tied and silent forms of Carlos and Hector Espinosa lying at his feet. He motioned for Little Abe to come help him with the squirming bundles.

Abraham immediately looked to Tressa, but she, after exchanging a quick glance with the stranger, motioned Abe forward.

So far not one word had been spoken and even as the two men dragged Carlos Espinosa from the room, the only sound was of Tressa hurrying to the desk to gather up the moneybags, which she stuffed in her satchel. Then already turned to the door, she stopped and hesitated for just a split second, before returning to the desk. Everyone knew Hector kept a pistol there. He would often leave the top drawer partially open, the weapon in plain view. When someone was called to his office he wanted it known he meant business, and that he wouldn't hesitate to take action should it be required. Tressa quickly removed the automatic pistol, and tucking it in her waistband, smoothed the apron over it.

In the parking area behind the office, Tressa watched as the stranger and Little Abe loaded the two trussed-up forms into the camper of Hector's pickup, spreading a tarp over and around them as an added precaution. Only then did the tall *Mexicano* look her way and nod as she moved to the door he held for her.

Little Abe, now on the passenger side of the truck opened his own door and got in thinking he had been right all along; Tressa had more to do with the intruder than she let on. Obviously the two had put their heads together on this. But who was this man and why was he helping them in so dangerous an undertaking? That was the question. Abe was even more puzzled that the man had, apparently, even left *them* the money.

The first thing Tressa said, as she settled herself between the two men in the front seat, was, "Abraham, this is Chuy Mariano, old Sancho's son...he is here to help us." She knew this wouldn't clear things up for Little Abe but felt it quite enough for the present.

Abraham, leaning forward a bit that he might see past Tressa, acknowledged the man with a cautious lift of his chin and couldn't help thinking, *Chuy? Why does there always have to be a "Chuy?"* The driver didn't acknowledge him, or offer the courtesy of looking his way, concentrating instead on the deserted back road. It was now three in the morning and with just a few hours until daylight, Little Abe was growing anxious. His hand strayed to the door handle as he considered jumping each time they slowed for a corner. Even to Abe, who had a certain amount of experience with such goings on, the entire thing seemed surreal. The thought flashed through his mind, he might be trapped in a bad dream—a nightmare. Whatever it was, it wasn't going away and was headed downhill fast. At this point he could only hope for a quick and painless end. At last, getting a grip on himself, he turned to Tressa and whispered in her ear, "I thought you said I could drive?"

Tressa, like Chuy, kept her eyes on the road and didn't answer right away, but when she did it was so harshly put as to offer little consolation. "You'll get to drive, Abraham, don't you worry about that," and then after a moment and even more sharply, "You'll soon have all the driving you can handle."

The truck swerved onto an isolated gravel road running south out of town and in only a few minutes the driver grunted to himself, doused the headlights, and leaving only the parking lights to guide them, turned abruptly onto a dirt road. Tressa caught her breath as she grabbed for the dash. Obviously, Chuy was familiar with where he was going and proved it by twisting his way through a small grove of cottonwoods hiding a ramshackle little clapboard house. The only sign of habitation was a tired old Ford pickup, sitting as though abandoned, in the front yard. Abe thought he caught a fleeting glint of another vehicle hidden behind the house. Chuy turned off the parking lights before shutting down the engine; the silence, cloaked as it was in near total darkness, was suffocating.

No one dared speak as the door swung open and old Sancho Mariano, nearly indiscernible in the light of a small lantern, studied them from behind a double barrel shotgun. Nearly a minute passed before the old man, apparently satisfied, moved the light in a prearranged signal. Only then did his son open the truck door and step out.

"*Hola Papá*," Chuy called softly on his way to the porch, then, still glancing back at the truck, walked slowly up to his father and with hat in hand spoke privately with the old man.

Tressa watched from the comparative safety of her seat and didn't move to get out. Little Abe, one hand already on the door handle, took this as a sign, and he, too, was reluctant to open his door. He was thinking it might be better to wait for some signal from Tressa. She might be only second in command now, but still, she knew more than he did.

After a while, old Sancho, raising the lantern higher, beckoned from the porch, but indicated with one finger that only Tressa was to come forward. She immediately got out of the truck telling Little Abe to stay put, then picked her way through the darkness wearing a strained smile.

The old man handed his shotgun and lantern to his son and met the woman with a fatherly hug, saying, "Ahh...*Mija* what you have endured these last months. It's beyond me how you got through it all...but here you are still alive and on your way back home." His smile turned to a look of dismay and caught her off guard, "I heard only yesterday you were in line for a most unpleasant time with those people and thought I should send Chuy right away to see what could be done. We've had plans for the Espinosas for some time and figured we might as well join forces." He looked past her to the truck. "We will do everything we can for you...along with your little friend, *también.*"

Tressa could only sob on the old man's shoulder as she mumbled a blessing for his compassion and understanding. "But for you, *Señor,* I should already be dead or a murderess or worse."

Little Abe, listening at the truck's open window, wondered to himself how one could possibly be worse than dead or a murderess, but knew if there were a way, Tressa would know about it.

In the dim glow of the lantern the three now looked toward the truck and lowered their voices, forcing Little Abe to strain his ears, yet try as he might, he could no longer make any sense of what they were saying. In another few minutes he saw Tressa being handed some small something, and watched as she gave the old man a final embrace. With only a wave for Chuy, the woman made her way back to the truck.

"Bring our things, Abraham; we are going in the other truck." She waved a hand at Sancho Mariano's disreputable old pickup. "He says no one will be looking for it, and in a few hours Hector's truck will be on every lawman's list."

Abe looked back over his shoulder and attempted to see through the camper shell's sliding glass. "What about these two *pendejos* in the camper?" He said this with a twist of his chin to indicate their two captives. "I can't see them very well, *pero* I think one of them is making a little squeak…or something…"

"Never mind about them, Abraham. I'm guessing they'll soon be making a big squeak. Chuy

111

and his father have something special in mind for those two—something far beyond what I was considering." She threw a glance at the porch and then indicated with a thumb that Abe should get moving. "I'll tell you all about it on the way."

Little Abe was speechless that anyone might contrive a more horrific end for the Espinosas than those so often described by Tressa. It would have to be something well beyond his personal experience, and being from Sinaloa, his experience was nothing to be sneezed at. He gathered their satchels and followed her to the other truck. He soon realized he had seen this old Ford parked outside Espinosa's bar, where it often drew laughter from the kitchen help, a few declaring even *they* would never be seen in such a wreck. Little Abe could not help having reservations. As far as he was concerned this pickup truck—as a getaway vehicle—posed serious problems.

He and Tressa stood on opposite sides of the truck, peering cautiously through the cab at each other. He knew Tressa was looking back at him in the darkness but was unable to tell by her face what she might be thinking. Abe opened the door and stowed their bags behind the seat, settling himself under the wheel. "I don' know, Tressa, maybe we would be better off taking Hector's truck...you know, just take a chance we won't be stopped by the *policia*. That other truck is only five or six years old and runs pretty good as far as I could tell. This old *cabron* is older than me…maybe a lot older than me."

"Just start the truck, Abraham. The old man said we would be better off with it. He said he wouldn't mind having it back someday if we make it to Mexico…that has to say something for it I think. *"*

"Ah, *si*, what he may be saying is we'll be lucky to make it to Mexico in such as this." Abraham sighed heavily, shook his head, and put the key in the ignition. When the truck rumbled to life, a strange little smile crossed his face. "This is not your regular old *abuelo's* truck, is it Tressa? He listened a moment to the powerful eight-cylinder engine burbling under the hood. "No, Tressa, this truck has been messed with I think." He put the four-speed in gear and as he flicked on the parking lights the dash lit up to reveal instruments he'd seen only in car magazines. He tapped the accelerator a few times and listened as the engine snorted, then snarled. Little Abe grinned over at Tressa, "With a little luck, we might make it after all."

The woman leaned over and patted him on the shoulder. "I'm glad you like it, Abraham. Try not to wreck it—Chuy said he would kill you if you did."

Abraham turned with a grim little smile, "Well, he will have to catch me first, and that's not likely with this truck."

It took a few minutes for Little Abe to work his way back through the cottonwood trees, but once out on the main road he headed south. Both he and

Tressa felt a wave of relief wash over them, but for Abraham, it didn't last long.

8

The Plant

Charlie Yazzie looked up from his desk to see the new receptionist wending her way back to his office. He frowned as the girl tapped at the windowed door. "Come on in," he called. *Gwen, her name is Gwen*...he reminded himself, and watched her fumble with the knob as she juggled a handful of papers.

"Sorry Mr. Yazzie, the intercom's out again. And the phones won't transfer either. This new system is crap."

Charlie shook his head and nodded. He remembered now, she was a Bitter Water Clan girl, some distant clan relation of Harley Ponyboy, or so he claimed. Her mother had been office manager when Charlie first applied for the job at Legal Services. He was right out of university then and thought he knew everything. It had taken a while to be disabused of that notion. It seemed like a long time ago now...and it was.

"A couple of these messages were on the recorder and looked like they might be important."

Gwen shuffled through the weekend stack and put several on his desk. "The repair guy is on his way from Farmington to fix the phone system." She stood there as though waiting for some hint she had done the right thing by taking charge all on her own.

Charlie tilted his head. "That's good. Gwen, it sounds like you have everything under control this morning. Thanks."

The girl smiled imperceptibly as she backed through the door. She was still smiling as she went about distributing the rest of the messages. Charlie had made her day.

One message was from the phone company's systems support people and he pushed it aside. The second said simply:

8:00 a.m.

"I am on my way to pick up my husband and his belongings. I will be there sometime this afternoon. I'll call. "

Tressa Tarango

Charlie had to read the note twice before it hit him, and when it did he felt a rush of feelings he couldn't have anticipated. His mind was still filled with it when he picked up the third and last message. He unfolded the paper and began reading Gwen's neat script, he already had the feeling it might be a game changer.

8:35 a.m.

Things are heating up...too much happening to leave on the machine. Your phone's not picking up. I'll try to catch you at your office at nine this morning. Bob

Charlie looked at the clock, *ten till nine—Bob Freeman wouldn't be late.* He swiveled his chair to look out the window. *This could get interesting...*

The sky was darkening toward Pastora Peak and though he couldn't see the mountain from here, he knew that was where the low-pressure system would be forming up for an end run toward *Teec Nos Pos.* The low bank of clouds would already be over *Tsaili.* The many ruins under the rim of *Canyon de Chelly* would be dreary and cold, but no rain would find them there. People would be keeping their sheep home this morning until they figured out what the weather would do. Feed was expensive this year and those sheep might well miss their breakfast.

...Unusual direction for a storm this time of year... Charlie was still thinking of sheep when he saw Bob's sedan pull into the back lot below his window. He watched as the DEA Agent opened his car door, studied the parking lot as though he might be on the lookout for someone, and then glanced up at Charlie's office window before heading for the back entrance. Bob wasn't wearing a hat and as the wind gusted around the building his hair caught up in

it, and for just an instant, in spite of the suit, he looked like a wild man.

Charlie was smiling as he turned back toward the reception area. The phone guy was already busy at Gwen's desk but looking a little puzzled as he listened to the receptionist explain her theory of what was wrong with the system. The Tribal Investigator watched as the two silently pantomimed their conversation. The repairman, frowning, nodding in all the appropriate places, shrugged finally and dug into his bag of instruments and tools.

Agent Freeman happened to approach Gwen from her blind side and the girl jumped a little as he tapped her on the shoulder. Charlie was still grinning as he met the agent at the door and shook hands before pulling the door shut behind them. The investigator pushed a seat closer to his desk then picked his way around to settle in his own chair. He reached down and unplugged the intercom, just as he'd seen Fred Smith do in the FBI office. He thought this a security measure he might do well to emulate. Who knew when the apparatus might suddenly turn itself on?

Neither man spoke for a moment. Bob opened a leather portfolio to remove a sheaf of papers, which he spread on the desk in front of him. He looked up at the Tribal Investigator, and cut right to the chase. "They fingered our guy up at Espinosas' in Colorado." The agent's voice remained calm, as though to minimize the gravity of what was to come.

Apparently the DEA doesn't spend much time crying over informants in trouble. The thought occurred to Charlie along with the unsettling revelation it could be a forewarning of what *he* might expect in a similar situation.

Bob answered before Charlie even asked the question. "Oh, he finally turned up this morning. Left for dead in a storage shed behind Hector's bar. A passing stray dog jumped the fence and was digging and barking at the door. That's what attracted our agents when they went to question employees." There was a hint of sympathy when he said, "Our guy had taken quite a beating. He's a big tough bastard though, and it looks like he's going to come through it all right." He pulled out a photo of the former enforcer taken just as he was found. Charlie glanced sideways at the picture and winced.

"He told our people he was nearly certain Tressa Tarango and Abraham Garza were on the Espinosas' hit list and might well be dead already. We still haven't been able to find what's become of them. Hector and his nephew, Carlos, as of this morning, are on the list of missing persons as well. The bouncer's cousin, a bartender there at the restaurant, told us he hadn't seen the Espinosas since late Saturday night, just before closing. He thought Abraham Garza and the Tarango woman must have disappeared about the same time. So far, there's still no trace of any of them."

Charlie could only imagine what effect this was having on the carefully laid plans of the DEA. He shook his head, offering a look he hoped might convey some understanding of what was at stake. The agent nodded and went on. "We don't know if the Espinosas have abducted Garza and Tarango…or if they made a run for it, in which case Hector and Carlos may be out tracking them down. None of the other employees would say anything…too scared." The agent almost smiled. "On the bright side, with a little help from his cousin, we do think we can flip the bartender. The man knows a lot about the operation and is already looking for a hole to hide in. Maybe we can turn him or maybe not, we'll see. Either way, when our guy is out of the hospital he'll be in witness protection. He might be there a long time before we get this case back together." Bob fidgeted in his chair thinking he might have overstepped in divulging even this much.

"What's your main objective here, Bob?" Charlie wasn't sure what the DEA was most interested in— Hector Espinosa or…

"Abraham Garza's our main concern. If we lose him, we lose any leverage we might have with his old man. Everything hinges on Abraham Senior coming around. He's one of the few weak links we've been able to come up with down there." Agent Freeman had made inferences to this probability in previous talks, but the investigator now had, for the first time, a better picture of what the DEA was up against.

The agent pushed back in his chair and rubbed his jaw with the knuckles of one hand; he hadn't shaved in several days and, to Charlie's mind, was actually beginning to look more like a DEA Agent was supposed to.

Charlie could see Freeman might make a good undercover guy—should he let his hair grow and lose the suit.

Bob ran his fingers through his thinning hair and grinned, "Right now, word out of Sinaloa is the Espinosa family has a recovery team on the way to Colorado—specialists, supposedly some of the best in the business or at least in Mexico."

"Recovery team for what?" Charlie was thinking this might mean it was all over for Tressa Tarango.

"Money, Drugs, even people. Who knows? Hector Espinosa was known to stockpile large quantities of product, and most likely reserves of cash as well. It will be critical for the Sinaloa people to locate their missing relatives and either bring them in…. or in the case of Abraham and Tressa…take them out."

Charlie narrowed an eye. "What's your chances of beating them to it, Bob?"

"We're working on that. Hector's home is under surveillance as we speak. He has a couple of wooded acres outside of town and a huge new home, plenty of room to hide stuff. Some of those caches we'd probably never find on our own. I imagine the

Sinaloa people will have a pretty good idea where to look and when they do, we'll be ready for them."

"It looks like all the action will be up there now, I suppose there won't be much I can do down here?"

"Well, Charlie, probably not, and I'm sorry it worked out this way. I was looking forward to working with you. But, in fact, I'm heading back up to Colorado this afternoon myself. I would like, at the very least, to salvage *something* out of the situation."

Charlie, on the spur of the moment, and not really knowing why, decided not to mention the note from Tressa Tarango, even though it was lying in front of him under the agent's own message. Instead he put on a face to match the agent's. "Bob, I'm sure working with you fellows would have been an interesting experience." Charlie rose from his chair and moved around the end of the desk, to hold out a hand. "Who knows ... maybe there'll be a next time?"

"I hope so Charlie, I do." And as the agent stood, they shook hands. Charlie couldn't help feeling doubtful of his further chances of collusion between the agencies, at least not with the way things stood now. Still, he wanted to leave that option open. He could see it was a tricky business and an unpredictable one. Given what he had learned earlier, Charlie felt something might still be possible, if not inevitable.

The Legal Services Investigator stood at the window watching as the Federal Agent opened his car door, removed his jacket, and then shrugged as though suddenly aware someone might be watching. When he turned to look up, Charlie raised a hand, and though he couldn't be sure, thought he saw the agent smile in return. It was a strange organization, the DEA, but one that seemed to know its business, and from what he'd heard, was still the front line in the war against drugs coming in from Mexico. He couldn't shake the idea of working with them but next time, if it happened, it would be on his own terms.

9

The Chase

Little Abe was clearly in his element. He played the old truck like a baby grand—one with a supercharged V-8 under the hood. Approaching turns he geared down then accelerated through the bend before ripping into the straightaways, foot to the floor. Occasionally the old truck fishtailed, tires squealing out of the skid. The suspension was state of the art as was the rest of the chassis, leaving only the vehicle's disreputable appearance to conceal the true nature of the beast.

The sun was just breaking the long grey line of the horizon when it occurred to him to ask without turning, "Who is that old man and his son back there. That Sancho Mariano?"

Tressa had been dreaming of Mexico and the *Dia de los Muertos*, she, decked out in costume and painted face, proudly bringing the remains of the village's most notorious son to its final resting place. She turned, slowly, from the dream and smiled in that way she often did when she meant for Little Abe to feel foolish. "Well, he's not just some old *Vaquero* out of lower Sonora. I can tell you that, Abraham. He's someone who knows how to keep his life hidden from prying eyes." She couldn't keep a sneer from her lips as she went on. "Not like that *ingrato* Carlos Espinosa, or his evil Uncle Hector—both of whom may already be paying the price of their wickedness." She smiled more broadly at the thought and then looked slyly over at Abraham. "Who do *you* think that old man is, Abraham?"

Little Abe took a deep breath and slowly exhaled shaking his head in resignation. "If I knew who he was, Tressa...I wouldn't be asking you." He grew testy, knowing he was once again being played. She was making him part of that little game she enjoyed. He gritted his teeth, determined to give her the least possible amount of satisfaction. Sometimes he indulged the woman...but not today. Things were going too well, and for the first time in a long while he felt he actually had a chance at life. He wasn't going to let her spoil it...not this time... but in only a moment he had relented, as he was often prone to do. Before he could again ask the question, Tressa's expression went from taunting to one suggesting a measure of excitement he'd never seen before. Little Abe could almost see her changing her mind. She turned, and slowly emphasized each word with the shake of a finger, as though speaking to a child. "He and his older brother are the head of the Sonora

Family, you silly goose. Did you think I would let some old cowboy be in charge of our lives? Why do you think Chuy let us keep all the money from the restaurant last night? That little bit of money don't mean nothing to them. They wouldn't dirty their hands with it, Abraham. No Señor, they are men of purpose, and might very soon control everything Hector Espinosa has built in that town. You are lucky he didn't keep you there with him, *Hombrecito*. Old Sancho knows who you are, and who your father is too. But, he is too smart to kill you just now—he said he is saving you, but he didn't say for what." Tressa fell silent for just a moment and when she finally spoke again her voice came softer and she leaned his way to whisper, "I had to beg to take you with me, *Amigo*. I told him I needed *you* to help take my Luca's bones back to our village." She gave a little sniffle. "I promised I would keep watch on you till we got to Mexico. Once we cross the border, we'll be in Sonora State. Sancho Mariano's other son lives just across the *frontera* and he will keep a finger on you from there. Sonora State is where we'll have to worry Abraham. If Chuy wasn't occupied with Hector and Carlos, *he* would have come with me, and you would have wound up with the Espinosas—and trust me—you don't want what's going to happen to them.

Little Abe's eyes grew wide, not so much with fear, but rather on hearing she would risk everything to keep him from so tenuous a fate.

"Why Tressa…why would you do this for me?"

She didn't answer, concentrating instead on the blurred line of fence posts rushing by in a graying dawn.

"Well, for one thing, Abraham, I trust you, as far as one person can ever trust another. I owe you *hombre*. I couldn't just throw you in the river. And, anyway…I guess, I'm a little afraid of Chuy, too. He only got out of prison a while ago and has a reputation for doing desperate things. He was not so bad a man as Luca Tarango, but he was bold enough to be his father's right-hand man, and old Sancho is happy to have him back."

Little Abe was seeing things in a different light. It had not occurred to him she might have such strong feelings for him. Finally, with a crooked smile, he said. "Don't you worry, Tressa," he said, finally, with a crooked smile. "I will take care of *you* down in Sonora. The Marianos don' know everything about my people in Sinaloa. Not by a long shot, they don't."

The sun was just touching the tallest peaks of the San Juans as they approached the little mountain town of Ridgway.

"*Tienes hambre?*" Little Abe was getting hungry and thought she might be too.

"I could eat." Tressa hadn't even thought about it but now that Abe mentioned it she salivated at the prospect. "We got to be careful though, Abe, we don't need to risk going into some restaurant." She glanced over at the fuel gauge and allowed they should fill the truck before tackling the mountains, and to this, he agreed.

Little Abe slowed the truck and when he spotted a combination service station and convenience store, he pulled into the pumps, shutting down the engine while peering inside to the checkout counter. "Only one old woman in there, this is a good time." He looked back down at the fuel gauge. "This little *truque* sucks down the *petroleo*. No?" He hadn't been keeping track of the fuel as he might have and now thought them lucky to have made it this far. *I better start paying more attention*, he chastised himself. The thought of them being stranded alongside the road and at the mercy of any who might come along weighed on him.

Tressa reached in her satchel and fumbled among the moneybags. Selecting the smallest, she extracted three twenties then opened her door. "You fill the tank Abraham. Old Man Mariano said it takes the hi-grade. I'll get us something to eat and some coffee. And pay for the gas, too."

"Hi-grade, eh? I'll fill 'er up but it's not going to be cheap. I think this has some kind of larger tank than a regular pickup. Must have been a transporter, this truck."

When Tressa came out with her arms full, Little Abe was still checking the oil and then proceeded to kick the tires.

"You don't need no tire gauge for that, Abraham? They got some for sale in there on the wall."

"No, Tressa, this is how we check 'em where I come from; it works okay once you get a feel for it. I don' like to waste money on those tire gauges."

She watched him kick the last tire, then stand back squinting at it as though still not quite sure. He shrugged finally and got back in the truck. Tressa made a mental note to pick up a gauge the next time they gassed up. A plastic cup-holder stuck out from the dash and she inserted the coffees in it, being careful not to loosen the plastic lids in the process. She had sweet rolls and breakfast burritos in plenty, but waited till Abe roared out onto US 550 and settled the truck on a course for Ouray. She unwrapped a burrito and passed it to him as they headed for the snowy peaks of the San Juans and the summit at Red Mountain Pass.

Tressa unwrapped a burrito for herself.

Carlos's Uncle Hector had brought them north this very same way. He had picked them up at the safe house in Phoenix only days after they crossed the border west of Nogales. These mountain roads scared her then and they scared her now. They didn't have mountains like these in Sonora State.

Little Abe had to slow down as they negotiated the winding road but, as he ate, finally had a chance to study some mountain scenery in daylight. His *Coyotero* had brought him up from Texas, mostly in the dark of night. These were the first real mountains he'd been able to see and he, too, was impressed and more than a little intimidated. As they entered the mountain town of Ouray, Abraham was amazed to see a large pond alongside the road, with steam coming off it—near naked people clearly visible in the mist. A few were already lolling around in the water, seeming to enjoy the chilly autumn morning.

"Why do you 'spose those people want to go out there half-naked, and this early in the morning, only to freeze their asses off?"

"The water is hot, Abraham; these mountain people probably think it feels good."

"Well, when they get out, they will freeze their asses off...I don' care how good it feels...or what kind of people they are."

High above the town of Ouray and past the steep switchbacks that left them wide-eyed and dizzy, the truck clung to the impossibly narrow two-lane etched into the sheer face of the cliff. Far below, when they dared look, a silvery thread of river flowed so deep among the towering ponderosas it only showed itself in bits and glimpses. A road sign declared it "The Million Dollar Highway" and noted it was built at a cost of one million dollars a mile in 1920 dollars.

By this time Little Abe had a death-grip on the steering wheel, and Tressa braced herself against the dash with both hands, eyes tight shut.

A Highway Patrolman, after a long night running the mountain, appeared from the south and turned his head as they passed—looking for a moment as though he might turn around—had there been a place to turn around. Little Abe, watching in the rearview mirror, thought he saw the *policia* frown, but couldn't imagine him being able to make a U-turn and follow them back up the mountain. Maybe, Abe hoped, the policeman would be thinking of his breakfast, or need to take a pee at one of the little blue outhouses scattered along the lower stretches.

In any case, Little Abe would be long gone by then. The highway was entering the alpine meadows after the pass and Abe put his foot in the carburetor.

As they approached the historic mining town of Silverton, Abraham was settling to his job but became entranced with the old frontier look of the distant buildings, slowing the truck for a better view, thinking he might spot some cowboys or saloon girls. Abraham was a great fan of American westerns and watched them every chance he got. He had improved his English in the process—not knowing some of those words and sayings had gone out of fashion. He kept an eye peeled behind them for the law and eventually came to believe the policeman hadn't noticed they were the sort of Mexicans who might need inspecting. He'd heard the law was prone to profile Hispanics in this part of the country. An activity that often proved beneficial to the state's coffers.

According to Tressa's map, Durango was just ahead, meaning they were nearing New Mexico, a comforting prospect. The fact that *Mexico* was part of the state's name made him feel closer to home.

It was nearly noon when they fell off US 550 onto 160 West and the more leisurely descent into Cortez—more of a hardscrabble farm and oilfield town than anything else. The beginning of Indian country and a welcome change from the upscale and bustling college town of Durango, with its ski resort and wealthy retirement community. The pair felt more at ease in the desert. Entering the business district of Cortez, they were comforted to see Indians, and people who looked like them along the streets. This put them even more at ease. It was only common sense they would be less likely to attract attention here, and that alone calmed their anxiety. For a minute or two Tressa thought they might be better off staying in Cortez until they figured exactly where they stood. But she wanted to talk to Charlie Yazzie as soon as possible, and time was running out; they hardly slowed down passing through town.

10

The Trouble

FBI Agent Fred Smith frowned as he picked up the phone and punched the button for his private line. He had absolutely no idea what he was going to say to Bob Freeman. The man had called twice already this morning and was beginning to sound peeved, according to the secretary. Fred had been tied up on the other line both times the agent called. His recent relationship with Drug Enforcement had become strained—iffy, at best, was how he might describe it in the vernacular of the Four Corners. Still, with a little effort, there was no reason to think he couldn't work things out. It wouldn't hurt to be the bigger person. And it wasn't that he disliked Agent Freeman, either. Bob seemed a good enough guy. Many thought him a straight shooter—at least that's what he'd heard—Charlie Yazzie, for one, thought so, and so did Billy Red Clay. Still, the FBI man's past experience with the DEA had been on a more complicated level and often left him frustrated, especially their notion of sharing. They never seemed willing to divulge the full scope of their work, even in joint operations, often pushy, expecting a lot in return for what little they were sometimes willing to offer. Fred admitted he might be wrong, but nonetheless remained slightly suspicious.

The drug problem on the reservation had become such an issue, the FBI Agent now felt the two agencies might soon be *forced* to a closer cooperation, one that might bring with it a better sense of trust and transparency. Fred was thinking that time might now be fast approaching.

"Bob! Sorry I missed your call earlier. It's been crazy here." Fred shifted the phone to his other shoulder and paid close attention as Agent Freeman updated him with a few choice bits on the Sinaloa Cartel's changes in operation, both in Mexico, and in Colorado. Fred already knew the bulk of that information from his own sources but listened politely and tried to sound interested. When the DEA Agent suddenly shifted gears and continued in a more confidential tone, Fred's interest grew more genuine. "No, Bob, I didn't know that. The Bureau had a briefing on Ashki's death yesterday, from our own people in Albuquerque, but there was very little about the recovery of the missing Tribal Police file, only that it had been found." He paused for a moment thinking Freeman might add something further, and when he didn't, went on as though it didn't matter. "So, you think it was Ashki who took it?" Privately, Fred was surprised the DEA had information beyond that covered in his own agency's reports. He was, however, quick to express his appreciation for Bob passing it along. His interest increased substantially when made aware that someone else might be thought to be involved in the theft.

"I see. Well that is news, Bob. We may be able to help some there. I'll get in touch with Quantico; they're pretty good at this sort of thing." Fred had learned something he didn't know, after all, and was certain Billy Red Clay would be just as surprised at the information.

"Yes, Bob, I'll pass that along to Officer Red Clay, I'm sure it will be a load off his mind to have a lead on that file. It will, at least, be a place to start. Yes, I can assure you, Bob, we'll lend every assistance."

When Fred finally hung up he had a slightly better opinion of Drug Enforcement, or at least of Agent Bob Freeman. The agency had certainly been forthcoming this time around. He recalled Charlie Yazzie saying it all along—ex-Councilman Robert Ashki wasn't capable of pulling off everything the DEA attributed to him. It looked like he might have been right. *At least Bob Freeman is man enough to own up when he's wrong.*

~~~~~~~

Charlie Yazzie and Thomas Begay saw one another coming at the same time and Charlie's first thought was he might be able to duck him by pulling into the convenience store coming up on his right. He should have known better. He was already overdue at the office; spending time jawing about the weather was not on the morning's agenda.

Being late for work went contrary to the investigator's nature. The flat tire had put him on edge, the second one this week. Charlie suspected it was more than just bad luck. Two other people in the office had flat tires in the last few days, too. There had been a rash of flat tires only a few months back, as well. The culprit turned out to be a disgruntled ex-husband in a domestic violence case, apparently taking the only revenge left him. The judge in the case, a clan relative of the man, let him off with a warning and suggested he go live with his brother in Albuquerque—see if he could lay off drinking and get himself straightened out. The man declared at the time he'd be back. Maybe he was. Charlie had to wait for the motor pool to send a mechanic with his spare—the one he'd taken in two days before. He made a mental note to request the big magnetic sweeper be brought in from Farmington; this wasn't the first time tacks had been spread in the gravel parking lot.

The Tarango woman wasn't supposed to show up until after noon, and would most likely call ahead, at least he thought she would—anyone else would. He didn't want Gwen fielding for him on this one.

That could turn out to be problematic to say the least. Gwen was a talker and kept no secrets.

Charlie Yazzie was never fully convinced Tressa Tarango needed his help retrieving her husband's remains. He'd felt from the start there was something more sinister there, and that was one of the reasons he'd considered throwing in with Bob Freeman and the DEA. A little professional backup by people with a vested interest might have provided a measure of confidence at this point. It only made sense; the more likely reason the woman contacted him was to find out how Luca died, who killed him, and who knows, maybe even get even. That's how it was coming together in his mind. The wife of Luca Tarango would have a plan.

Charlie already had the nozzle in the tank and was watching the numbers roll across the meter as Thomas got out of his truck and ambled over, not saying anything or even looking directly at him. The lanky Navajo leaned against the front fender of the Chevy and watched as the pump tally mounted. Charlie considered his friend from under the brim of his hat. Thomas had always been a leaner, even when they were kids, as though his long frame needed to be propped up just to counter gravity. Nothing was farther from the truth, of course, Thomas was quick on his feet and with lightning reflexes when a situation called for it. The problem was, the situations calling for it were often of his own making.

"How much does that damn thing hold anyway?" It wasn't really a question. Thomas knew exactly how much the truck held so Charlie didn't bother answering, pretending instead to focus on the meter.

After a while the pump shut itself off and Thomas threw Charlie a look as he whistled at the amount. "Too bad we can't run drip-gas in these new trucks, you know, like we did when we were kids." Thomas was referring to the natural gas distillate known locally as Drip, covertly available from wellhead locations all over that country—assuming one was willing to take the risk of getting caught or blowing himself up on some isolated well location. Back then they, and most of their friends, were willing to take that chance. Store gas was, after all, 36 cents a gallon at the time. The *Diné* are, of necessity, frugal, but remain born gamblers—helping explain why Charlie had now been without a spare tire for two days.

The reference to drip gas made the investigator smile in spite of himself, and he was still chuckling under his breath as he finished writing down the figures for his expense account. "Those were the days, all right. I don't know how we made it through those little adventures without one of us getting killed...or at least spending a night or two in jail."

Thomas grinned, "Ah, good times, huh? Do you remember the night Tommy Natallii's engine froze up at the well—he didn't even make it off the location." Thomas slapped his leg, "I had just told him the day before that the Corporation Commission was sugaring those wells closer to town." The two stood looking at one another and smiling, their minds lost in a far different time and place.

Charlie shook his head, "No word on the old man yet?" He hoped if there was it wouldn't be bad. Paul T'Sosi was one of the last of the old time *Hataaliis* and took a protective interest in the Yazzie family from day one. Paul considered himself the family's personal guardian when it came to traditional pitfalls and concerns. It made the old Singer no difference that the Yazzie's didn't always believe in the old ways.

"No," Thomas grew more serious. "Lucy's afraid if we don't hear anything in the next few days, we never will. You know how it is with these old ones when they get that thing in their head...start believing they're done for...that's when they come up with their own way out." Thomas looked across the parking lot, gazing for a moment at the trailing clouds of discharge from the coal-fired generators between them and the river—misty white now in the morning sun. Some thought they let the heavy stuff out after dark. The new scrubbers appeared to have made a difference, at least during the day. When he turned and refocused on their conversation, it took Thomas a moment to pick up the thread of what he'd been saying. "Paul is sick, and he doesn't think he will get any better. I'm sure that's what he's thinking. I can understand that, too." He looked back toward the generators and grimaced. "I hope I have the guts to do the same thing when the time comes."

Charlie shook his head; it wasn't what he wanted to hear. "Let me go in and pay for this gas. You want anything from inside?"

"Naaa, you go ahead...that left front tire of yours looks a little low...I'll check it for you."

When Charlie came out, he watched as Thomas finished rolling the air hose back up, hanging it on the hook by the pump just next to the water hose.

Thomas looked over at him and smiled. "What's up today, college boy, you just wandering around town this morning...or did they shut down Legal Services, and let you go."

"No, I've got something going on and I need to be getting back to it."

"What is it?" Thomas was not shy about his curiosity no matter how private the matter—but that didn't mean he would get an answer. "Or is that more of your *privileged* information?" Thomas, if he was attempting a smile, wasn't putting much effort into it.

Charlie took a deep breath and let it out in a long sigh. "Tressa Tarango is supposed to be in town this afternoon. I'll probably have to meet with her. I don't know what she really wants for sure, but I'm thinking it might concern your uncle, John Nez. Those court documents were sealed and only one other person, outside you and I and Harley, knows for sure what really happened that day up on the mountain."

Thomas nodded and narrowed his eyes in the direction of Pastora Peak. "Will she be alone?"

"From what I'm told she may be traveling with someone; the DEA Agent let me in on that when we talked recently."

Thomas had no doubt Charlie would eventually tell him what was going on. Among the Navajo, close friends and family think they need to know even the tiniest details of each other's lives. Thomas and Charlie had known one another since they were kids and Thomas could keep a secret—not to mention, he'd been there and saw Luca Tarango killed. "Where are you going to meet up with her?"

"I'm not sure yet, but I'd like for it to be my choice and not hers."

"You don't trust her, do you?"

"She's Luca Tarango's wife—would you trust her?"

"No, I guess not. The man killed a lot of people here on the reservation. You and me and Harley just missed being some of 'em, too." Thomas broke into a grin. "I'm free this afternoon. How about I tag along with you in case you need a little advice, or something?"

It was the *something* that bothered Charlie. Asking Thomas to go along was the farthest thing from his mind, but he didn't have time to argue him out of it—that usually took some doing. "What is it …you looking for something to take your mind off things at home?"

"It's been hard," Thomas, admitted, "this thing with Paul has everyone on edge. Lucy has convinced herself Paul's decided to take the long trail. As you well know, there's nothing anyone can do about it, if that's what has happened.

Charlie looked down thinking it had been a mistake, not trying harder to avoid his friend when he first saw him coming. Getting rid of him now would be a long and likely futile, exercise, but maybe that's why he let him in on as much as he already had— maybe he did want a little company. He raised his head finally and nodded. "You suit yourself, *hastiin*, but don't blame me if you wind up wasting what could otherwise turn out to be a nice afternoon."

"I'll meet you at your office…and Charlie, don't try leaving without me."

Charlie waved him off, but with the niggling little thought he'd just made a decision he would come to regret.

On his return to the office, the Tribal Investigator went the long way around to see if Billy Red Clay was still at his desk. He wasn't. By the time Charlie pulled up in front of Legal Services, Thomas Begay's diesel truck was already sitting empty in the parking lot alongside a beat up old pickup with Colorado plates. Charlie's first thought was, maybe he ought to have given Gwen a heads up.

As he came through the reception area, Charlie was met by the secretary, eyes wide with questions as she held up a warning finger but seemed unable to get the words out of her mouth.

Charlie nodded as he blew past the frustrated woman without comment—he already had a pretty good idea. Looking toward his office he could see three people gathered around his desk and they did not look happy.

Thomas Begay was leaning against the wall, the man across from him fixed in a gimlet-eyed stare. The man seemed frozen in place—a sheep held in the grip of a Border collie's eye. The woman by his side gazed out the window seemingly amused by her companion's predicament.

Though surprised to see them, Charlie Yazzie knew instantly who they were and was faced with the realization he'd been outflanked. As Tressa turned his way, he couldn't help noticing her uncommonly good looks. Her face striking enough to catch the average man off guard and even reveal embarrassing chinks in his loyalties.

Tressa Tarango took her cue from the flicker of recognition on Thomas's face when Charlie came in and spoke first.

"Charlie Yazzie. I'm Luca Tarango's wife. I've come to take what there is left of my husband back to Mexico." Her voice was clear, her tone amiable enough to counter suspicion. Holding out a wrinkled letter, she smiled. Charlie recognized the paper as the one he'd sent the woman after Luca Tarango's death. She nodded toward Thomas Begay. "Your friend here said you'd be along shortly. I hope you don't mind we decided to wait."

Thomas moved aside, releasing Little Abe from his hypnotic scrutiny, and repositioned himself to allow Charlie back behind his desk.

"I assume everyone has introduced themselves?" The investigator asked dryly, though looking only at Thomas.

Thomas shook his head, "No, I was just getting around to that."

Charlie reached across the desk to shake hands with the woman, and then turned to the man beside her, Abraham still appeared somewhat befuddled by his encounter with Thomas Begay.

Charlie offered his hand to Abraham, "Mr. Garza I'm guessing?" He knew this might sound a little formal but thought it would please Little Abe and he was not far off. He made a mental note for future reference. Charlie indicated Thomas with a glance and introduced him as well. The tall Navajo nodded to both people before murmuring something no one quite caught.

While Tressa Tarango looked a bit weary she had obviously taken some pains with her appearance that morning, her natural good looks still radiant despite her last few harrowing days. The woman's aura of confidence and straightforward manner added a certain something, and Charlie couldn't help being impressed. Tressa was not at all what he'd envisioned. For one thing she had obviously made a serious effort to learn English during her time in Colorado. He remembered Luca Tarango's broken attempts at the language and marveled now at how well this woman expressed herself. There was still an accent, of course, but she sounded more Americanized than he'd expected. He was, of course, unaware Hector Espinosa demanded everyone under his roof to learn and continue to improve their new language. It was the way forward, he told them, and it was good for business.

Tressa studied the Investigator—the person who first took the trouble to notify her of Luca's death. He was younger than she'd imagined though still older than her and not so officious as she might have thought, despite the title on his letterhead. "I have a few questions about Luca's death."

Here it comes, Charlie thought, but remained silent and waited. It was her can of worms and he'd let her open it her own way.

"I'd like to know how he died, and what brought him to it?" Tressa already had a pretty good idea— her husband's business was not unknown to her—but still she wanted to hear it from someone with firsthand knowledge.

Charlie was considering how he might answer and still retain some anonymity for those involved. He didn't get the chance. Thomas Begay stood up, and leaning menacingly toward the woman, said bluntly, "Your husband killed some good people here on the reservation—a good many, in fact, considering how few we are to begin with." Thomas knew it wasn't his place to confront this woman but was thinking of the young girl with the sheep and her old grandmother who swore undying vengeance. That girl wasn't the first to be murdered in Luca Tarango's rampage nor had she proved to be the last.

Charlie frowned over at his friend, but when he turned back to the woman he fixed her with a look that carried little sympathy. His tone made it plain that he had no regrets when it came to Luca Tarango. "My friend here is right. Law enforcement did make an effort to bring your husband in alive but that proved impossible. From what I know of the man, he died pretty much as he lived."

Tressa's eyes flashed fire and Little Abe steeled himself and made ready for anything. He watched Thomas for some hint of the man's intentions. In his view, Thomas was the one to watch.

Tressa's uncles hadn't told her...if even they knew...what sort of havoc Luca had visited on the Navajo people. Put to the test of so relentless a pursuit, and by people he'd previously perceived to lack his skills, had only served to increase the fugitive's frustration and then his rage, which he'd focused on whomever crossed his path. Eventually, however, he came to see his pursuers for what they really were—much like himself when pushed to the edge of endurance—and this had infuriated him even more.

Charlie gave Thomas a warning glance, accompanied by a shove of his chin to indicate Little Abe should be taken outside so Charlie might speak to the woman in private. The Investigator rose slightly from his seat and leaned across the desk, thinking he would take the psychological high ground.

But with a glint in her eye, Tressa edged her hand toward a bulge in her jacket pocket, a thing the investigator had not previously noticed.

Charlie quickly sat himself back down. Clearly, Tressa Tarango was unwilling to endure the slightest intimidation. She had, apparently, had her fill of it since coming to the U.S.

"There are people looking for you," Charlie finally offered, now on the defensive."

The woman didn't change expression. "What people?" She moved her hand closer to the pocket.

"Well, there seems to be an assortment—some of whom mean you no good." Charlie edged his own hand toward a desk drawer. There wasn't a weapon there, but he didn't want her to think him totally defenseless. He made yet another mental note, this time to bring up office security at the next interagency meeting. The thought had never before crossed his mind; he'd never considered Legal Services the sort of office that need consider security of this sort.

A flicker of interest crossed her face. "Who's looking for us?"

"Well, for starters, it seems the disappearance of Carlos and Hector Espinosa has caused quite a stir down in Sinaloa. It's thought they have people on the way up as we speak…or maybe they're already here." Charlie raised an eyebrow and his voice at the same time, "You did know the Espinosas were missing, didn't you?" He attempted a more ominous tone as he declared, "These people from Sinaloa are not the sort you would want to have find you…or Abraham Garza either… I'm sure Mr. Garza would agree."

Her eyes went dead. "Who else?"

Charlie studied a moment before deciding he might as well push his advantage. "There is a government agency interested in your whereabouts." He watched and saw he now had her full attention.

Tressa didn't ask what agency; secretly guessing it was *la migra* he was referring to. Immigration was the only agency she was aware of who might have an interest in her and Abraham. But, then, *la migra* was looking for everyone she knew; that was no big deal. Both she and Little Abe had green cards obtained for them by Hector Espinosa, he was not so foolish a man as to risk so much for so little a trouble as documenting his employees. Whether or not the cards were genuine was another matter altogether. "So, why have you not turned us in?" This was said in so casual a matter as to indicate she cared little, one way or the other.

"Oh, I will. I believe it would be in your best interest and, at this point in time, might even be your only option." Charlie was bluffing, of course, the DEA wouldn't want these people to fall into the hands of Immigration. From their viewpoint that could only complicate things.

"Tell me, Charlie Yazzie. How could being turned into Immigration be good for us?" Tressa had the hint of a smile tugging at a corner of her mouth, obviously on to him now.

Charlie let her go on thinking it was Immigration looking for them—which by now was probably true anyway. "Well, it might keep you from getting killed for one thing, or spending a long time in jail." Charlie's tone became more insistent. "You might want to talk to your friend Abraham before making a decision. If he is as well connected as I've heard, he might have a different slant on the thing."

"Little Abe? Connected?" She laughed. "He's a busboy and a dishwasher. Who would he be connected to? He has no connections, as you call it. Not in Sinaloa...or anywhere else that I know of." Now *she* was the one bluffing and Charlie knew it.

"Hmm..." he smiled, "Maybe I was misinformed..."

Charlie's demeanor worried her. Even so small a show of confidence as this, caused Tressa doubt. *Maybe he does know something,* she thought, *he obviously knows more about the two of us than I expected."* In the past, Tressa had often been misinformed by men with agendas and had, of necessity, come to leave herself a little leeway when dealing with them. She somehow doubted this Indian would turn her and Little Abe over to Immigration. Even if he did, it would likely prove a temporary inconvenience, and in the end, most likely come to nothing. She and Abe were, after all, *trying* to get back *into* Mexico. None of this, however, appeared to be getting her any closer to information regarding her husband's death. She was beginning to worry she might never find who killed him, and that was unacceptable. Taking revenge on Luca's killer was an integral part of her plan. If this investigator was telling the truth, she now had to worry about someone else on their trail. She thought they'd gotten away clean and might be able to make it to Mexico in time for the great celebration of the Day of the Dead. Those few days preceding the holiday were some of the busiest crossing times of the year, the very best time to venture across the *frontera,* and with the least amount of trouble, too.

"Maybe you could help me with getting my husband's remains ready to take back. We'll need papers, I think…should we get stopped here in the States, and maybe at the border, too…or so I'm told." Tressa gave him a look. "You know how it is at the border?"

"I can only imagine." Charlie *could* only imagine, he'd never been closer to the border than a couple of hundred miles.

As far as going back into Mexico, Tressa knew it wouldn't be anywhere near as complicated as getting *out* of Mexico had been, that was for sure. One major stumbling block—the papers for the truck—were already in order and safe in the glove box. Old Sancho Mariano had seen to that, he had, in fact, pretty much thought of everything. Tressa was well aware, even for a person of moderate means, there were ways around Mexican Customs, minor officials would pose little problem.

They wouldn't be the only ones taking a deceased family member back to Mexico for *Dia de los Muertos*. It was a common enough request from older family members, even from those who'd spent many years in the U.S. They still wanted to be buried at home among their own people and childhood friends. There was some inimitable lure in those dusty little plots where they might do proper penance for whatever sins they'd incurred.

Charlie was ready for this aspect of her visit. "I've taken the trouble to speak to the Medical Examiner," he said, passing her the Coroner's card, "He tells me there is no longer what we call, a potter's field in San Juan County. There is no designated place for the burial of indigents and criminals. Apparently, when next of kin cannot be located within a reasonable period of time the remains are now by law, cremated." Charlie saw a shadow cross the woman's face and quickly added, "But, the ashes are kept for up to two years as a precaution against late claimants." He nearly smiled before catching himself, "You're lucky. Luca's ashes were scheduled for disposal in less than a month's time. And the Coroner's Office still has his personal effects on hand as well. He'll turn those over to you as well."

Tressa closed her eyes but was unable to keep her lower lip from trembling. "Where are they now...Luca's ashes, I mean?"

"The cremains are stored by a local Farmington funeral home." The investigator's voice took on a kinder tone as he saw the bewildered look on the woman's face. "It's probably better this way. I'm told they will come in a small sealed box with all the official data printed on the outside. Overall, they will be much easier to deal with. All you will need in order to claim them is a release form from the Medical Examiner's Office." Charlie hesitated for a moment. "I suppose I could witness for you if need be." He fidgeted in his chair. "I was present at the death and recovered the letter you sent him." Charlie probably wouldn't have revealed that information had she not already been aware it was he who informed her of Luca Tarango's death...and, of her husband's last words. The investigator had no intention of telling her more than this. He was not going to involve anyone else if he could help it.

"No...no one has to come with us," Tressa declared. "I have our Mexican marriage license and my identification is all in order." She looked in the investigator's eyes and thought she saw some small hint of pity. "I am thankful for all you have done, but

Little Abe and I can handle it from here." She considered the investigator for a final moment and wondered if it was him who killed her husband. She intended to know, one way or the other, and before leaving for Nogales, too.

Charlie reached in his desk drawer and drew from a far corner a single crystal on a leather thong. When he looked up he saw Tressa's hand inside her pocket, her eyes now cold and watchful. Startled, he quickly pushed the talisman across the desk. "This was your husband's. I've kept it here in case you came for his remains. I didn't want to risk someone losing it."

Tressa picked up the leather string and held the crystal to the light. "What is it?"

"In your husband's last moments he held this crystal and recited some sort of chant or incantation. When he finished, he asked if I could still see him. He seemed to think this might make him invisible."

Tressa gave a fierce shake of her head. "Luca didn't believe in anything, not religion, or anything else. He believed only in his own abilities. Why would he trust in this crystal?"

"I wouldn't know," Charlie answered honestly. "But I've heard desperate people sometimes put their faith in desperate solutions."

"You mean he still didn't pray to God even in those last moments?"

"No. There was only the amulet and the incantation, as far as I could understand. We think a witch-woman gave it to him. The chant sounded like Piute...the witch was half-Piute. Your husband killed her, too."

A now more subdued Tressa put the amulet in her pocket and stood to go. The investigator gave her directions to the Coroner's Office in Farmington and pointed out the address on the card. "The people there will give you the proper paperwork and direct you to where the ashes are stored. The funeral home may request you reimburse them for certain 'extra' costs, but if you stand firm they won't push it and you should not have to pay anything. Their contract fee has been paid by the state...six hundred dollars for this sort of thing, if I remember right." He took on a kinder tone, "Nothing more should be required of you." He nodded to emphasize his point. "Have them call me if you run into trouble." Charlie hesitated as he watched her start for the door. "Tressa...the government agency that's looking for you and Abraham, is not Immigration."

This stopped the woman dead in her tracks. "Not Immigration? Who then?"

Charlie didn't answer directly, but instead offered one further piece of advice. "It won't take long to finish your business in Farmington. If, you are heading for Nogales and the border, you'll have to pass back through here. I might have additional information for you by then. I can only tell you there are people interested in your wellbeing. They may be able to help if you'll let them." Charlie touched her arm as he opened the door. "Make no mistake, Tressa, both your and Abraham's lives may be in danger. You should be very careful from here on out."

Charlie and Thomas followed the pair through the outer office—Abraham casting cautious glances back at Thomas Begay who remained inscrutable and menacing as ever, at least in Little Abe's reckoning of the man.

The two *Diné* moved to the front window where they watched as the pair got in their old truck and headed out of the parking lot. Thomas grimaced, "They'll play hell getting to Mexico in that rig." He mentally sorted through the probabilities, and then amended the statement. "I expect they'll be damn lucky to make it to Farmington and back."

Charlie shrugged and watched as the couple started toward the larger town. "I'm afraid they have more to worry about than that."

Back in his office the investigator made a call that went to an unlisted answering service, and then sat back in his seat as he watched Thomas Begay doze off in the chair across from him. He never ceased to be amazed how easy it was for the man to fall asleep at the slightest opportunity and in most any surroundings. He'd actually seen him nod off while standing up, leaning against a haystack. He'd occasionally thought the man might be afflicted with some form of narcolepsy.

Not more than ten minutes passed before his phone lit up and he answered to hear the voice of Bob Freeman. "What's up, Charlie?"

Still uncertain how he should approach the matter, Charlie cursed silently under his breath and decided to come clean with the agent. "Tressa Tarango and Abraham Garza were just in here, Bob. They're on their way to the Coroner's Office in Farmington and then to the funeral home to pick up her husband's ashes. After that, I guess its Mexico. I figured it might make things easier if I talked to them first... maybe put in a good word for you. I get the feeling she trusts me to some extent. There are no warrants out for either of them at present...I checked."

Bob seemed to consider this; "We already have a deal in mind for Abraham Garza, Charlie." He again hesitated. "I doubt he'll turn it down when he hears what's become of his father in Sinaloa. As far as the woman goes, we have no real interest in her at this point." Again, the agent paused as though calculating some unforeseen odds. "I can't promise you anything, Charlie. But, I can tell you right now; we can't let Abe Garza leave the country. I'm afraid the situation has changed drastically over the last few hours."

Charlie glanced over at Thomas, now wide awake, and taking in the one-sided conversation with obvious interest.

The investigator nodded grimly at Thomas. "What happened, Bob?"

The agent didn't hesitate. "Several hours ago our people found Hector Espinosa and his nephew, Carlos, dead in a burned out pickup at a rural residence in Colorado." The agent paused. "Well, actually, the fire department found them after getting a call from a neighbor who said it sounded like a small war going on up there and then reported the fire. We don't have a positive identification on the two bodies as yet, but the truck belonged to Hector Espinosa, and what's left of them seems to match their descriptions. We're not sure who killed them. They found an old man inside the house, barely alive. The medics did what they could—staunched the bleeding as well as they could and loaded him up with pain-killers—but they doubt he'll last very long. His name is Sancho Mariano; we think he's one of the head people in the Sonora family. Both of his sons are major players down there. We know the younger one is in the states right now, Chuy Mariano. He has connections all over the southwest. He's known to be a very bad boy, probably the equal of, or worse, than the people out of Sinaloa."

"Chuy Mariano, huh? What's the other son's name?" Charlie was making notes.

"He's known as El Gato, or just Gato to his friends. His father sent him to school here in the states. He's the educated one, but I wouldn't discount either of them when it comes to street smarts. Chuy's been the front man for the Sonora family for several years now. The old man told our investigators that his son had been there earlier, but left before the attack. He was able to tell us the assassins were from Sinaloa and was certain they would have interrogated Hector and Carlos before killing them. We figure Sancho had the same thing planned for the pair but was waiting for his son to get back."

"Sounds like the Sinaloa people had their hands full?"

"He must of put up a hell of a fight; there were shell casings everywhere, windows shot out, and plenty of bullet holes. The old man told agents he was hit once right off, but still managed to wound one of his attackers…as least he thought he did."

Charlie interrupted. "Damn Bob, how many of them were there?"

"The old man wasn't really sure…maybe only three…but they were well armed and knew what they were doing. He said he was still returning fire when he was hit the second time and went down—he played dead when they came in, but thinks it was the fire sirens that saved him."

"I'm surprised he said as much as he did!"

"The medics had him flying high by the time we got to the hospital. I doubt he'd have talked to us at all without the drugs. The old man was convinced he was dying but was even more worried about his son and wanted us to warn him. Chuy apparently left before daylight to contact someone higher up—not very long before the shooting started—probably sometime just before dawn. It's several miles to the nearest public phone." Charlie could hear Bob cover the mouthpiece and say something to someone else in the room. "I'm at the hospital, Charlie. The Doc just said Sancho might have a fighting chance. They have the bullets out and the bleeding is mostly stopped."

Bob paused to take a breath and Charlie Yazzie did the same. Charlie spoke first, "He must have got the drop on them from the start."

"As I was saying... When the Sinaloa people showed up, Sancho, afraid his son might return and try to help him, didn't even try to negotiate—he just opened up on them. He says they will be after Chuy now no matter what. Sancho Mariano's a tough old bird, Charlie. Chances are he won't make it through. If he does, he might prove a valuable source, especially if anything happens to his son—he's hellbent on revenge at this point, and will do anything to stop the other side from getting to Chuy."

For a moment Charlie was at a loss and held up a hand to warn Thomas who seemed about to say something.

"Local law enforcement is afraid the two factions are headed for a blood bath. They are convinced now is the time to move in and clean things up. They might be right from their vantage, but it could put our investigation in jeopardy. Our goal is to strike at the highest level and that's in Sinaloa. We need to act now, Charlie, and it looks like you might be in a position to help."

"How about protective custody for Tressa and Abe? Maybe the FBI could handle it for you, Bob."

"I don't think so, Charlie. If the FBI gets in the middle of this, it's going to cost us. That whole process—even assuming we could win them over and build some sort of trust, which I doubt, would just take too long. In our people's estimation Sinaloa and Sonora are going to the mats no matter what, and soon. That means we need to take our best shot right now." The agent cleared his throat, obviously undecided how he should broach his next thought.

"I don't know, Bob, I may never see these people again."

"Charlie, there may be more in this for you than you think. The stakes are far greater than before, and I might mention, so are the rewards." Once again Bob Freeman covered the mouthpiece and listened to someone else in the room. "Charlie, I'll have to get back to you on this—just think about what I've said. And Charlie, please don't let these people get away from you. At least stay with them until we can get someone out there, we have a plane warming up as we speak." The phone clicked off without waiting for a reply.

Charlie was momentarily taken aback by the intense and forceful exchange—one-sided though it was. Bob Freeman certainly didn't seem to be holding anything back. Charlie pondered what he now considered to be his only options. He still couldn't fathom what Freeman meant when he mentioned "rewards." Was he alluding to the DEA, to him, or both working as a team?

11

Blood Ties

Chuy Mariano slowed the truck and pulled to the side of the road into a scatter of trees. Shutting off the engine, he rolled down the window to listen. He should never have left his father. On the rise toward town blue and red pinpoints of light flickered in the dark as a soft orange glow suffused the hillside to his left. He listened to the distant sirens, barely discernable over the sound of the pumpers already grinding up the road to the house. That was his Papá's house on fire. It was clear what had taken place…but too late to fix it now. The realization brought no outward sign. Chuy had learned over the years that emotion was the direct enemy of decision-making. Even in the worst of times, he was able to rise above the sort of mind numbing anguish that might immobilize another man. His own father had cautioned: "Never commit yourself to a lost cause." It was something he'd been taught as a child.

Chuy had warned his father these men would be coming. The old man knew it, too, but insisted.

"There is still time to take care of these Espinosas ourselves and not leave them to someone else's justice. If it comes down to it, we'll make the Sinaloa people a present of Hector and his nephew." He'd chuckled at his little joke. "You go make the telephone call. I'll watch these two. Your brother needs to know little Tressa and her 'friend' are on their way." Sancho Mariano had survived many a dangerous encounter and thought he was still capable of handling this one himself.

Chuy, lost in thought, was about to start the engine again when he noticed the glint of parking lights, almost hidden, as they made their way through the underbrush headed for the highway. *Those people must have been warned by the sound of the fire engines*, Chuy thought, and only escaped by leaving just ahead of the *bomberos*. They came by way of the overgrown track behind the house. Chuy was fond of keeping his own vehicle parked there and for just such a reason. He wondered now if the assassins might even have watched him leave before moving in? A glimmer of teeth, his only sign of a now deadly resolve. *God is watching over me after all,* he thought, and crossed himself with a quick, *Gracias a Dios.* Releasing the brake, he let the truck roll backwards a bit to be hidden by the trees.

His papá was dead, he was almost sure of that, but was just as certain the old man would have sold himself at a terrible price. His father would not have given up no matter the odds or threat of torture.

The law would be there any minute and there was nothing left to do but make sure his Papá didn't make this last cold journey without the warm shroud of revenge. He would not let his Papá down this time. The full wrath of the Sonora family would soon be upon the killers, and that would include anyone who might get in their way. He waited and watched as the vehicle worked its way off the hill and onto the highway. These men would be the best the Sinaloa people had to offer, there was little doubt of that. Their *Familia* was known to be meticulous in its choice of specialists and was, therefore, almost never disappointed. None of this deterred Chuy Mariano, he was of a like breed, and not without his own set of skills. He gave the black four-wheel drive a reasonable lead, knowing full well where they were headed. Carlos Espinosa would have cracked like an egg, blubbered anything he could think of that might lead to the capture of the woman and Abraham Garza. But that would not have saved Carlos—any slight revenge he had taken on the pair was most likely short lived. The Sinaloa Cartel would not stand for being compromised and the Espinosas, and everyone connected with them, would now be considered a serious liability.

Chuy had no real reason to feel protective of Tressa Tarango, or Abraham Garza either for that matter, but his Papá had been adamant they should be allowed to reach Mexico and wanted them safely across the border. His Papá had plans for young

Garza but had neglected to let Chuy in on what those plans might be. Possibly his older brother, Gato, knew, and that might be the reason the old man had been so determined that Gato be informed the pair were on their way. His brother would be in charge down in Sonora now, and Chuy the one responsible for moving forward with business in the States. Taking over the Espinosas' holdings would be just one step along the way, and this was Chuy's domain. First, however, these jackals out of Sinaloa must be dealt with, and in such a way as to prevent further incursions.

12

Insurrection

Charlie had to wait for Billy Red Clay to come on the line and while waiting, tried to envision some rational way in which Robert Ashki might have come into possession of the Tribal file on Luca Tarango. He couldn't help wondering, again, if Billy Red Clay might know more than he was saying. *Someone damn sure did.*

"Billy? Charlie Yazzie here; I just got off the phone with Bob Freeman and wanted to be sure you were in the loop. I imagine you've already heard about the death of Robert Ashki…and, about your missing file being found?"

"Yes, I have, Charlie, but only about an hour ago. Fred Smith gave me a courtesy call and again, wanted to know if I had any leads on how the file might have wound up in the hands of Robert Ashki. He thinks he might have a murder on his hands down there."

"I think he might be right, Billy. So, do you have any idea how Ashki got ahold of it?"

"Not a damn clue, Charlie."

Billy's voice was pained and the Legal Investigator felt the policeman had already gone over what little he had with a fine-tooth comb.

"You wouldn't be calling with some possibility we haven't already discussed would you, Charlie?" Billy was only half-joking.

"Well, we already know it had to be an inside job. I'm thinking it's someone right under your nose." Charlie hadn't meant to sound facetious but was instantly sure Billy took it that way.

"I'm pretty much aware of that, Counselor." Billy hadn't missed the inference in Charlie's tone and wanted him to know it. "Captain Beyale and I just spent the last hour in a heated discussion about that very thing."

Charlie waited for him to go on, but after a pause grew antsy and asked, "…And?"

"And nothing, Charlie. I'm on my way out to Emma Bittsii's place north of town. She retired here several months ago but before that was the office manager with full access to the file room. She was the one responsible for checking the files in and out."

"You say she's been gone a while now?"

"Yes, but that file could have been taken any time in the last year or two." The policeman lowered his voice almost to a whisper, "I may have told you before… the Captain feels she's beyond reproach. She'd been here for over twenty years, in one job or the other, and now I know why."

Charlie could hear some sort of commotion going on in the background and Billy stopped talking. "…Uh…so why, Billy?"

"We'll have to talk later, Charlie, there's people running around all over the place out there, something must be going on…I'd better see what's up."

Charlie looked at his phone as though it might be the cause of the commotion. He frowned and hit the intercom button for the front desk. "Gwen? Has Dispatch heard anything about an emergency over at Tribal?"

Gwen glanced over at the cubbyhole housing the Dispatch Operator, put her hand over the receiver and called over, "Hey, Carla, anything going on over at Tribal?" It was Carla's duty to monitor Tribal as well as handle Dispatch traffic for Legal Services.

Gwen had been asked not to yell across the office on several occasions but the concept of confidential messaging seemed beyond her grasp.

"She says nothing's come across that's out of the ordinary." Gwen's voice was uncommonly loud, as though she might have only the one volume available. Now, everyone in the office was alerted and made aware something might be going on over at Tribal.

Charlie sighed, shook his head, and wondered what it might be like to work in a downtown office like Fred Smith's. More sophisticated FBI digs—with polished furniture, waxed tile floors, and refined office personnel. Government service might not be so bad. Maybe he should have applied for something like that right after graduation. Of course, then he might not have met Sue and that would be sad. *Maybe it's not too late...I'm not so old after all, there might be something else out there for me yet.* Then, too, there was that thing still lingering at the back of his mind about the "rewards" Bob Freeman mentioned in their earlier talk. As he sat staring out at those gathering around the water cooler, he watched the animated conversations and couldn't help considering he might have chosen the wrong career path after all. He'd enjoyed his studies at UNM and after a certain adjustment period, even became used to living in Albuquerque. Sue had initially mentioned it might be nice to take a look at opportunities in the city. She had no real experience with that sort of living, but Charlie thought her to be the type of person capable of thriving almost anywhere. Certainly, the children were young enough to assimilate into a more diverse culture, and would no doubt gain from the more progressive educational advantages.

His phone buzzed and Charlie picked it up before Gwen could catch it. He saw her snap her fingers in frustration, and frown at the intercom lights.

"Yazzie!"

"Charlie, it's Billy. Captain Beyale had a heart attack! At least they think that's what it is. I knew he was getting pretty worked up as we talked earlier but had no idea it might lead to this. The clinic's ambulance was on another call along with the only Fire and Rescue unit. Lieutenant Arviso has him in our van and on the way to the clinic. It's not far—I should hear something pretty quick—I'll get back to you, Charlie."

The phone clicked off but continued buzzing until Charlie finally realized he still had the receiver to his ear and hung up. *Dammit!* Captain Beyale was barely forty years old and in good health, as far as a person could see. He was known to work out on a regular basis and insisted his officers stay in shape too. He'd almost fired Hastiin Sosie for being too fat. Beyale had been letting him slide, until one day during a highway traffic stop, Hastiin went back to his unit, and in the process, inadvertently missed his footing and slipped backward into the ditch—a deep one. Rolling nearly to the bottom, he came to rest wedged between two small junipers. He was stuck, unable to disentangle himself. The detainee watched from the highway and only when he quit laughing did he go down and pull Hastiin loose then help him back up the hill. The laughing cost him. The red-faced officer gave him a ticket despite his help. Needless to say, the incident got around and excited a good bit of interest at headquarters.

Charlie was still thinking about the Captain when, right in the middle of everything, Harley Ponyboy up and walked into the office. Didn't stop at the front desk, or even take notice of his cousin Gwen's protests. Being his younger cousin, Gwen knew better than to try stopping him. She knew that would not have turned out well. Harley stood in the doorway clasping and unclasping his hands and frowning at the Legal Services Investigator.

"What is it, Harley?"

"Why didn' someone tell me Old Man Paul was missing?

"You don't have a phone, Harley. That's why." Charlie's patience had worn thin, and he was having trouble controlling his voice. He hoped he didn't lose his temper right there in the office. Several employees were already looking their way.

Harley didn't quit. "So...no one knows where I live anymore? Same old place I been living over fifteen years."

Charlie rubbed that little place between his eyes, a headache was starting up again; he almost never had headaches. This one might be a doozy. "You've been working with the professor, Harley, out of town half the time. Have you not seen Thomas today?" It was rare for the two of them to go twenty-four hours without talking to one another. "If he didn't tell you, who did?"

"I haven't seen Thomas. I been over ta Doc's helping him catalog some specimens...but when I do see Thomas Begay, he'll get a piece of my mind too." Harley scrunched up his shoulders and squinted his eyes. "Sue's the one who told me...if I hadn't run into her, I guess I still wouldn't know!"

Now Charlie knew it was going to be one of those days and wondered if he was up to it. "Harley, I've got about a dozen things going on this morning, and I don't need you busting in here disrupting the entire office. What does Gwen have to do—tackle you? We have a protocol here that everyone follows…except you…and Thomas." Charlie's voice became a little edgy, "And you two don't even work here, although a couple of the staff were surprised to hear it." The investigator narrowed an eye and barked, "Call ahead, Harley, or at least check in at the desk before bulling your way in like this."

"Oh, so now I'm not welcome here—is that it?"

Before Charlie could calm himself enough to offer a civilized answer, Harley Ponyboy had spun on his heel, slamming the door on the way out. He took no notice of the open-mouthed staff as he marched himself through the front office. He did give Gwen an apologetic little wave and everyone was surprised when she whispered, "Bye Harley." Gwen, nor anyone else, had seen Harley Ponyboy lose his temper before, nor had anyone heard Gwen whisper.

Charlie stood helplessly clinching his hands and trying to calm down. *Before this day is over I'll be damn lucky if I don't have a heart attack myself.* When the phone rang he was almost afraid to answer.

Fortunately, it turned out to be Sue. "Has Harley been there yet?"

"He just left and before you ask, no, it wasn't pretty." Charlie and his wife were at the point in their marriage they often knew what the other was thinking, sometimes anticipating what the other would say, before they said it.

Charlie knew Sue was trying to keep from laughing when she said, "Harley let me know he was going to give you a piece of his mind."

"Well, he did that; by the time he left here I doubt he had much left." Charlie was beginning to see the humor in the thing himself.

Sue could hear the smile in her husband's voice and chuckled at the thought of a confrontation between Charlie and his old friend. She knew Harley didn't stay angry with anyone very long, and almost always made up for it one way or the other. The last time this happened he'd brought them half a goat he'd bought from a man parked alongside the highway in town. The man set up for business knowing full well there was an ordinance against it. Shortly after, Hastiin Sosie came along and made him take down his sign and go away, but he was unable to catch Harley for his share of the warning. Most people thought the new ordinance unfair and were sure local businesses were behind it—afraid perhaps, it might somehow cut into their trade, though none carried goat meat on a regular basis.

~~~~~~~

Charlie kept one eye on the clock as he grappled with the Tressa Tarango situation. Finally picking up the phone, he dialed DEA's Bob Freeman. After a short time on hold, the agent came on line sounding out of breath. "Hey Charlie, what's up?"

When Charlie explained he was unsure how to keep Tressa and Abraham around should they show back up, Bob had to think a moment before answering. "Didn't you say they have to stop off at the funeral home to retrieve her husband's remains?"

Charlie confirmed that was the case, and when asked, gave the address and name of the director.

Bob hesitated before admitting, "I called the Coroner's Office after we talked and had the Doc stall them by saying he was having trouble locating Tarango's possessions. I've been thinking about it, too, and sort of anticipated you might have a problem with them sticking around. Let me see what I can do to make this easier for you. How about I try this…"

~~~~~~~

Despite Charlie's vehement protests, the DEA Agent finally won out, insisting Charlie was the only one the fugitives trusted and it was imperative they play on that. It was agreed; the Investigator, being closer, shouldn't wait for the pair to return, but should instead intercept them in town. Hopefully Bob and his partner would arrive in time to back them up at the funeral home should it be needed. Bob, after a quick calculation, figured he was less than an hour away. The wind in Farmington had been so bad their light aircraft had diverted to Durango where the pilot still had to come in nearly sideways. When Bob finally hung up Charlie was still wondering how far ahead of him Agent Freeman might have been all along.

13

Lucky 7

Tressa Tarango sat tapping her foot and shifting position on the cold hard bench outside the Medical Examiner's Office. She was pretty sure she knew why they had to keep it so cold in there. It had been over thirty minutes since the Coroner met them at the door and went into a lengthy explanation of the steps required to claim her husband's remains. The Doctor hadn't spared her the details of Luca's autopsy report, and Tressa became even more distraught as she listened to the graphic account. She'd done her best to prepare herself beforehand, but now felt a growing sense of unease at a process becoming more frustrating as time wore on—certainly not the pain-free process Charlie Yazzie led her to believe it would be.

Finally, the Doctor sent an assistant for what few personal possessions Luca Tarango had on him when the body came in. As time passed, Tressa was beginning to wonder if the package was worth the wait. *But no, it would be important to have some small something of Luca's on the Day of the Dead.* She had nothing left of him, not even a picture, and it was customary to leave something of the deceased with the remains or at the site. This wasn't a tradition to be taken lightly and Tressa was resolved to do the right thing by Luca, to do otherwise would risk the unknown, and in the case of Luca Tarango, that risk could be far reaching.

Little Abe watched from drooping lids and idly judged Tressa to be nearing the point of throwing a fit. The woman was a study in contradictions and one never knew how such a thing, once begun, might wind up. He couldn't help being a little nervous at the prospect. Abe had no idea what was involved in a procedure such as this, or how long it might take. He wanted her to think he was a person who remained calm in the face of hardship, a rock she could lean on in times like these. He couldn't help thinking his support through these adversities would eventually help bring them closer and to a more binding relationship.

The Medical Examiner eventually emerged from his office bearing a small package: a brown paper envelope enclosed in a plastic bag and bearing a case number in black marker. Tressa appeared somewhat mollified that things were at last on track, and stood, motioning the sleepy-eyed Abraham to do likewise.

The white-coated Doctor remained unapologetic. "There was some difficulty locating these items due to the length of time since closing the case. This particular item," he said, patting the package, "had already been set aside for disposal. That's why we couldn't find it right away."

Tressa eyed the man skeptically, as though still not understanding.

The doctor frowned. "When a body is unclaimed for so long a time as this, their personal effects do occasionally get misplaced." He held the package up. "You're lucky," he said, again frowning at the brown paper package as though it should have made itself more available. "Yes, you are quite lucky indeed." He looked over the top of his glasses at Tressa. "I'll have to watch as you verify the contents and sign off, of course." The Medical Officer led the way to a small table where he opened the wrinkled envelope, spilling the contents onto a metal tray.

Tressa was surprised to see a rather large folding knife fall out with a clunk, followed by a shower of smaller items. The Doctor glanced at the writing on the package. "Hmmm…'seven items', it says. There are only six here, that I can see. Upending the envelope, he gave it a good shake, and then smiled as a tiny obsidian arrowhead fell out. He picked it up and held it to the light. "A fine example, I'd say." The Doctor then stroked his chin for a quick moment before turning his attention to the heavy folding knife. "I recall this being the weapon used in several of the murders committed by the deceased." He puckered his face into a frown and scratched the lobe of one ear. "There was never an actual trial as such...you know...only a Coroner's Inquiry sanctioned by the courts. It was all pretty well cut and dried. I suppose that's why we still have this." He studied the knife with obvious distaste before pushing everything toward Tressa, indicating she should examine the objects as well. "If you'll just verify the contents of the envelope..." He passed her a form to sign, along with the official release required to claim the cremains at the holding facility.

Tressa looked briefly at the items, which other than the knife and arrowhead included only a few coins, and a small turquoise ring. *How little there is to show for a life...regardless how bad a life it might have been.* She picked up the ring and examined the stone. *Maybe Luca was bringing me this as a present.* She couldn't help wondering this, regardless how unlikely it might actually be. She was well aware how improbable it would be for Luca to pick out such a thing, even for her. She couldn't imagine how he might have come by it but could only suppose it belonged to one of his victims.

One thing Tressa was sure of—her husband was not a thief, and wouldn't have stolen it unless, of course, the owner was already dead and had no further use for it. She hoped this wasn't the case but held the ring more gingerly than before. She did her best to push such thoughts away, fearing they might somehow taint her carefully nurtured dedication to what she saw as a duty...and in fact, a mission.

Slipping the ring into her pocket, Tressa turned her attention to the folding knife. Without a word, she handed it to Little Abe who was quick to take it, and eagerly opened it, and held it up to examine the blade. It occurred to him there might still be traces of gore, should the stories be true. He seemed almost disappointed, seeing it clean and well-polished with a razor edge. This husband of Tressa's had taken good care of the weapon, as one naturally would should he believe his life might depend on it. Where Little Abe came from, a knife engendered a certain respect or at least envy, and he was proud to have it regardless what its former job might have been.

"You can keep that, Abraham, just you remember who it belonged to, and try to put it to some better use." Tressa put the stray coins and small obsidian arrowhead in her jacket pocket with Luca's crystal amulet but on the opposite side of the automatic pistol. Now both she and Abe were armed, and though she had never fired a gun before, it seemed a simple enough thing to do. She'd often seen women shoot pistols in movies. Women you wouldn't think capable of shooting a person, but they did and made it look easy, too. Should she sometime have need of this pistol of Hector's—a thing she deemed unlikely—she would at least have the element of surprise in her favor, at least she hoped it would be a surprise.

~~~~~~

Little Abe pulled the old Ford truck up to the funeral home and cautiously examined the building. *So this is where the ashes of the notorious Luca Tarango are stored.* It was almost churchlike, even had a small steeple, which for some, he thought, might evoke forgiveness, perhaps even a hint of redemption.

A newer grey Chevy Suburban with dark windows was parked on the opposite side of the street, and Little Abe glanced its way briefly, dismissing it almost immediately as a vehicle which might reasonably be associated with the funeral business. There was no one visible inside, as would be expected, given the impenetrable limo tint.

Walking up the steps, a clearly emotional Tressa, unsteady on her feet, and already trembling, put a hand out to Abraham, who was quick to take her arm. The woman was obviously distraught at the thought of being so near the mortal remains of her former husband and she waited as Little Abe pulled one of the big double doors open and held it open as she entered. He hesitated a moment, turning slightly, to reconsider the Suburban across the street. The vehicle was of the same sort that would draw suspicion back home. The Mexican Federales—almost all government officials and drug cartels, too—found that particular model's intimidating appearance indispensable in the pursuit of their various and nefarious enterprises. Abe fingered the Buck knife in his pocket and for just an instant imagined he saw a shadow, or at least some sort of movement behind the suburban's opaque side window.

~~~~~~~

Charlie Yazzie backed his truck into the drive of a vacant house with a For Sale sign on it, yawned, and turned off the key. Far down the street the funeral home made the old Ford truck look out of place. It seemed Bob Freeman's plan to stall Abe and Tressa had worked.

What appeared to be one of the mortuary's courtesy vehicles was parked just across the street from the establishment. "We'll wait for them to come out and then I'll try to make a case for Bob Freeman's offer of immunity...if that's what it turns out to be."

Thomas lolled back against the seat. "I don't know why Drug Enforcement didn't just call the FBI to handle this little job. I mean I'm sure it's fun for you to play undercover agent and all, but it seems a little silly to me."

Charlie touched his tongue to his front teeth and thought about that. "I suspect Bob doesn't want the FBI involved just yet, and I imagine that's because the Bureau goes strictly by the book. Once the FBI steps in, they'll take charge—Bob won't have as free a hand to work his own agenda." While this was mainly speculation Charlie thought he had Bob Freeman figured out, at least in that regard.

Thomas sat quietly for a moment. "So, I guess the local law wasn't informed for the same reason? I guess those boys would screw things up for damn sure.

"Probably." Charlie thought this a reasonable assumption.

Thomas fidgeted in his seat trying to cover all the empty bases in his mind. "How long do you think this is going to take? I told Lucy, Billy Red Clay and Tribal are doing everything they can to find her father, but she still wants me to go along with her and talk to those people at the Episcopal Mission. Lucy still don't do too good with white people. Paul did work there for a long time and she's got it in her head he might have gone for a visit and someone there might know something." Thomas still wasn't sure why they had to go at all. "I told her to just call 'em up. But she said, 'No, there's a lot of people there who knew him and might have heard something. We need to talk to as many people as we can find.' So now she's determined to talk to all of them I guess..." Thomas stopped short and came upright in his seat. "There's someone getting out of that Suburban."

Charlie had been watching the other direction, hoping Bob Freeman might make it in time to take part. Now, he turned his attention to the man headed for the mortuary's front door. He didn't look like a funeral employee to him.

"I thought those guys all had to wear suits...even the drivers." Thomas had no real experience with the occupation but *had* observed a funeral service or two from a distance. Even from a long way off, cemeteries made him nervous.

As the two Navajo pondered the mechanics of the funeral business, the Suburban started up, crossed to the side entrance, and then disappeared behind the building.

"Must be making a pickup, I guess." Thomas pursed his lips and narrowed an eye. "Or a delivery."

"Maybe." Charlie, too, was beginning to think all was not right. The first man, now standing at the front door, seemed to be waiting for someone...or something.

Charlie started the engine.

~~~~~~~

Inside the mortuary's rather somber reception area Abe spotted a small desk nearly hidden among a grove of potted plants. Tressa and Abe both jumped slightly as a timorous voice called across the foyer. "You must be the couple who've come for the cremains. The Coroner's Office called ahead..." An older man in a dark suit—small of stature and with a slight limp—crossed the small space rubbing his hands together, as though he might be cold...or nervous.

Tressa Tarango eyed him with the same caution she reserved for anyone she thought might present a problem. Nonetheless, she took the man's proffered hand, cold and limp though it was, and introduced herself with as much confidence as her state of mind would allow.

Little Abe, eyes slow to adjust to the dim light of the funeral parlor, clasped his new knife more tightly in his pocket and revealed his cautious nature by standing back, ignoring the odd little person entirely. There was something wrong—even he could see that.

The funeral director, if that was what he was, spoke almost in a whisper, as though afraid he might wake someone. "You people wait right here while I nip back to the repository for the box. We'll soon have you fixed up," he assured them, as he turned anxiously toward the back of the room and a door standing slightly ajar.

As the man walked away Little Abe nudged Tressa. "I don't like this Tressa. There's something wrong about that little man, I think."

Tressa, without turning, nodded, and not taking her eyes off the doorway, said, "You may be right Abraham. Something smells fishy to me too." She watched as the man partially closed the door behind him.

"Oh, I think that's just the formaldehyde. My cousin worked in a place like this in Sinaloa, and he always smelled like that." Abe was nervous and didn't try to hide it.

She turned to him, gritted her teeth, and said severely, "I didn't mean it that way Abraham. I was only agreeing...something's not right."

"That's what I said Tressa...something's off." Abe had no more than uttered the words this second time, when the old man reappeared in the doorway holding a container smaller than a shoebox. Coming toward them he handed the container to Tressa without even a mention of paperwork. Still not saying anything, the man quickly turned and retraced his steps, again disappearing through the half-open door. The faint sound of a scuffle was heard from the back room, then silence. Abe and Tressa looked at one another but remained rooted to the spot

A very different figure appeared in the doorway, big and ominous, hidden in the shadows. Tressa was just making out the man's face when the lights clicked off leaving them in virtual darkness. Almost instantly the room brightened as the *front* door of the establishment flew open to reveal yet another person—one quickly lost in the darkness as the door swung closed behind him.

Little Abe pushed Tressa behind him, shielding her with his own body, knife already in hand, blade open and moving in a small circle.

"I think they got guns Abraham?" Tressa, now wide-eyed, was thinking the knife might prove a poor defense and was about to offer Abe her pistol but was so stricken with fear she could hardly speak.

Abraham Garza followed his first instinct, which was to draw back his good right arm, and with all his might, throw the big folding knife at the shadowy figure blocking the front door, the nearest and most obvious route of escape. Abe had a powerful arm and could send a projectile to its target with amazing force; a skill learned as a boy growing up where rocks and sticks were not only the implements of a playful pastime, but also, should things get out of control, a handy weapon. Unfortunately, he was unpracticed in the more delicate balance of a hunting knife. The heavy butt of the weapon struck the man above the right eye, bringing him to his knees, pistol skittering across the polished floor to hide among the potted fronds.

Little Abe yelled, "Stay down Tressa," just as a shot rang out from the back of the room—the bullet clipping off a large palm leaf above their heads. Abe grabbed Tressa's hand and dragged her toward the front door, where he paused only long enough to kick the fallen man in the stomach as the assailant struggled to regain his feet. As Tressa opened the front door, she looked down and pointed to Abraham's knife, lying in the thin shaft of light. Little Abe scooped it up as he pushed his way out dragging the panicked Tressa behind.

Yet another shot was fired—this time from somewhere behind them, but too late. The pair had spilled out across the steps and the heavy door swung shut behind them. The gray Suburban was nowhere in sight, but their old pickup was.

The pair made a run for the Ford.

Little Abe snatched open his door, but dropped the keys and fell to one knee to retrieve them; by the time he leapt into the cab and had the engine started, Tressa, was already inside with her door locked.

The white pickup truck seemed to come out of nowhere and pulled alongside with Thomas Begay at the window.

Wide-eyed, Abe recognized both Thomas and Charlie and despite being suspicious couldn't help feeling a wave of relief.

Thomas leaned out the window and shouted, "Follow us!" as Charlie Yazzie urgently motioned them to go.

Abe's foot was already on the accelerator as he shot Thomas a wary look.

"Sorry we're late," came the yell as the Chevy truck pulled slightly ahead. Head hanging out the window, Thomas's wild grin left Abe thinking the man might have lost his mind.

Abraham gunned the engine and the Ford again pulled even with the Chevy. Tressa glanced back at the funeral home in time to see the front door open and a momentary glimpse of a familiar face. She smiled to herself. They were not alone in this...at least there was that.

"We almos' got killed in there!" Abe announced, as though Tressa might not understand the full gravity of the situation. He shifted gears, gaining speed as they headed, he supposed, out of town. "You know that was Chuy Mariano covering us back there, right?" Abe was panting.

"I do now, Hombrecito. Once again, we owe him...and his father... our lives. As long as old Sancho lives I think we will be under their protection." Tressa didn't appear nearly as worried as Abe thought she should be. He gave her a questioning shrug and jerk of his head toward Charlie's accelerating truck. "Do we keep following those two?" He was pretty sure he knew the answer but hoped he was wrong.

"I don't see we have any choice," she said without looking him in the eye.

In the white pickup, Thomas frowned as he turned to Charlie. "If the cops had gotten there first, those two would be in jail right now," then grimaced to himself and thought, *Well, that might happen yet—we'll see how this next part works out for them.*

Charlie couldn't put his finger on it, but something about Abraham Garza irritated Thomas and it was only getting worse.

14

Salvation

Chuy Mariano was not at all pleased with himself. Twice in two days he had let the Sinaloa assassins slip through his fingers. Granted, it was mostly of necessity, dictated by circumstances beyond his control. Still it was not the way he would have handled it given better options. He had, at least, stopped them and probably been the instrument of salvation for the woman and Abraham Garza. That was good enough for now. He was certain the one quick round he got off had clipped the main shooter and just in the nick of time, too.

There had been a third person outside in the Suburban; seriously wounded, and burning with fever; the man carried the putrid odor of death. He was no longer a problem and Chuy knew he had done the man a service. His Papá, a deadly adversary under any circumstance, had put his mark on that one, and

Chuy knew the old man would expect no less of his son.

In any case, there was now one wounded, a second with a cracked head along with a couple of broken ribs, and a dead man they would have to get rid of, and quickly, too. These people were no longer a priority as far as Chuy was concerned, but he would be foolish to count them out.

His job now was to get the woman and Abraham Garza to Sonora and into the hands of his brother, Gato. He, himself, would settle with those last two assassins when the time came. Even in their present condition they would not simply go away, not empty-handed and knowing they would suffer even greater pain in Sinaloa should they fail. In any event, they wouldn't be hard to find. He would let them come to him, and he knew for a fact they would. They were professionals and though they'd had bad luck today, these *cabróns* would stay with it to the last man.

Chuy watched from hiding as the two pickup trucks sped away from the front of the building, growing gradually smaller even as he bobbed his head and smiled.

The Suburban in the alleyway roared to life and headed in the opposite direction. Chuy ran to the corner, thinking he might risk a last shot. But the locals were likely already on their way and in the end he decided against it.

The tall Mexican walked calmly around the corner to his own truck and drove away unnoticed.

That night in his cut-rate room at the edge of town Chuy tried again to telephone his brother. He'd had no news of his father since the attack in Colorado, and while convinced there was little hope for his Papá, he would still have liked to know one way or the other. He had much to prepare and many plans yet to be made. When Gato was ready...*he* would be ready, too. Only one other person remained above them in Sonora State now, and that uncle was old and might not be in charge much longer—not if Gato had his way. The elder Abraham Garza would be the key to bringing down the Sinaloa Cartel, and for that they would need Little Abe.

Chuy didn't bother trying to tail his Papá's old Ford. He'd seen the logo on the white Chevy and knew all he need do was watch the offices of Legal Services. The white truck would lead him to someone; it was just a matter of time.

15

The Offer

Charlie hoped Thomas was right about Alfred Nakii's old place being empty. Isolated, and a good distance out of town, it was perfect for anyone who had nowhere else to go. After Alfred died, one of his cousins had moved in and remained for almost a year. Thomas claimed the cousin cleaned the place up and left behind a nearly full propane tank, a huge plus as far as Thomas Begay was concerned, not to mention the two barrels of water, which he considered an even greater inducement. Harley Ponyboy told Thomas the cousin was a school bus driver and allowed to keep the bus right there at the trailer. The county even plowed the drive from time to time. It only made sense, Harley said, as that was the beginning and end of his route.

"It's all just temporary," the cousin told anyone who asked. His ultimate goal, he said, was to find a job in Albuquerque. "I'm too young to waste my talents on the reservation; the city's where the people are." Even his mother was unable think what talents her son might be referring to. The entire family was skeptical and surprised when they heard he'd actually done it—moved to the city and found a job in an all-night eatery off Old Town Plaza. As the son later assured his mother in a one-sentence letter, "I'm in Albuquerque—that's the main thing!"

In the beginning Charlie had been a bit apprehensive about Alfred Nakii's place as a hideout. It had, after all, been a woman that led to poor Alfred's death there two years ago, and even now the investigator was left a little queasy by the thought of it. But after hearing how the cousin had fixed the place up he thought it might serve the purpose. They wouldn't need it for long.

When the two trucks drove up to the mobile home the sun had slipped to one side of the valley, putting the shabby dwelling in a warmer light.

Tressa Tarango got out of the truck clutching her box of ashes and stood a moment, one hand on her hip, chin tilted to one side, as she considered. She surprised everyone by saying, "I've seen worse. At least it's nice and quiet and I don't plan on being here that long." This was more for Charlie's benefit than anyone else.

Little Abe had grown up in one-room houses where you could see through walls and might sometimes share space with a curious chicken or goat—he had not the slightest concern.

Charlie immediately sent Thomas down the hill to Harley Ponyboy's place to see what sort of grub he might rustle up. They could replace it later, he assured Thomas.

Harley was known to be a frugal shopper but generally kept something on hand, even if it were only beans and rice. When he was working it might even be more than that. The door was always unlocked at Harley's place and everyone knew he was a soft touch should a person be in need.

Harley's truck wasn't there and Charlie hoped their business would be finished before he returned. Charlie was still not sure what sort of humor Harley would be in after their earlier little set-too.

Tressa and Abe sat down on the couch. Tressa, still clutching the box with Luca Tarango inside had refused to leave the ashes in the truck. Thomas mentioned it was not a good thing to have burial remains in a house owing to the likelihood of attracting *Chindis* or other evil things. He glowered silently when the woman, not knowing what *Chindis* were, acted like she didn't hear.

The Legal Services Investigator brushed Thomas's complaint aside and began relating the latest happenings in Colorado. Stressing the fact Tressa and Abe might now be suspects in the double homicide of the missing Espinosas. He proposed, again, they cooperate with agent Bob Freeman and his DEA task force. Bob was someone, he assured them, who would do everything in his power to help.

"So, Carlos and his Uncle Hector are dead?" Tressa looked over at little Abe and scowled then sneered, "I'll bet it wasn't easy for 'em either."

Charlie was a little surprised by the comment. "You're right, it wasn't easy for them...and it won't be easy for you two either if the people who killed them, catch up to you. They *are* looking, you know... probably the same gunmen you ran into at the funeral home."

Abraham looked pensive. "It's the Sinaloa people isn't it?" Little Abe had known all along it might go this way, and again thought of his old father in Mexico. *His* head would now be on the chopping block, as the old man liked to put it.

"That's how it looks right now." Charlie thought this a good time to ask, "You two didn't have anything to do with killing the Espinosas...did you? If you did, it's going to come out—no doubt about that. Sancho Mariano has been talking."

Tressa gave a little jerk of her head and coughed. "No. Not really, we were more or less just along for the ride." She frowned, "Those two were still alive the last time we saw them. I'm glad to hear they got what they deserved though. They had it coming...the both of them."

Little Abe was more diplomatic, hoping to lessen the impact of Tressa's possibly incriminating opinion. "They were bad people and we weren't the only ones to have it in for them. Plenty of people will be glad to see those two are gone."

This reminded Charlie Yazzie of his own thoughts when Bob Freeman informed him Robert Ashki was dead. Everyone was glad to see *him* gone, too. Charlie couldn't help wondering how Billy Red Clay was coming along with his enquiry out at Emma Bitsii's place. He was more than a little curious what might come of that—just one of several reasons he should have already been back at the office. He knew Thomas was anxious to get home as well. He still intended going along with Lucy Tallwoman to see if the Episcopalians knew anything about her father; he'd once worked for the missionaries, off and on. Hopefully the old Singer had already shown up somewhere, but if not, Thomas would probably be in trouble.

Fixing Tressa with as stern a gaze as he dared, Charlie Yazzie made the thrust of his final argument. "At the moment, Tressa, you seem to be a minor player in this. The authorities are most concerned with Abraham. No one, other than Thomas and me, know where you are—certainly not whoever's trying to kill you. Some very competent people are trying to find those men and when they do, they will stop them. In the meantime, you'll be safe here. Should you take it in your head to leave—then all bets are off. You understand that, don't you? You will be on your own, you and Abraham." He looked over at Little Abe. "You understand all this don't you, Abe?"

Little Abe made a face. "Yes, I understand..." Secretly Abe was thinking *...and you, Señor, seem unaware someone else may be looking out for us, too.*

Charlie allowed himself to sound slightly more optimistic when he said, "Hopefully everything can be quickly sorted out and you two will be in a position to get your lives back in order," then the investigator's voice took on a slightly more ominous note. "Make no mistake, you *are* in danger, and cooperating with Bob Freeman and his people appears to be your best way out."

Thomas returned with what little food he could find at Harley Ponyboy's place. Bacon and eggs, along with a half-stale loaf of bread and a few potatoes made up the bulk of his find. It would have to do until they came back for the pair.

While Charlie went on with his recruitment plea inside, Thomas took the opportunity to ensure the old Ford truck wouldn't start should the fugitives become fidgety. He and Charlie had discussed disabling the vehicle on the way there and the investigator had agreed it was a good idea. Thomas didn't even get under the hood—only slammed a raw potato up the exhaust, then kicked it in good and tight with the toe of his boot. Thomas had no idea what sort of engine the truck had under the hood now, but he knew it wasn't the original. Either way, whoever next tried to start that truck, would be in for a big surprise.

~~~~~~~

On their way back into town, Thomas couldn't help mentioning that Harley would be unhappy when he returned home to find himself without the makings for his breakfast.

"I'll find him and make that right with him." Charlie said this knowing the finding of Harley Ponyboy might be a job in itself, but since Harley commonly took many of his meals either at the Yazzie or Begay house, Charlie was not overly concerned with this little incursion into the Ponyboy larder. "I'm sure one or the other of us will hear from Harley at some point today and can make it up to him."

Thomas hoped so. He didn't like to think of his little friend going hungry just so strangers even *remotely* related to Luca Tarango, could fill their bellies.

16

Resurrection

Old Man Paul T'Sosi dreamed again the ancient dream of those who came before.
The next day he gave away his saddle.
It was time.

Paul never intended to have a curing ceremony. It was clear as rainwater what he needed to do. Henry Bill and his *Blessing Way* hadn't been his idea in the first place. Henry, himself, after the barest of consultations, had agreed—he didn't think there was need of a ceremony either—telling Paul's daughter that, however, would only have made things harder. There would be more tearful pleas for Paul to go to the clinic or see an old people's specialist in Farmington.

The venerable Singer had led a full life, and for the most part, was satisfied with the way it had played out. He didn't intend being remembered as a doddering old fool. He'd had all night to rethink his decision, but in the morning was more determined than ever not to have a curing ceremony; there was no cure for old age. He was tired and he was sick;

and he was sick and tired of people who didn't understand— insisted on trying to fix something that couldn't be fixed.

They would look for him a while, of course, but would finally realize he wasn't coming back—then they would give up looking—there wouldn't be any point in it after that. No one wants to find a dead person...at least not any who have kept the old ways.

~~~~~~~

A man and wife from New York stopped for Paul T'Sosi that morning, thinking it would be interesting to meet a real Indian. Paul was a good talker when he wanted to be, and knew what white people liked to hear. He told them he was on his way to attend a burial ceremony but didn't mention it was for himself. The couple became caught up in his stories and would gladly have taken him even farther just to hear more. The old Singer insisted, however, he needed to get off at Mexican Water.

It took him a while but he finally hitched another ride, this time with a one-eyed man taking a load of bucks to that rough country just south of the San Juan. The ewes, the man allowed, were a little early coming into season this year, and if he intended to have spring lambs time was growing short.

When Paul mentioned where he was headed, the man glanced down at the little bundle wrapped in a blanket and tied with a rope.

"That's not much camp to take back into that rough country." The man looked to be Piute and had a pretty good idea what this old Navajo was up to.

The sheepman had spent a lifetime cheek by jowl with the *Diné* and knew very well what was on the old man's mind.

"No," Paul agreed, "But I won't need much camp...I expect this will be plenty."

"Not many people up that way anymore," the man cautioned. "What few ever lived there are mostly gone now...moved closer to town to be by the schools and the stores. My wife is Navajo and she and I are about the last ones left on the lower Chinle...at least as far as I know...and *we* won't be here either, come winter."

Paul nodded. "Is it running water? The Chinle I mean, is it running water now?" It really didn't matter, but water would be pleasant to look at he thought.

"I believe it is...but not too much... I crossed it horseback a few days back; we've had some rain since then, so it could be more." Water and the exact amount of it was an important topic of conversation in that country and it was important to report it exactly right. "Are you headed back in that far? A little late in the day for it...don't you think?"

"Maybe..." Paul turned and for the first time looked the Piute over more carefully. It was said, in olden times, many of the Great Basin Piutes were barely over four and a half feet tall. It was poor land for a poor people and didn't encourage growth of any kind. This one-eyed Piute had gone some better though, nearly as tall as Paul, who being old himself was not as tall as he once had been. When the *Diné* finally answered the man's question, it was with a hint of frustration, "Yes, I'm a little later than I planned. It took me a while to catch a ride this morning."

The Navajo have generally gotten along with what few Piutes lived along the northern reaches of the San Juan. Those people were never so warlike as their Shoshoni and Ute cousins. And they didn't join Kit Carson as scouts in that great purge of the Navajo people—leading eventually to the Long Walk across New Mexico to the reviled Bosque Redondo.

"Well, I guess you were lucky I came along then." The sheepman noticed Paul watching the bucks in the rearview mirror. They were big rangy Suffolk; the kind Indian stockmen could only afford to lease from a Tribal-sanctioned breeder of terminal sires. The Tribe occasionally offered help to local sheepmen who wanted to increase the quality of their flocks. "Are you a sheepman?"

"We run a few *Churros*," the old man's reply was noncommittal, as though uncertain of the exact number of sheep his family might have on hand. "My daughter is a weaver." He said, thinking that might explain them having the ancient breed.

"Ah, not many have that old kind of sheep no more. I guess it was up to the weavers to keep them going."

"Yes, they are getting hard to come by now." Thinking about the sheep had confused Paul—who was taking care of them today?

The two jounced along in silence to the top of a rise, where the driver slowed the truck to a crawl and pointed down to a thatched shelter alongside a mud and wattle dwelling. There was a rickety set of corrals to one side of the structures and a woman appeared to be sorting a band of ewes. "That's our place down there; we're only here till the pasture gives out and then we go too. We've had a good summer as far as rain goes, ordinarily we would be gone by now. There's still good feed here though, and I don't see no point feeding these bucks what little hay we have put by at home. In another two weeks the ewes should be covered. Then we'll take them all back down to the home place for the winter."

"Your people... They been in this country a long time haven't they?" It was more a statement of fact than question, and Paul smiled as he watched the man consider how he should answer. The Navajo had always maintained this strip along the San Juan was rightfully theirs—but seldom begrudged the few Piutes a place here; it was hard country and few *Diné* ever called it home for very long. Besides, this man was married to a *Diné* and thus had Tribal rights by marriage. Paul idly wondered what clan the man's wife was but didn't bother to ask.

The sheepherder, seeing the look on his face, finally chuckled. "We Piutes been here since time began, according to my grandfather. He said we always been here." The man knew that's how the Navajo thought, too, and expected he might get a rise out of the old man. The one-eyed man grinned as he wrestled the truck over a rough spot. "I guess it's good to have a country no one else wants." He turned his one good eye on Paul and nodded as though making up his mind to something. "You're welcome to roll out your blanket in the brush shelter for the night. I'm going a ways up into that same country in the morning to get a load of firewood; I could take you back in a little farther, if that would suit you?"

Paul T'Sosi was worn out and doubted he could make it much farther on foot this day anyway. He nodded and smiled his appreciation before looking away.

The next morning, the man's wife brought the two men coffee and fry-bread with slices of bacon on top. The Piute said goodbye to the woman with a glance in Paul's direction. The woman seemed sad as she stood watching them go. When they were well above camp she waved goodbye, even knowing they wouldn't see it. Her own father had chosen to end his life in just such a way. She shook her head and called up the dogs before opening the corrals to turn the bucks in with the ewes. Life went on.

The truck clawed its way nearly to the rim above the San Juan before grinding to a stop. Chinle Creek was just over a slight rise to their left. When Paul got down from the pickup the two men barely looked at one another.

Shouldering his bedroll, the old Singer thanked the Piute for his trouble and when asked, assured the man he didn't have far to go. It was a place, he said, that could only be reached by foot but close enough it wouldn't take him long. Paul mouthed a brief goodbye and turned his face west, searching with rheumy eyes for the little feeder canyon that would take him cliff-side and the hidden ledge still so clear in the far reaches of his mind. In less than an hour more he had reached the trail down and given his muddled state of mind, was somewhat surprised it hadn't been harder to find. Elmore Shining Horse had shown him this place when the aged *Hataalii* was still strong enough to get around in such country. Paul had been back only one other time in all those years...he remembered it all right.

One would think twenty-five thousand square miles of reservation would afford plenty of places for an old man to leave his bones. *Maybe...*he thought, *but not good places like this one.* Many of the best places he knew already had bones in them...some bones on top of bones. *That's no way to spend eternity.* He didn't want that.

The entire Four Corners area was little more than a vast burying ground. Paleo-Indians were likely first to migrate into the country—more than ten or even twenty thousand years ago. Their posterity may have slowly evolved there, culturally speaking, eventually taking up residence under the tribal names of Ute, Piute, and maybe a few other isolated bands of Great Basin Shoshonian rootstock. Then the Anasazi came, and later, when drought forced them out, they resettled in other places to become what is believed to be the Puebloan people, the Zuni, Hopi, and others. And then the Navajo and their Apache cousins began filtering down from the North Country in yet another wave of those hardy adventurers who crossed the land bridge now known as the Bering Straits. They didn't come all at once, of course they trickled down in ragged little groups, some interacting with different peoples along the way. By the time the *Diné* finally reached the Four Corners they had only a few hundred years to settle in before the Spaniards came exploring—and the Mexicans up from the south, determined to carve out a place for themselves in that harsh land. Later, the Mormons, and other white settlers began flooding through. They all came, died, and were buried here.

Now, in a more modern and diverse society, they fenced their dead into little dead-people villages with only stone markers to remember them by. At least, some said, they did not leave them lying about some isolated nook or cranny where honest folk could run afoul of those spirits left in their wake.

Paul wondered how many of his own people's bones lay hidden…forgotten over the centuries. That was the old culture—all about survival of the fittest, and sad though it might be, there was neither time nor resources to be spared for those too weak, old or disabled to keep up. There eventually came a time when those unfortunates must, of necessity, be abandoned and left to their own devices. Many were the taboos to forbid, or at least discourage dwelling on their memories.

Those left to carry on did their best to forget the ones they'd left behind. It must have been hard trying to erase memories, or visions of loved ones appearing in dreams. There was no way around that, of course, and recurring dreams came to be considered omens— and not always good ones, either. There are traditionalists who think it best to disconnect from their people when that time has come. They feel loved ones should move forward unburdened. It was not so long ago families still had to make that hard choice; the stories are not unknown. Paul wouldn't want it to come to that. Although he knew his own family would never go so far as to abandon him in such a way.

The alcove was not much below the rim, hidden by a huge slab of sandstone calved almost vertically from the roof to hide the front of the cave-like interior; it was not an uncommon phenomena. His uncle Elmore Shining Horse, on an expedition to gather medicinal plants, had shown him this place and it remained stuck in his mind. The old man first found it as a child chasing a rabbit that sought refuge there. His uncle had grown up in that country and often mentioned what a good place this would be to spend the afterlife. The climb down, while not so steep, was rough with fallen rock and scree tiring for an old man who was not quite himself.

Once inside, Paul T'Sosi found the recess much as he remembered it more than a half-century earlier. Odd how easily those old memories came now, yet how hard it was to recall what happened only the day before. The walls and ceiling here were still free of soot or other hint of human discovery, the floor clean of any sign, leaving only a layer of sand to record the end of his own story. There was a little space at the end of the alcove where one could lie protected while still looking out over the country, down to the river of shining water, and feast on that vision until he knew no more. *Not many could afford such a tomb as this*, Paul thought.

The west-facing slab, now bathed in the glow of a setting sun, radiated warmth, and allowed a comforting, almost ethereal light to filter in. Being dead, he wagered, was not the hard part. It was the process of dying that remained in doubt…a certain mental fortitude might be required for that. His own father died in his sleep only to be found the next morning with a smile on his face. His father's brother, Elmore Shining Horse, thought this a great blessing, saying, his brother might have been thinking of something…but would never say what he thought that might be.

Paul settled himself on his worn blanket and sorted through the meager pile of dried plants and medicinal herbs beside him. They would make the end easier, or so it was said. The water bottle he set aside, certain it was enough to sustain him through the simple ritual.

He had not meant to eat that morning but the look on the face of the Piute woman was so sad he felt obligated to take at least a few bites when it was offered. He had purposely brought no food; the idea was not to prolong the process, but to allow a natural progression of events to eventually bring things to a close. Maybe, he would at last recall those shadow dancers at the back edge of his mind. It would be good to see those people again.

As the sun sank beyond the river, Paul fell under the spell of a last trickle of light touching him with a final blessing. Truly, he had chosen the right place.

17

The Supposition

Charlie Yazzie had almost convinced himself he had done the best he could by Tressa and Little Abe Garza. They were safe where they were...if they stayed there, but he had no real control over that and it was all he could manage for the present; other duties needed tending. He dropped Thomas off and by the time he reached the office it was nearly time for everyone to shut down for the day. He sat in his chair for a few moments quietly watching the exodus, mentally listing those things yet to be done, so many, he felt guilty and wondered how he would ever catch up. Billy Red Clay had radioed him on his way into town asking if they could meet after work—he had some news, he said.

Charlie watched the clock and guessed Billy was closing his own office about now and probably wouldn't be long doing it. He looked toward the reception area; Gwen had obviously left early. Charlie made a mental note not to let that pass without comment the next morning. He still hadn't heard from Bob Freeman at DEA. That was strange he thought *Bob seemed so anxious to stay on top of the situation earlier.* Charlie knew the agent was probably enroute and likely out of radio range. Still it bothered him.

The investigator, to busy his mind, sorted through his in-box thinking Gwen might have left something for him...a note or excuse for her leaving early perhaps...but obviously not. Things had apparently gone well enough without him. Charlie sighed and after glancing out the window to check the parking lot, decided a restroom break was in order. Returning back down the hall he could see Billy Red Clay at the reception desk, looking undecided, as though waiting for Gwen to appear and check him in.

Catching his eye, Charlie motioned him on back and was already seated behind the desk when Billy came in, frowning up at the clock, and saying, "Your people don't waste any time clearing out after work, do they?"

"No," the investigator couldn't deny that, "but I intend having a little talk with the chief instigator tomorrow morning; She's been gaining a few minutes on me every day—if I let it go on unchecked she won't be coming in at all."

Billy took this to mean Gwen might soon find herself out of a job and nodded his encouragement. Temporary services had sent the woman over to Tribal a couple of times and they hadn't gotten along.

It seemed as though Gwen figured anyone with so small an office as Billy's probably didn't deserve much consideration. The young policeman shook those thoughts away and recovered his sense of purpose. He was again focused when he said; "I went out to Emma Bitsii's place today. She lives a damn long way out there, too, so far, in fact, they used to let her ride the school bus back and forth to work before she retired. She never learned to drive and had very little schooling of any kind. Everyone always thought Captain Beyale had something to do with Emma being hired in the first place...along with a couple of other things no one could figure out.

Charlie raised a questioning eyebrow. "Such as...?"

Billy scratched his jaw, and stroked his sparse chin whiskers. "Such as being on the books as Office Manager when all she really did was keep the Captain's office straightened up and the file room in order—along with being in charge of checking the folders in and out."

This was the sort of nepotism that went on in every facet of the Tribal hierarchy and Charlie wasn't surprised. His was one of the few agencies taking an aggressive attitude toward hiring in that regard. So far Charlie had managed to keep a lid on it but was sure there were instances flying under the radar. When his own wife wanted to come back to her old job—after the babies were up and running around— he had to tell her it was no longer possible. "Things have changed at Legal Services," was all he said, and didn't mention being the instrument of that change. The sad thing was, Sue was the best Office Manager they'd ever had.

Nepotism had long been rampant on the reservation and few thought anything of it. Everyone seemed to be related, either by clan or blood, and there was little to be done about it as far as Charlie could see. It was a frequent cause of jealousy and suspicion among the rank and file, and a constant worry for administrators. The subject was critical enough to occasionally be brought up at Council meetings, but nothing ever came of it. Things just continued to rock along as they always had—blood and clan were not to be denied when it came to allocating jobs on the reservation. Billy Red Clay was as aware of the situation in his own organization as Charlie Yazzie was in his, and neither man bothered to pretend otherwise.

For a moment the Tribal Officer seemed almost reluctant to continue. "Emma Bitsii wouldn't say much in the beginning, but I went prepared and when I told her I'd been looking into her past over around Cameron, she changed her tune." Billy pulled his chair closer as he turned to peer out the open door, checking to see who might be lurking about. Satisfied, he went on. "Charlie, I have irrefutable proof that Robert Ashki was Emma Bitsii's illegitimate son." He paused to gauge how the investigator would take this and was surprised at how little reaction he saw.

Charlie doesn't believe me, was his first thought, but he pressed on more determined than ever to verify the facts of the business. "The information wasn't hard to find... once I knew where to look. There wasn't a centralized record repository back then; when babies were born at home they didn't always get added to the tribal roll, sometimes not until they started school."

Charlie raised an eyebrow; somewhat surprised Billy would follow through with his investigation over his boss's protests. He could see the reasoning behind the young policeman's decision but hoped he had more than what he'd heard so far to back up this astonishing claim. "Okay...how did her relationship with Ashki not come out before this? The woman's been around for a number of years?"

"That's where it gets a little sticky... When Emma up and left her hometown, on the other side of the reservation, she somehow wound up here and took up with another man who later became her new husband and he already had a son. And here's the kicker, Charlie..." Billy Red Clay paused for effect. "That little boy, as it turns out, was Captain Beyale." Billy feared this might stretch his credibility beyond any hope of acceptance. He kept his eyes on the investigator and wouldn't have blamed him had he not believed the story.

Charlie rocked back in his chair and stared across at Billy as though he thought he might be drunk...or crazy. Clearly, Billy was neither. Charlie pondered a moment more, attempting to digest this latest information, then gave a low whistle. "You've verified all this, Billy—there's no possible mistaking any of it?"

"It's verified, and then some, Charlie. Yesterday, when I finally began putting my research together, it was pretty obvious Emma was at the center of it. When I went to the Captain for permission to question her I didn't say anything about what I'd been up to. I wanted to talk to Emma first you understand, make sure I was on solid ground. Even before hearing what I'd come up with, he refused permission, immediately became argumentative, and went on the defensive. That was when I knew for certain there was something there. Things became heated and I could see Beyale was getting worked up. I tried to back off a little and let him calm down, but too late. He went into some sort of cardiac arrest right before my eyes; you know the story from there—he's in the hospital in Farmington now—they had to transfer him a couple of hours ago."

"How is he? I got in touch with the clinic after you first called but couldn't get a straight answer." Charlie couldn't believe he hadn't thought to ask Billy right off. He'd always gotten along with the Captain, and his concern was genuine enough, though he wanted to support Billy Red Clay as well.

"It was a stroke, Charlie, the worst kind, the doctor said, and I can only guess that led to the heart attack, if that's what it was." Billy looked down at the desk and when he spoke, Charlie could barely understand the whispered words. "According to the doctor in Farmington, they're doing everything they can, but they think there's not much hope." The officer hung his head. "It's my fault, Charlie, I caused it—I shouldn't have pushed him—but there was just so obvious a connection I couldn't help trying to get to the bottom of it." Billy took a ragged breath, "Emma Bitsii considered both those boys her sons and loved them both in her own way I suppose, but still when the chips were down, Robert Ashki came first, I guess being her own blood he counted most."

When Billy paused to look him in the eye, Charlie nodded for him to continue.

"While in prison, Ashki corresponded with his mother on a regular basis, and was eventually able to convince her to get hold of the Tarango file for him. She said Robert became obsessed with getting some sort of *evidence* on Thomas Begay's uncle, John Nez. He was certain that file was the key. As you know, he and John had long been at odds in the Navajo Mountain District. John has always been fairly prominent up there—once even threatened to run against Robert for Council. And after Ashki was sent to prison, John not only ran but won Ashki's seat on the Council. Robert couldn't stand that and swore to get even when he got out."

Charlie was by now shaking his head and holding up a hand, trying to put it all in perspective, "Whoa! What are you getting at, Billy?"

When Billy looked up it was obvious he, too, was struggling with the improbability of his own conclusions. "When I confronted Emma with the birth records she broke down completely...talked for nearly an hour about the two boys and what different paths they had taken. Yet, she felt they were both her sons, and it tore her apart to have to choose between them. Robert Ashki, of course, ever the master manipulator, persuaded her he had been wrongly accused and could vindicate himself if only he had the file on the Mojado case. What he actually thought, was that it might be the deciding factor in ousting John Nez from the Council."

Charlie's mind shifted into overdrive. "How in the hell did this stay quiet? It's just the sort of crap people love to talk about around here... I've never heard a whisper of it." Charlie's voice rose, "How could anyone not know?"

"Emma wasn't from around here, Charlie, she was from over around Cameron, at the far edge of the reservation. Ashki's father wouldn't let her take the boy with her when she left, she was drinking again and running around a lot, let's just say her reputation wasn't the best. The woman was basically hounded out of that country by the father's family who kept Robert, saying Emma wasn't fit to care for a child and that he should be raised by his relatives.

Normally that would have been the mother's relatives, but Emma's parents were dead, and her one aunt wanted nothing to do with the woman. Emma said she began drinking even more after that, and by her own admission became impossible to get along with. She eventually left her new husband, too, basically abandoning her stepson in the process. She lived in Flagstaff for a few years. You know how it is there Charlie—well, it was worse back then—a bad drug scene even back then, many of the young people who hung out in town got lost in it."

Charlie shook his head. "Only on the reservation." It was clear Billy was taking no pleasure in the telling of these things and Charlie thought he detected a bit of sympathy for Emma Bitsii. "It's no secret how women who leave their kids, are thought of here on the reservation, Billy. It's always been that way. Mothers abandoning children—that's one of the unforgivable sins among the old people. They call those women, *Yóó'a'háaskahh*—one who is lost."

Billy Red Clay winced. "We both know there are plenty of men on the reservation who leave their families, but there's always been a different standard for women, hasn't there? Fair or not, the expectations are higher for women." Billy threw up his hands in frustration and looked to Charlie for some sort of affirmation, but the investigator only indicated the young policeman should continue. Billy sighed, "Emma kept track of both boys, and as they got older she would come to one or the other, occasionally, for a little help. Finally, Captain Beyale, who had been with Tribal only a short while at that point, still managed to get her a part time job. With his help, she began straightening herself out, but never let one son know about the other, at least not as far as I could find out. The Captain may never have had any idea Robert Ashki was his stepbrother and apparently Ashki didn't know about the Captain either. Both of their fathers have been dead for years." Billy Red Clay looked tired and Charlie Yazzie felt sorry for him. If not for Billy's curiosity, and dedicated police work the truth might never have come out, but Charlie could see uncovering these secrets had taken their toll on young Billy.

Charlie looked up from the notes he was scrawling across a legal pad. "I guess that only leaves one thing we *don't* know."

"Right. Was Robert Ashki's death really an accident?" Billy was again thinking out in front and Charlie could see the wheels turning.

"Well, it's pretty clear Ashki was on his way to Albuquerque, and probably to find someone who could use the file to discredit John Nez...a lawyer maybe. Robert must have had some deranged thought he could pressure the Council into recalling John's seat."

Both men now sat back in their chairs. Charlie Yazzie was first to speak. "No matter how all this turns out, Billy, I want you to know I think it was a damn good piece of police work on your part. We may never know who killed Ashki, but I'm betting we haven't heard the last of it."

Billy nodded, "The reservation keeps its secrets all right, but I'm not through yet. I expect there's more to this story than we can even imagine. Why is it nothing is ever what it seems out here?"

This was one of the few times Charlie didn't have an answer for the young officer.

After Billy Red Clay left the office, Charlie closed up his desk and locked his file drawers, a precaution he had only recently implemented. He was about to take down his hat and Levi Jacket when the phone rang and he thought it could only be his wife, wanting him to stop at the store on the way home...or, it might be Bob Freeman, already long overdue checking in. It proved to be the latter, and as usual, Bob didn't waste any time getting to the point.

"Charlie, I know you expected to hear something sooner than this; needless to say, we ran into a little snag and, apparently, just missed you at the funeral home. We got there just as Sheriff Schott and another of his units pulled up. There had been reports of shots fired, he told us, and wondered how we just happened to be in the neighborhood. He was pretty quick to point out local law enforcement was on a different radio frequency than the Feds and wanted to know what we were doing there." Bob chuckled. "In fact, Sheriff Schott seemed more interested in how we came to be there, than in what the shooting was all about. When I didn't bother to answer, he sort of blew a gasket; said they'd had reports of a high-speed chase along with gunfire and he intended getting to the bottom of what was going on...then he accused us of operating out of our jurisdiction."

Charlie could hear the smile even over the phone. "What did you say to that, Bob?"

"I didn't say a *damn* thing, Charlie, it was Federal business and he wasn't on our 'need to know' list. I'll probably hear about it later, of course," Bob chuckled again, "we'll see."

Charlie shifted the phone to his other shoulder as he pulled his note pad closer. "I guess you're wanting to know what happened with the Tarango woman and Abe Garza? I really wish you could have been there, Bob. We could have used some backup. There were gunmen inside the funeral home and the two of them, Abe and Tressa, barely escaped with their lives...that's how Abe tells it anyway." Charlie figured this was the real reason for Bob's call and the DEA Agent had only used the story of Sheriff Schott's intervention to deflect any blame that he hadn't been at the funeral home in time to help. Bob was good at that sort of thinking and Charlie wondered if it was part of his training, or just came naturally.

"Of course, I want to know what happened, Charlie. I figure you have those people stashed somewhere, and that's good; I don't even want to know where right now. I haven't had much sleep for the last twenty-four hours and I'm going to catch up on that while I can. We've got people all over this, and there could be a break anytime. Can you shake loose early for coffee in the morning, at the *Diné Bikayah?* Agent Smith from FBI wants some sort of sit-down…along with Billy Red Clay, of course. Fred thinks the Tribal cops are feeling a little left out of late."

"It'll have to be early, Bob, before my people get here. I'm thinking it's going to be a full morning; the Cafe opens at six, let's make it then."

Charlie was almost to his car before he remembered he should have asked if old Sancho Mariano was still hanging on, up in Colorado. He was somewhat anxious to see how that would affect Bob Freeman's pursuit of the Sinaloa investigation, and more importantly, what charges, if any, might be filed against the pair hiding out at Alfred Nakii's old place. Despite himself, he couldn't help thinking like a lawyer. He also wondered if Harley Ponyboy had returned home to find his vittles missing. That was another can of worms he'd have to face eventually.

18

The Follower

Tressa Tarango was not the sort of woman to wait around to see what was going to happen. If necessary, she thought, she'd *make* something happen. She wouldn't allow herself and Little Abe to fall into another trap.

Abraham Garza was still asleep, though how that was possible she couldn't fathom. She had been banging around getting breakfast and cleaning up for half an hour. She could only attribute it to his breeding. It was different blood that flowed in her veins, bluer blood, the blood of *Conquistadores* and she was determined to do it justice. Their future must remain in their own hands and despite Charlie Yazzie's apparent good intentions—ultimately it would be up to them, or rather to her, to take charge. *I am the only one who knows what's best for us.*

"Abraham! Get up..." Tressa turned from her work at the stove to yell at the snoring figure on the couch. "It's almost daylight, *Hombrecito*." She knew Abe hated being called "little man" but felt it might at least hurry him along. She continued cutting up the last of the potatoes, dropping them into the hot bacon grease from the night before.

There were still three eggs and when she thought it was time, she cracked them on the edge of the skillet before gently easing them to one side of the pan, where they immediately began to sizzle and pop. Toast was browning under the broiler and she watched it like a hawk. She doubted it would make any difference to Little Abe who'd known little better. She, on the other hand, *had* known better…much better; Luca had been a good provider when once they'd left the squalor of the village, and she'd gotten used to that new life. She meant to have those comforts back…and soon, too.

Tressa was not convinced she and Little Abe should entrust their lives to a federal agency in exchange for cooperation—she had seen how that sort of thing turned out down in Mexico. Of course, this was the United States; still, she had heard stories. There might not be much difference—at least not as much as one might be led to believe. She knew enough about the DEA to guess they ran their business pretty much to suit themselves.

As far as Tressa knew, all the authorities had on *her* so far were rumors and loose talk. According to Charlie Yazzie, they did have something more concrete on Abraham Garza. She was convinced that once they had Abe in their power they wouldn't let him go back to Mexico at all…that was almost certain. Little Abe might not be turned loose for a long time. Maybe never. He had become crucial to her plan. No, the two of them had to make their move now. No one else had *their* best interest at heart—no one.

She heard Little Abe stir behind her and turned to see him sitting up, wrapped in his blanket with one corner over his head like a hood; he looked across at her and frowned as he rubbed the sleep from one eye. "I wish you wouldn't call me *hombrecito*, I'm almos' twenty-two years old, you know" He stretched and made rough noises in his throat.

"Yes, yes you are, Abraham, and it's time you started acting like it." She waved an arm toward the back of the trailer. "Go wash up in that tiny little *baño*." Let's see what you can make of yourself this morning." She turned back to the stove but could hear Abe muttering as he grabbed his clothes and shuffled off to the bathroom.

"Just once I would like to see a little respect," he whispered under his breath, knowing he had not been so idle as Tressa thought. He'd lain awake half the night trying to figure a way around their dilemma. He had even tried formulating some sort of plan, but just when he seemed close to something, he had been rudely awakened, which caused him to forget the most important part. No matter, it would come to him eventually. In the meantime he, also, was not so sure about Charlie Yazzie and his overbearing friend. In his mind he and Tressa owed their escape to only one man—the ever-dangerous Chuy Mariano. Abe believed as Tressa did, they must still be under the protective wing of Chuy's father, Sancho—whether the old man was alive or not, was quite another matter.

Tressa looked up as Abraham came back to the table, hair slicked back, usual grin in place. She sat the fuller of the two plates at his end of the table and motioned him to sit. "It's not much, but there will be better days once we are in Mexico."

"I been thinking about that, Tressa. Why do you think Chuy Mariano wants us to make it to Sonora so badly?"

"Because it's what his father wants."

"But don't you think there is something more to it than that?"

"The old man likes me, that's all."

Little Abe thought about this, *everyone likes Tressa. What's not to like?* But Abe was smart enough to realize the danger of being caught in enemy territory. The Mariano family controlled Sonora State, and much of Western Chihuahua as well, still the Sinaloa Cartel were making significant in-roads. It was only a matter of time before the two factions came to war. How that played out would decide who controlled the most lucrative stretch of the border, and the bulk of the U.S. market.

Tressa took a small bite of egg and potatoes. "We need to eat and get out of here, Abraham, before those shooters catch up to us again."

"I don't see how they could find us here, Tressa. This is a long way from anywhere, and I'm pretty sure we weren't followed. One of those hired guns got hit, too, I'm pretty sure of that. The one at the front door wasn't feeling so good, neither. It's probably going to be a few days before those two are up to doing much."

"That's exactly why we need to be getting out of here while the *getting* is good. We might not get off so easy next time."

Little Abe chewed this over along with his eggs and studied the box on the shelf behind Tressa—the box containing Luca Tarango's ashes. "Maybe there won't be a next time Tressa. You do know it was Chuy Mariano that fired that last shot yesterday."

"I know. There's not many like him. He's a good son to old Sancho…to carry out his father's wishes.

"Well, what about those *Indios*? That Charlie Yazzie said it would be safer for us to wait here until he got back."

"I'm only thinking of you, Abraham. You are the one Drug Enforcement wants to get their hands on…not me."

"That may be true, Tressa, but if they decide to tie us into the Espinosa murders—which they could probably do if it suits them—then we might both be better off to cooperate." Abraham Garza was not without basic knowledge of how the DEA worked its business. Flipping people was what they did, and he'd known plenty who took advantage of it, a few came out all right, but not everyone. *What if they knew about the suitcase his Papá had him bring into the country?* He'd hoped that secret died with Hector Espinosa—but who knew? It was a hard and dirty business no matter how you looked at it, and in the end, few walked away better off.

While Tressa was cleaning up she couldn't help thinking that Abe had given her something else to worry about. She hadn't considered there might be conspiracy charges related to the death of the hated Espinosas. *So, it's cooperate or go down, and for something we had very little to do with—Little Abe could be right.*

"Get the truck ready, Abraham, we're leaving."

"Are you sure that's what we should do, Tressa? It's going to get rough down in Mexico. I've thought about it, and I'm pretty sure it's going to get lively down there."

"It's rough everywhere, Abraham, I'm finally catching on to that." Tressa began taking down the few things she'd washed the night before—it wasn't much and in minutes she was ready to go.

Abraham stood helplessly by, not really sure what he should be doing. Exasperated, he grabbed up their two small bags and opened the door. "Uh…Oh," he whispered barely loud enough for Tressa to hear. "A pickup is coming…" It was a truck he'd not seen before.

Tressa, just behind him, poked her head around to see what she could make of it. "Maybe it's just the neighbor checking out our truck."

Abe nodded but thought if it were the neighbor, he might be there to get his food back, or barring that, at least get paid for it. *What did they say his name was? Harley Ponyboy, I think.* Little Abe stared harder at the truck as it stopped in a cloud of dust then eased forward a bit, almost touching their old Ford's bumper.

When the dust cleared, and the door opened, Tressa said in a barely audible voice, "Whoever it is, he's an Indian...and a pretty good sized one, too." The man vaguely reminded her of someone, but she couldn't quite decide who; she didn't know that many Indians.

The man walked right up to the steps like he owned the place. There was something about his attitude—and then it came to her—this was an older, heavier version of Thomas Begay. Not quite so tall as Thomas, but definitely older.

"How are you folks today? Doing all right I hope?"

Tressa pushed past Little Abe who she could see already had his hand in his pocket.

"We are doing fine, thank you. We were told we could spend the night here last night and were just getting ready to be on our way."

The man came closer and though Tressa was standing on the upper step, he was still about eye level. "Ah, yes, I know all about that…and who you are, too." He smiled briefly, "I was told to take you somewhere else. Someone thinks you might be better off in another place."

Tressa gave Little Abe a significant look. The sun was just moving up behind the man now, and Tressa had to squint a little to make him out. "And who might you be then?"

"Oh… my name is John Nez from up around Navajo Mountain. My nephew is Thomas Begay. I stopped by to see him last night and when he heard I would be coming this way he asked if I would drop by and maybe take you somewhere else. He said you're strangers around here and might need a little help this morning."

"Well, that's very thoughtful of your nephew, and of you, too, but we're fine up here and as I said, we're just getting ready to leave—we have a long way to go today."

"Yes, well my nephew has a phone now, and it was Charlie Yazzie who called and said he would like for you to be taken to a different place until he can have another little chat with you."

"Do you intend to force us to go with you, Mr. Nez?" Tressa's voice took a slight edge. "Because if you do, my friend Abraham here might have something to say about that." She nudged Abraham hoping he might make some kind of tough talk and maybe take charge of the situation.

Little Abe hadn't said a word and apparently didn't intend to. This was a big Indian and Abe couldn't be sure the man didn't have a knife in his own pocket.

Tressa was looking at Little Abe to see what he intended to do about this John Nez from Navajo Mountain. Almost a minute passed, and though Abraham postured and screwed up his mouth a little, he still hadn't said a word. Finally, Tressa decided to speak for him. "If you don't move your truck and let us out, Abe here will kick your ass." She tried to sound matter-of-fact, as though she had good reason to believe Abe could do such a thing should he take a mind. She felt this was the sort of talk that might bolster Little Abe's courage and cause him to take a stronger position in the matter.

Abraham blinked his eyes a couple of times, thinking he had simply not heard her right. The last thing on his mind was kicking this big Indian's ass. He'd had a light breakfast and was feeling a little weak as it was.

John Nez looked from one to the other of them and said, "I see… Well, I hope it doesn't come to that. If it does I'll have to knock him down." He turned his attention to Tressa Tarango. "And if you don't get your hand out of your coat pocket I may have to knock you down, too. I've never knocked no woman down before, but I can see you have a gun in there, and I don't feel like getting shot this morning. I've been shot before, and it hurts."

Abraham looked down and could clearly see the outline of a pistol in Tressa's pocket. "Tressa, I didn't know you had a gun. That might have come in handy yesterday." He took his hand out of his own pocket and handed his knife to the Indian. "I think we better do what he says, Tressa. If he's anything like his nephew, he probably means business." He looked at her again but this time with a hurt expression. "I could have used that gun yesterday..."

Tressa glanced up at him and after hesitating only a second or two, took her hand away from her pocket.

John Nez nodded and moved right up in her face. "That's better," he said calmly. "Now if you'll just turn a little toward me I'll take that out and hold it for you. You can have it back later—I already have one. You've done the right thing here," John assured her. "You wouldn't have stood a chance in hell."

Tressa turned slightly and John fished out the handgun and put it in his own pocket.

Abe shrugged and whispered in her ear, "He didn't really have a gun, Tressa...but now he does."

Regardless of who was or wasn't armed at this point, Tressa could see she and Abraham were no match for this man...not under any circumstance. When she turned to go back into the trailer for the box with Luca in it, she thought it only polite to mention, "Mr. Nez, I don't have anything to offer you to eat this morning; we are fresh out of everything."

"That's all right. I've had my breakfast and there's plenty to eat where we're going—we should be good till Charlie Yazzie gets out to talk with you."

Tressa and Abraham gathered up their possessions and stood by their truck waiting to see what travel arrangements this Indian had in mind.

"I see your truck has Colorado plates on it."

"Yes," Abraham said proudly. "It's a built truck, you know, like for...I dunno, racing maybe, I guess that's maybe what it was for. It's fast."

"I could see that from the exhaust pipe, have you tried to start it today?"

"Not yet, uh...why?"

"It wouldn't have started."

"Why not?"

"It has a potato stuck in the exhaust...I saw it right off. If you'd tried starting it you might have damaged your engine...or worse."

"Worse?"

"Well, if it blew out while one of you was passing behind...it might have killed you."

Tressa canted her head slightly, "How did a potato get in our exhaust?"

"I expect my nephew jammed it in there to keep you two from leaving. He did it to my truck once when he was a kid."

"What happened?"

"Nothing happened to the truck, but plenty happened to him."

Nobody said anything for a short moment, but it was plain everyone was thinking about that potato and how someone might have gotten killed by it. No one wanted to get killed by a potato shot from a thirty-year old truck. There wouldn't have been anything funny about that.

John Nez pointed at his own truck and then to Abraham. "You'd best follow us in my pickup, it's not very fast at all. This lady and I will take your racing truck."

19

The Meeting

Charlie Yazzie spent most of his night thinking how he would approach Bob Freeman regarding Little Abe and Tressa Tarango. While he still figured a deal with Freeman might be to the pair's advantage, now it was getting complicated. It might only be the kind of lawyer he was coming out, but he was beginning to feel some sense of responsibility for the two and didn't want it on his head should they come off badly dealing with Drug Enforcement, whose methods he was beginning to think somewhat questionable.

Sue Yazzie woke several times to find her husband staring into the dark. When the baby woke and toddled into their bedroom it was Charlie who put Sasha in bed between them. Ordinarily he would have returned the baby to her own bed across from little Joseph Wiley, but on this morning he appreciated a little company from someone neutral on the subject of him helping these people reach Mexico. Charlie tried to convince Sue it was only an option and probably wouldn't happen; at least he hoped that would be the case. He had already decided, however, that should Drug Enforcement take Little Abe into custody without a deal that included equal protection for the woman, it could change the entire dynamics of where he was in the matter.

Sue generally got up to make Charlie's breakfast when he had to go in early, but not today. He considered making oatmeal and toast but after noting the time, he didn't, making do instead with only a cup of coffee and the thought of something more substantial later at the cafe.

Sue had mentioned she and the children would be busy packaging dried peaches. The Yazzie's little row of peach trees had begun bearing in earnest this year, and all things considered, the harvest had been bountiful. She dried more peaches than they could use she told him and intended to take some to Lucy Tallwoman and Charlie's aunt, Annie Eagletree, if she had enough time. Peaches and apricots came to this part of the country with the Mormons, she'd been told, though, some claimed they were already there, brought by the Mexicans. Either way, the dried fruit had become a favorite winter staple for the canyon dwelling *Diné*.

Sue's mother had grown peaches and as a young girl she had helped. Her favorite treat, as a child, was hot fry bread filled with stewed peach filling—the Navajo version of peach pie.

~~~~~~~~

The wind was coming up and the little metal-roofed porch rattled and shook as Charlie looked out the window and watched a plume of dust swirl down

the drive before slipping across the highway to the river. The clouds, banking well to the north were sending wind-blown scouts ahead to promise a nasty day…maybe in more ways than one.

Charlie left for the meeting at the *Diné Bikeyah* still hungry, and was already thinking of *huevos rancheros* as he pulled into the parking lot. He headed directly for the big back table next to the window.

Bob Freeman was already there, as was Officer Billy Red Clay who waved Charlie on back, as though the investigator might not have noticed them in the nearly empty room. Billy held up a cup to alert the waitress and grinned as Charlie pulled out a chair.

"*Yaa' eh t'eeh,* Counselor." The young policeman pushed the stainless coffeepot toward him with a smile.

Bob Freeman signaled a greeting as well and then motioned toward the door where Fred Smith was making an entrance—knocking the dust off his hat and frowning back at the approaching weather. The FBI man appeared a little out of sorts, which was not the amiable lawman's usual demeanor.

Bob raised a finger in salute and regarded the agent before speaking. "Good day for working on reports back at the office, huh, Fred?" He was glad a suit and tie weren't always required in his line of work.

"I just had my car washed last night, too." Fred waved it off with what he hoped came across as good humor.

The waitress appeared with yet another steaming pot of coffee and filled everyone's cup before taking orders. The girl seemed to be on good terms with Billy Red Clay, and the two bantered back and forth a few moments before she left for the kitchen; obviously, this was not the pair's first encounter.

Charlie nudged the young policeman. "Nice," he teased, and stirring his coffee, didn't remark further.

Billy turned a shade darker and was glad Thomas Begay wasn't there; his uncle wouldn't have let the subject go so easily.

Fred Smith looked over at his Tribal Liaison Officer but only nodded. Fred was an old hand with the Navajo and knew Billy well enough not to make too much of it and then even moved to help him out. "So, Billy, how's Captain Beyale coming along this morning?" Fred was aware he checked on Beyale's condition several times a day.

"Not very well, I'm afraid. I talked to the floor nurse first thing this morning and she said he was still hooked up to support and isn't showing any improvement. I'll get back with the doctor later—maybe we'll know more then."

Charlie could see Billy still felt responsible for the captain's misfortune. "So, Lieutenant Arviso's in charge now?"

"Pretty much, but it's like a ship without a captain. I think they are waiting for something more from the doctors before actually appointing Joe; that could come any time now if there's no improvement."

Fred Smith held up a hand. "Right, down to business. Quantico sent us the results from the paint sample taken from Robert Ashki's truck. They believe it's from an older model Chrysler product. But that's as far as it goes...really nothing new that points to foul play. Our people say the paint damage could have happened anytime, not necessarily at the time of the wreck, and there's no real proof anyone forced him off the road. The final autopsy shows death by head trauma, and the coroner thinks that might well be attributed to the wreck itself." Even Fred appeared surprised they had nothing more to go on than this. "It's beginning to look like a blind alley."

Billy Red Clay looked up. "They returned what was left of our file...a few pages were missing...maybe lost out of the wreck and carried away by the wind for all anyone knows."

Charlie felt compelled to add, "Robert Ashki was obviously complicit in the theft of the file and just as obviously, had some reason for taking it to Albuquerque with him." He paused and looked at Billy. "One thing is for certain, there's no lack of people who might have wanted the man dead. But that doesn't mean that's what happened."

Fred Smith held up a cautionary finger as the waitress brought their tray, and no one said anything further until she distributed the food, smiling all the while at Billy Red Clay who concentrated on his breakfast and didn't look up. No one appeared to notice and when the girl left everyone busied themselves with the food for a few minutes.

The DEA's man didn't seem inclined to discuss the case from his agency's perspective, and he was glad when Fred Smith took up the conversation again. "An interesting report came in yesterday evening... maybe one of you might know something about it?" He reached for the syrup and gave his pancakes a good dousing. "It seems a body was found last night dumped in a patch of weeds south of town. Hispanic male about thirty years old, shot in the chest with a load of double-ought buckshot, but at a distance they doubted was lethal. The preliminary says infection was the eventual cause of death, a slow and painful way to go by all accounts." Here, Fred put down his fork and looked up to three blank faces. "There is one more thing—on the inside of his left wrist was a small tattoo, the mark of the Sinaloa Cartel. There was no other identification." The FBI man glanced at Bob Freeman and smiled, "Our people checked with your people, Bob, and they confirmed the tattoo indicated an affiliation with the Sinaloa bunch. I assumed they let you know."

"I've been a little busy, Fred, and I haven't seen the morning briefing as yet, that generally doesn't go out until the Albuquerque office opens at eight. I'm guessing the Bureau thinks this might be connected to the shooting at the funeral home yesterday; anything new on that, Fred? I expected the FBI to be all over it by now."

"We *are* 'all over it,' Bobby, and as soon as we find something we can hang a hat on, I'll be first to let you know." The FBI man grimaced, "Sheriff Dudd Schott found the funeral director tied up in a closet. The man was incoherent and his story still doesn't add up. We are trying to get that straightened out right now."

Charlie thought things might be going off track between the agents and changed the direction of the conversation. "Bob, what's the latest on Sancho Mariano—still hanging on I hope?"

The DEA Agent redirected his gaze toward the Legal Services Investigator and smiled. "It was touch and go last night, according to the hospital. The doctor didn't see how the old man could last till morning—this is the second time he's thought that. Mexicans can be incredibly tough people. I expect you know that from your past run-in with Luca Tarango." He smiled at Charlie. "Much like Indians, I guess."

Billy Red Clay couldn't help grinning at this and lifted an eyebrow at the investigator.

Charlie fixed the agent with a thoughtful gaze of his own. "Well, I hope you're right about that Bob…I know a couple who may be about to find out how tough they are."

Fred Smith looked up at the big clock above the cash register then with a frown, double checked his watch as he pushed his plate back and announced, "Gentlemen, I've got to get back to the office. We have some high-level people coming in from Albuquerque this morning." He gave them all a searching look before going on. "At the moment, the Bureau is not directing any major attention to yesterday's incident at the funeral home. The local authorities seem to think they have that well in hand. We won't interfere unless we hear otherwise." The FBI man winked. "…But that could change."

Billy Red Clay took this as a cue and wiping his mouth on his napkin he, too, pushed back his chair and rose from the table, eyes now fastened on the retreating back of the Senior FBI Agent. Billy took his job as Tribal Liaison Officer seriously. "There's something I need to go over with Fred on the Ashki

241

matter." He looked down at Charlie. "We'll talk later, maybe by then I'll know more about how the Captain is doing." And with this, Billy headed for the front entryway—just as Fred looked back and held the door for him. A cold blast of sand-laden wind peppered both men, causing Billy to curse as he caught the door and then slammed it shut behind them.

When they were alone Bob Freeman appeared more at ease as he smiled and looked across the table at Charlie. The agent pointed a finger. "You've still got our package I assume…" then watched as Charlie took a sip of coffee and swallowed hard.

The investigator coughed, pretending the drink was hotter than it actually was. He touched a napkin to his mouth and nodded at the agent. "As far as I know Bob, they are safe and secure—last I saw of them anyway. I'll be heading that direction right after breakfast."

Freeman frowned. "No one's with them now?"

"No, Bob, if you'll remember, you wanted my part in this kept confidential. That's what I'm doing. I can't be everywhere at once, I do have a job you know." Charlie kept his tone as agreeable as possible but hoped he'd made himself clear in the matter. He had a feeling Bob had something else he hadn't touched on yet this morning; he intended to remain noncommittal until he found out what that might be.

"Charlie, I had a long talk with the federal prosecutor yesterday and he's willing to cut a deal for Abraham Garza. *If* he offers full disclosure of his connection to the Sinaloa Cartel, we'll have some touchstones to guide us in assessing the veracity of that, and I'll make clear to him the ramifications of not adhering to his agreement."

"So, the prosecutor would be offering government protection to both Garza Sr. and his son?" Charlie thought that had been the DEA's original goal.

Bob Freeman fidgeted and looked away for a moment. "That's what we *were* asking for, Charlie—immunity for both father and son. Unfortunately, about midnight last night we were informed Abraham Garza Sr. was found dead in a field outside his home. Neighbors said he was lured out by calls from someone he took to be his son. From all reports the old man had been drinking and was not his usual cautious self." Bob couldn't disguise the bitterness in his voice as he went on, "That leaves us with just one card—Abraham Jr.—he's all we've got now and that might not be enough. We still have the Espinosas' bartender on ice and his cousin, too, of course, but they were not privy to the kind of information Garza Sr. had...or the son either, for that matter." Here the agent's voice took on an air of satisfaction. "The cousin, who was the bar's bouncer, and found badly beaten if you'll remember, is willing to testify he picked up Little Abe at the border, along with a suitcase full of narcotics, and delivered him to the Espinosas'. We've got Junior dead to rights, Charlie. One way or another he's not going anywhere...just one more reason for him to do business with us...or face some pretty serious time. You might let him know that. I honestly think you have a chance to persuade the man, and that's why we're giving you first shot at him. It might take us—God knows how long—to convince him to cooperate, and as you can see, my friend, time is truly of the essence."

Charlie remained quiet as he processed this new development and how it might affect everyone involved, including himself. It was obvious now the DEA was not going to let Abraham Garza go anywhere...not if they could help it. Agent Freeman, despite his vote of confidence, would most likely be tracking Charlie when he left the café this morning.

Freeman sensed the investigator's hesitation and was quick to point out, "We figure Little Abe might be more willing than ever to cooperate—revenge being what it is for those people down there. But it might take two or three days to bring him around. You can do this, Charlie and save everyone a lot of wear and tear."

Charlie Yazzie just looked at him. "I notice there's no mention of protection for Tressa Tarango?"

Bob sighed. "We don't have any intention of charging the Tarango woman with anything at this point...though if she comes up in the investigation of yesterday's shooting, the local law might detain her for questioning or maybe even longer as a witness. Old Sancho Mariano was adamant the woman had nothing to do with the Espinosa murders in Colorado. If she's out of here pretty quick she could be totally in the clear once she's in Mexico."

"What about those shooters yesterday? It looked to me like they were out to kill both her and Abraham. We don't know where they are now or where they might show up, including Mexico." The question remained in the investigator's eyes even after he grew silent.

"That's pretty much out of our hands. We have the prosecutor's word for Garza Jr. and that's it." Bob cleared his throat and became even more reticent, "The woman's situation could, admittedly, involve some risk, however, there's still one thing we haven't touched on. From the early ramblings of Sancho Mariano, our agents believe his son, Chuy, may have been sent after the pair as a safeguard." The agent narrowed an eye at the investigator. "The deposition from the funeral director seems to indicate the presence of a third party; the day of the shooting, someone may have intervened on our little friends' behalf. If that's true, and I'm not altogether sure it is, we would be interested in *him* as well. Chuy Mariano is well up in the Sonora hierarchy, and while he's flown under the radar for years, he and his brother recently came to DEA attention as this clash between the two families heated up."

"You think this Chuy Marino is shadowing Abe and the woman with a view to keeping them safe?" Charlie sounded doubtful. "Even if Abe goes under witness protection—do you really think this man will continue looking out for Tressa?" Personally, Charlie thought this highly unlikely, but was interested in what spin the agent might put on it.

Freeman chuckled. "Chuy Mariano, is as tough as they come, Charlie...more than a match for the Sinaloa boys. As for Fred's report this morning, the one regarding the discovery of the Hispanic male's body, I'm inclined to think there are only two of those attackers left out there...and at least *one* of the two may be wounded as well. Chuy Mariano is sure to hold those boys responsible for what happened to his father; there's no doubt in my mind about that." Bob smacked the table. He'll try to take those two out and that's for damn sure." With a wry smile the agent went on. "With a little luck, Ms. Tarango could get clear of this entire mess…wind up scot-free south of the border."

Charlie toyed with this thought for a moment, considering the information in the spirit it was offered, which is to say, in the best interest of Drug Enforcement. It didn't take him long to come to a conclusion—one he'd had in the back of his mind for some time. "Let me talk to them this morning, Bob, they've come to trust me I think…at least to a point. Maybe I can convince Abraham that coming in *is* his best option given the alternatives." He didn't sound convinced and his hesitation was clear when he said, "If Abraham Garza's amenable to your offer, I'll bring him in to you this afternoon. I tend to agree it's his best way out."

"And if he's not interested?" Bob leaned forward in his chair. "I can come with you Charlie, you might need a little support out there; I may be able to help you convince him. "

Charlie immediately shook his head. "No, Bob, that probably wouldn't work—if they see you with me, they'll think I've *already* sold them down the river."

Bob saw a kernel of wisdom in what Charlie was saying and nodded finally. He did, however, have one final inducement he thought might further encourage the investigator to sway young Abraham Garza. "You know, Yazzie, our office in Albuquerque has an opening coming up soon. Field Supervisor at that...not like starting at the bottom, Charlie...hell, not like that at all. A man of your training and experience would be a shoo-in for the position; especially with just the right words of recommendation here and there." The agent paused. "I could promise you, the pay would be well above what you make now. I expect our agency would jump at the chance to have you on board." Bob Freeman watched carefully to see what sort of impression this might be making and was secretly pleased.

~~~~~~~

Charlie smiled to himself as he left the Drug Enforcement agent still standing in the parking lot staring after him. He thought Bob looked a little grim and knew for a fact the agent would attempt to follow him. *Bob Freeman means to take Abraham Garza regardless,* and Charlie was glad he'd taken the precaution the night before—asking Thomas Begay to move both Mexicans to safer quarters—and could only hope that had been done.

The Legal Services Investigator considered Bob's job offer genuine, despite the motivation behind it. It would please Sue to think he was coming around in regard to relocating off the reservation. Still, he was afraid she had it in her head they could always come back should things not work out in the city. Charlie himself knew otherwise. Deciding to make so drastic a change would indeed open new horizons for them—but there would be no returning to anything like the life they'd left behind. It might be a decision they would come to regret down the road.

Charlie would be giving up a position that took years of hard work to attain; he would never come back to anything like it. Granted, the move could be good for the children, but they might lose in some respects, as well. A number of Charlie's Indian friends at university had grown up in Albuquerque and he knew very few who retained any semblance of their native culture. It was a conundrum widely debated in sociology, and even in anthropology classes, but never with any real conclusions reached. Moving would be a life-altering decision for his family and once done would change everything forever, especially for the children.

20

The Run

Dark clouds billowed out of the northwest spitting what eventually would turn to snow. *Too early for that,* Charlie thought, but there it was. He turned on the wipers and settled in for the drive to Alfred Nakii's place. He thought it might be worth risking a quick stop at Lucy Tallwoman's house to see if Thomas had taken care of their problem. The investigator sometimes had to remind himself it was not Thomas's house; even Thomas would have thought such thinking unseemly, if not outright presumptuous. For the more traditional folks it would always be Lucy's house—regardless how great her husband's contribution. Thomas Begay would always live there only at his wife's indulgence, and subject to being divorced or ordered out, should she become displeased enough with him. Considering Thomas's past, however, and the fact he was still there at all, made this an unlikely scenario going forward. At this point in their relationship, Lucy considered them "stuck together" as the old people would say. For the traditionalist this was how the *Dinés'* matriarchal culture was structured and in their world, it remained the way of the *Diné*.

Charlie turned off the highway and was nearly halfway to the house when he saw Thomas making his way up from the corrals. He'd been watching for his children to bring the sheep down and just happened to see Charlie turn off the highway. The investigator eased his pickup into four-wheel drive and allowed it to labor through the slippery adobe mud in first gear. The investigator rolled down the passenger side window; Thomas leaned in, removing his wet hat in the process and tossing it in the seat. He rested his arms on the window frame. "You're headed up to the stash-house?" Thomas, lifting a forearm to brush the rain from his face, smiled briefly at his own joke,

Charlie nodded and motioned the tall Navajo to get in. Thomas unfolded his long legs and relaxed back against the seat with a sigh. "Harley Ponyboy came by here yesterday. That's after he had that little blowout with you about Paul T'Sosi—he told Lucy he might know where her father is." Thomas scratched his head and watched the ridge above the corrals as his kids brought the sheep skittering down through the slop.

"So, where's Harley now?"

"I dunno'. I had the sheep for a while yesterday and missed seeing him, otherwise I'd have gone with him—whether he liked it or not. You know how tight they were. Harley considers Paul his spiritual advisor. He depends on him to help keep his *hozo* in order, and on the *beauty path*...just life in general, I guess. We all do I suppose." Thomas paused, recalling some fleeting thought from the past. "Do you remember that time when the two of them came into all that money and no one could figure out where it came from...most still don't know? Well, only last week, Harley told me it came from money and jewelry buried by Paul's uncle, Elmore Shining Horse. Elmore had been dead a while at that point and I guess when they were digging it up, Paul told Harley the old Singer didn't want it to go to his wife and her kids." Thomas smiled. "They were all drunkards, he told Harley. When the older Singer passed away no one even knew he was gone for a long time—his wife and those kids buried him at night. She never would tell no one where, neither. Everyone knew Elmore had plenty of money and when Paul finally figured out where he buried it, he said he and Harley might as well have that money...it wasn't doing anyone any good where it was."

Thomas looked around the clearing. "That was when Paul told Harley where he wanted to wind up when he died—the same place Elmore had wanted to end up. Told him how to get there too. You know, in case he couldn't make it by himself." Thomas pulled out a handkerchief and blew his nose.

Charlie watched from the corner of an eye, without saying anything other than "Hmm..."

Thomas put the hanky away and clearing his throat, went on. "You know how Harley is when he likes someone; he didn't want to hear that kind of talk from the old man, but Paul told him anyway." Thomas shifted his wet jacket against the Naugahyde seat covers and went on with his story. "So, Harley tells Lucy he thinks he knows where her father might be...and why. He said Paul told him a long time ago where he wanted to go when his time came. That's when Harley told her he was going up there to see if he could find him." Thomas shook his head and couldn't say much for a moment. "Harley thinks a lot of that old man."

Charlie put his head back against the seat and rubbed his forehead with the back of one hand. He thought he felt the precursor to another headache coming on; the second one in two days. He didn't say anything as he waited for Thomas to continue his story; he already had a pretty good idea where it was going.

"Anyways, he refused to take Lucy with him when she asked. He said Paul wouldn't want that.' Harley was pretty sure, at that point, he was going to be too late to help Paul anyhow."

Charlie nodded thoughtfully. "Well, that's just a bitch, isn't it? Did Harley say how far he thought it was...or how long he thought he'd be gone?"

"Not really, but he mentioned it would take him all day just to get up in that country. That's even knowing where the old man was heading; he still figured it would take some time to locate him after he got there." Thomas spit out the window. "You know Harley...if the old man's up there, he'll find him."

Thomas seemed lost in thought for a moment, but Charlie got the impression there was more to it than that. After a long pause, his friend finally got around to it. "I know you asked me last night to go move those two people someplace different until you could get some sort of commitment from the DEA. But Lucy was so upset over Paul; I almost called you back and said I couldn't go. That's when Uncle John dropped by...right out of the blue, I guess you'd say. John mentioned he was on his way back from Shiprock—Council business, he said—and thought he'd just drop by and see us. He didn't seem to be in any big hurry, so I ask him if he would mind running up to Alfred's place and see what he could do about moving those two desperados somewhere safer." Thomas chuckled, "You know Uncle John; when someone needs help he can't refuse. He said he'd do it—said he'd always been curious what kind of woman Luca Tarango's wife was for the man to go to all that trouble trying to get her back, killing all those people and all."

"So, what was he going to do with them?"

"Well, he wanted to know where he should take 'em." Thomas raised a finger and shook it, "You told me to use my own judgment...I thought about it and said for him to take them to Annie Eagletree's place, until you could figure what to do." Thomas waited to hear he'd done something right for a change, and when that didn't happen, asked straight out, "You had someplace better in mind?"

"It's not that. I'm pretty sure Bob Freeman has been tailing me since I left the office. I imagine he's watching us right now—just waiting to see where I'm headed."

"I know…I been watching him in the side mirror. He's pulled over on that last big rise, behind the rock outcrop on the right."

Charlie checked the rear view mirror but was unable to see the blue 'sneaker' unit from that angle. "Well, I'd better get with it then, or he'll be coming up here thinking *this* is the place."

Thomas got down from the truck with a grimace, already stiff from sitting wet and cold. "I don't know how long Uncle Johnny can keep his bluff in on those two, but I'll bet he's got 'em plenty scared for right now."

"I'll be back," Charlie called, putting the Chevy in reverse and flinging mud every which way as he sloughed the truck around and got it pointed toward the highway.

Thomas Begay leaned into the wind and yelled through the rain. "Don't you worry—me and Uncle Johnny have everything under control." It was a good thing Charlie couldn't make out what he said. He'd heard Thomas say he had things under control on a number of occasions, and not one of them ever ended well.

Thomas stood there in the rain and the mist until he was sure the Legal Services Investigator was well on his way. Down on the highway there was no traffic to speak of, and it wasn't hard for someone familiar with every rock and arroyo to make out the front end of the blue sedan, though it was nearly hidden by a squat little juniper. He saw the agent hold back until Charlie was out of sight and then ease out onto the highway.

~~~~~~~

Charlie Yazzie was not the sort to believe in premonitions, but he had one this time, and it wasn't about Agent Freeman. He knew Bob was keeping just out of sight somewhere behind him. No, this was something else. He hoped Thomas's uncle wasn't tempted to wreak some personal vendetta on his two charges. Navajo are taught revenge is not healthy for a person's *hozo* and some consider it a mental aberration particular to whites. John Nez, however, was a Vietnam vet trained by the military to override what they took to be cultural deviations. That made John Nez a hard person to figure out.

The investigator caught no sign of Bob Freeman until he was already past Harley Ponyboy's place and well up the road to Alfred Nakii's trailer house. Almost there, he chanced to look up at the right time and caught sight of Bob's car in the rear-view mirror. He was struggling with the sedan as it fishtailed through the icy mud. Charlie watched and smiled as he eased up to Alfred's with his truck in four-wheel drive. No vehicles in sight, nor was there any other sign the place might be occupied—not a single fresh track in the muddy yard.

Charlie got out of his truck and leaned against the hood as the DEA Agent pulled alongside.

"Where are they, Charlie? I'm guessing this is where you left them?"

"Well, this *is* where I left them, Bob." Charlie replied truthfully enough, "But, since their pickup's gone I've got to believe, they are too." Charlie tried his best to look worried over this but was unsure how it came across to the agent.

The DEA man thought this over as he ran the tip of his tongue across his teeth and squinted one eye at the Navajo investigator. "Are they back there where you first stopped? I was about to pile in on you right then, but you pulled out and headed upcountry so fast I figured I better stick with you. Are they back there at Begay's, Charlie?"

"Not that I saw, Bob."

Freeman got out and glanced up at a grey sky. The snow was tapering off leaving patches of ground fog to drift below the ridges. The agent picked a spot next to the investigator, lazily stretched and flexed his shoulders, before brushing traces of snow off the hood with a coat sleeve and leaning an elbow there. He looked back across the muddy stretch to the highway. "Well, I kind of figured this might happen."

The agent looked suddenly tired and there was disappointment in his voice. "It probably won't do any good to go back to your friend's camp and check, will it?"

"I doubt it, Bob, I don't think you'll find them there."

The agent nodded pleasantly enough, but sounded a bit sad when he said, "I'd hoped for better than this Charlie. I hoped we might someday be working together in Albuquerque." He raised his chin and closed one eye. "I think you might have liked it down there."

The investigator nodded back. "I thought so, too, Bob...at least for a while I did. But I guess I've been out here too long now for that. I expect I'm probably better off where I am. I did think about it...on the way out here this morning, but it finally came to me the reservation is where I can do the most good." Charlie turned his head toward the agent. "This is pretty much where I belong I guess."

The two men stood silently, each with his own thoughts, until finally Bob Freeman lifted himself away from the truck and turned to Charlie. "You know I have to take that Garza boy in, don't you? We'll get him, one way or the other. It will be the best thing that could happen to him, too, you'll see, Charlie. Otherwise, someone's probably going to kill him, either here, or in Mexico. Neither of the two cartels has any reason to keep him alive now that his father's gone—he's a liability now." Bob looked down at the mud. "Does he even know about his father yet?"

"I doubt it, I didn't know myself until you told me this morning at the meeting. Abe Garza could be anywhere now—but Bob, if I do see him again, I will advise him to turn himself in. In all honesty, I can't help thinking you're right about that. I'd hoped you would take the pair of them under your wing and try to get them through this together, but if you can't...you can't."

"I tried to make that happen, Charlie, I really did, but my people wouldn't go for it; for one thing, they think he'd be harder to deal with." The agent rubbed his hands together and blew his breath on them. The snow had stopped completely but left in its wake an icy breeze sweeping down off the ridge toward the sage flats. "If Chuy Mariano has talked with his people in the last few hours he might know old man Garza is dead. Chuy was probably the one who saved the pair's bacon at the funeral home. There won't be any reason for him to safeguard Garza now...there's no leverage in it for the Sonora people at this point. "Just something to think about, Charlie, I mean...if you should see him again." The Federal Agent stuck out his hand with a wry smile. "I'll be seeing you Investigator—no hard feelings—me and you are still good as far as I'm concerned."

Charlie Yazzie shook the agent's hand with a firm grip and looked him in the eye. "We're good,

Bob. I wish it could have turned out differently, but no…we're good, you and me."

The Legal Services Investigator sighed heavily and looked on as the agent's mud-splattered sedan slid almost sideways in the icy muck and turned down the track. There was no denying it. He liked Bob Freeman.

21

Capitulation

Charlie Yazzie poked around in Alfred's old trailer making sure John Nez left no bodies behind, and not finding any, was impressed the place had been left so orderly—the propane was turned off, that was important. Back outside it occurred to him John Nez should already have the pair up at Annie's place, and he hoped it had not inconvenienced his only aunt. Annie Eagletree lived alone now, her second husband, Clyde, having been banished the last several years due to his drinking and overly generous investment of Annie's money in his lifestyle.

Charlie took advantage of several four-wheel drive roads on the way to Annie's place insuring the blue sedan wouldn't follow.

~~~~~~

When he pulled up in Annie's yard, Charlie saw the tailgate of the old Ford pickup, just visible behind her abandoned lambing shed. Not as well hidden as he'd hoped, but he suspected Thomas Begay might have taken care of that part. John Nez probably had his hands full with their detainees.

Annie Eagletree peeked from the window and smiled at her nephew as he came up on the porch. Charlie was careful to scrape the mud off his boots on the new piece of hardware by the door. It was obvious what it was for, though it was the first one he'd seen. It looked like a big hedgehog...or a small porcupine. Charlie wondered briefly where his aunt got it, and why—Annie's place was mostly rock and sand—the mud on his boots, he'd brought with him.

Around Annie's big table, four sets of eyes fastened on him—two of the people looked unhappy. His aunt, who loved company of any kind, regardless of reputation, was the only one smiling. "Come on in Charlie," she chuckled, hefting the big coffeepot in greeting as she passed him on her way to the table.

Tressa Tarango and Abraham Garza sat side by side, under the watchful eye of John Nez, and of course, Thomas Begay, who had beaten Charlie there by a comfortable margin. The tall Navajo fiddled with his cup and raised one eyebrow as he gave Charlie a lift of his chin in greeting. Everyone busied themselves with their coffee, giving Charlie Yazzie the side-eyes thinking he was the one in charge now—but no one asked what he had in mind. Annie Eagletree had been made privy to a portion of her new guests' story and had immediately taken their

R. Allen Chappell

part. She loved rooting for the underdog and was known to take the side of all but the most heinous offenders in her favorite cop shows. She saw no link between what Tressa Tarango's late husband might have done, and the couple here at her kitchen table. She motioned her nephew to a chair with an air of approval; Charlie was doing the right thing in helping these people.

Charlie glanced around the table, finally settling on Little Abe. "Mr. Garza, you and I have something to talk about...in private." He rose from the table and indicated Abe was to follow. Tressa started to get up, but the investigator motioned her back down with a wave of the hand. No one said anything, only stared into their cups and watched from the corner of an eye as the two men went outside. Not a word was spoken among them until the door reopened and Charlie, followed by the now sad and dejected Abraham, came back to the table. Little Abe sat himself down—not looking directly at Tressa, or anyone else.

Thomas Begay watched as the investigator doctored his coffee and from long experience knew Charlie was pondering his next move. Thomas admired his friend's ability to think things through on the fly and was curious to hear what had passed between the investigator and Little Abe. He hadn't missed the crestfallen look on the younger man's face. That alone seemed to put the Navajo in a better mood.

Tressa Tarango, however, had no trouble at all guessing the outcome of the private conference and

262

turned an icy gaze, first on Little Abe, and then away, toward the window, where she raised her chin and refused to acknowledge the glances thrown her way. She knew she was alone now and grasped the box with Luca's ashes more closely.

Charlie took a long sip of his coffee and looked around the table. "I have just informed Mr. Garza of the unfortunate death of his father in Sinaloa. And have further advised him, though not in any legal capacity, that his best course of action may now be to accept drug enforcement's offer of immunity in return for testifying on behalf of the federal government."

Charlie's Aunt Annie, an inveterate follower of television crime shows, immediately saw various implications in such a move and wasn't shy about her thoughts on the subject. "What, then, is going to happen to this poor woman here?" She was looking at her nephew as she asked but tipping her head toward Tressa Tarango.

Charlie was just getting to that and hadn't quite come up with the best way to couch the answer.

Annie's phone rang, and everyone's attention turned toward the sound. Charlie sat back with a frown knowing his aunt demanded telephone calls take precedence over any other form of human communication. She was sixty-five years old before the phone lines finally reached her section of the reservation and even then, was the last person at the end of her particular run of wire. The woman was inordinately proud of the device and often, by virtue of the optional twenty-foot cord, took it along with her from room to room. The last thing she wanted was to miss a call. She hated it when she ran out of cord and when that occasionally did happen she cursed both the phone, and the phone company.

After she'd said hello, Annie listened quietly a moment or two before moving to the privacy of the living room where she turned and signaled Thomas Begay the call was for him. She handed him the phone, and what was left of the cord, as she shook her head and frowned, before making her way back to the kitchen.

Charlie gave his aunt a questioning tilt of his head, and in return, she mouthed, "Lucy Tallwoman."

When Thomas finally hung up and returned to the table his face was ashen. "My wife says Harley Ponyboy has found her father."

~~~~~~~

Charlie Yazzie concentrated on his driving. As evening fell, the late fall storm had, as predicted, revitalized, and sent yet another wave of rain mixed with snow to hamper their way south. The old Ford truck burbled along happily enough—the laid-back pace leaving the big V-8 loping along without effort. Old Sancho Mariano and his sons knew how to build a transporter.

Charlie was clear that taking his official vehicle across an international border was out of the question. He *was* the boss, but there were limits to what perks that provided.

The phone call from his wife had pretty much ruled out Thomas Begay going along with him—that might cause more drama at home than he could handle. He didn't fill everyone in on the call, but did whisper to Charlie, that things didn't look good.

When asked if he could, on his way through Shiprock, drop Abraham Garza off with Agent Bob Freeman, Thomas agreed, though not without reservations. Nor was Little Abe pleased with the arrangement, but he was in too deep to back out. Charlie called to make sure the Federal Agent would be on hand for the transfer.

A sullen Tressa Tarango sat as far away as possible…placing the cremains of her late husband on the seat between them, thinking they might at least provide some small psychological barrier.

John Nez followed closely behind the pair in his own truck, Tressa Tarango having been adamant she return old Sancho's truck as promised. Thomas's Uncle John hadn't hesitated when asked if he'd go along, even when told it would likely be a risky venture…or maybe that was *why* the ex-Marine was going along. "Why not…I'm caught up with Council-work for the next couple of days. I wouldn't mind seeing Mexico."

They drove steadily through the night and made the Mariposa crossing in time to wait for the 6 a.m. opening. Getting into Mexico wasn't hard, but the Kilometer 21 Customs Facility was a mess. Long lines of returning Mexican nationals were bent on making their town's Day of The Dead celebration. The parking lot was full of U. S. plated vehicles from a number of states, all lined up for the holiday migration back home. As is common on the day before a Mexican holiday, traffic was backed up. The parking lot was crowded with entire families leaving their vehicles for a chance to stretch, buy soft drinks made with real Mexican cane sugar, and look for old friends they thought might be returning as well. They chatted, and complained about what would, one day become a much more complicated process.

The Navajos kept to their trucks, both men easily passing for Mexicans as long as Charlie kept his mouth shut and let Tressa do the talking. John Nez spoke enough Spanish to get by.

Finally, bumper to bumper, the trucks idled through the last military check station, picking up speed as they headed south on Federal Highway D15 toward the city of Hermosillo and the rugged but alluring country that lies beyond. On the long arm of the Sea of Cortez, isolated villages have scratched out a precarious existence for more than a thousand years. Tressa could almost smell home in the breezes wafting off the damp mesquite, Luca Tarango had never wanted to leave this place...and after tomorrow, he would never have to.

They had eaten little, other than what snacks they'd picked up with their coffee at fuel stops—both men were worn out and ready for a break and a meal. When a trucker's eatery appeared alongside a government run Pemex station, they filled up the trucks and, at the woman's urging, pulled over to the cafe. A few cars and pickups were scattered among the big rigs, which Tressa considered a sign the food would be decent. Though she had slept a good bit on the way, she, too, was ready for a break. John Nez picked a booth at the back of the room; one facing the door, and Charlie took this as yet another similarity with his nephew and was careful to look around before he seated himself to one side. There was the usual assortment of diners one might expect in such a place, but only two Charlie thought might bear watching. John Nez picked them out, as well, but after only a glance directed his attention elsewhere. The two men's gold chains were, alone, enough to make them suspect, that and the fact they seemed more than a little interested in Tressa.

The waitress came from nowhere to take their orders—there were no menus and the woman announced in Spanish what was available. Tressa was comforted by the familiar local dialect, and as the woman shuffled off to place their orders, Tressa watched as one of the men with gold chains touched the passing waitress's arm and spoke behind his hand as he looked their way.

John Nez hadn't missed the exchange and gave Charlie the kind of look one might expect from a man who had, in another life, made a habit of sensing danger. John had, in fact, killed more people than Tressa's husband but for different reasons. Charlie sometimes wondered; what exactly, in the final analysis, made them so different. In the end killing was killing. He didn't think very long on it for fear he might decide they were more alike than he cared to admit.

The waitress returned with their orders; she leaned close to Tressa and whispered something in her ear that made her smile and give a quick toss of her head.

The food was good, not too spicy, which Charlie thought might be the case having never eaten Mexican food...in Mexico. The migration of Tex-Mex to the greater southwest was most likely responsible for that misconception, Tressa explained when he mentioned it.

After paying the bill and waiting for Tressa to return from the *baño*, the three of them headed for the door—preceded by the two men with gold chains. The pair filed out ahead of them, got into a convertible sporting a set of bull's horns on the front, and with a wave, smiled back at Tressa. They turned the car north, toward Nogales, and their wives and children.

John and Charlie looked at one another, and still standing near the door, watched until the car was out of sight. Neither man commented, and Tressa only smiled. She thought, *Welcome to Mexico amigos.*

The three were so focused on Tressa's two admirers they completely missed the gray Suburban hidden between two eighteen wheelers at the rear of the parking lot—nor did they feel the two sets of eyes that followed them when they left.

They hadn't gone far when John Nez moved up alongside and indicated with a backward jerk of his thumb that they were being followed. They saw the ex-Marine smile and shrug his shoulders as he fell back and let Charlie stay in the lead. A few miles later, when Tressa directed them to turn right on a feeder road to the coast, they could see the Suburban slow and gradually fade from sight. This told them two things: these men were not in a hurry and there was no other way out. There remained the remote possibility that seeing where they were headed, the men simply decided it wasn't worth it.

According to Tressa, there was still a ways to go. The heavy traffic and long wait at the border had eaten up a lot of time and would put them into the village late in the afternoon.

Her village, she said, would host its own *Dia de los Muertos* and would draw many people from the smaller communities in the coastal mountains. Some would already be gathering, so as not to miss any of the next day's festivities. The real fun, the dancing and drinking, would begin that very night. The three passed a few old cars and trucks full of people—and even a few Seri Indians on foot or horseback. The Indians generally kept to themselves, relegated to the banks of the little stream from the mountains. That trickle of water from the Seri reservation to the north was the villagers' only supply, and for that reason alone the Indians would be tolerated—the locals guessing what might happen to their water supply, should the Seris be given cause.

As they drove down the dusty main street, small groups stood and watched them pass, some already lined up at those houses where women were selling food through the open windows of their kitchens. Suspicious dogs surprised by the sudden influx of strangers, took up defensive positions in alleyways and behind fences, where they barked nonstop until old women were forced to come screaming out of their houses to throw sticks at them. Roosters crowed from backyards, cutting their wings at the ground as they did their little dances, listening for rivals to crow in return. A pall of dust and smoke from cooking fires hung heavy in the air, but only those now living in the north took any notice.

Children were everywhere, chasing, screeching and laughing; a few already wearing the costumes meant for the next day. Vehicles with U.S. plates parked along the street, or in front of relative's mud-brick homes. Several of the women were unpacking black plastic bags filled with used clothing—items shrewdly bargained from northern yard and garage sales—the better things, some still in style, were from *gringo* thrift shops and church fundraisers. Lucky relatives of these travelers came out to the street to pick through the best of the booty. The remaining items would be sold on the streets the next day. What rags were left would be given as an act of kindness to the Indians.

"There is really no place for you to stay here," Tressa warned, "My cousins have been living in my old house, but now they have gone to Guaymas to find work, and only their old father is left. I will introduce you—he is a good old man but lonely and welcomes company. He worked up north, in the fruit, when he was young. He likes *Americanos* for some reason. He will be happy for you to stay and rest up before you start back." Tressa considered the two Navajo for a moment and her tone softened, but only a little. "I have relatives to see and things to prepare before morning. The men of my family will watch out for me now." With that, the woman turned and slipped away up the street; Charlie watched to see which house she went in.

John Nez kept an eye out for trouble and when he did finally speak, it was to say he thought they shouldn't wait, but leave right then. Charlie was considering this when Tressa returned to the trucks.

"I have spoken to the old man and he will take care of everything, even bring you some food later. You can leave Sancho Mariano's truck where it is;

my uncles will come for it. I promised old Sancho he would have it back." Almost as an afterthought she added. "I will go to my sisters-in-law for the night and after I settle with Luca tomorrow, I will figure out what to do from there." The woman, looking mostly at Charlie Yazzie, said, "You have done what you came to do...though you owed me nothing...and I appreciate that." Tressa let her gaze fall to the ground. "But I will probably not see you again before you leave. Were I you, I would be careful for the next few hours—stay inside. The old man will watch while you sleep and wake you when it's time. Those men in the car, from the funeral parlor, are not who you have to be afraid of. They don't know what they are getting into down here...when they figure that out, they may not show up at all, but if they do they will be taken care of."

The partying had begun with music and drinking already underway, singing could be heard from several directions.

Charlie nodded back the way they'd come. "John thinks we should go now?"

"No, that would not be a good idea. Once people hear who you are it will be safer for you right here. Besides, no one drives at night on Mexican highways, there are no fences and the horses and cows are all over these roads at night. It's dangerous. And if your truck should break down there's no telling who might come along and cause you trouble—the *Policia* most of all. In the daylight everything is different down here…you'll see."

~~~~~~~~~

The old man brought them steaming bowls of green chili and pork *caldio,* with freshly made tortillas wrapped in a cloth. Although Charlie had never had the soup he thought it good after learning to watch for the pieces of neck-bone from the young pig that went into it. John Nez didn't care for it but ate it just the same; he'd eaten a lot of things he didn't care for over the years. There were cots made up, but before that the old man brought out a bottle of something with no label and sat it on the table in a further show of hospitality. Neither man refused and each took a good swallow as a matter of courtesy. The drink, rough going down, left the oily aftertaste of barbershop Bay Rum. That was what it tasted like.

They talked with Tressa's uncle for a while as he had several more drinks, and they listened to the party grow louder outside the windows of the old adobe. The old man finally went to bed in the other room, and John Nez picked the cot closest to the door and lay down with a sigh. The trip had taken more out of him than he'd thought, and he suspected he might finally be getting old. Charlie's bed was farther from the door but not by much. The two discussed how they would go home after crossing the border, and it was decided they should go pretty much as they came. Shortcuts on a map are not necessarily quicker. They would already be later returning than they'd hoped, but were not totally unprepared for that eventuality. Charlie was signed out for a few days of vacation time and coupled with the weekend, thought that would be enough. By two in the morning the party outside was winding down with only the occasional shouted obscenity left to mark its passing.

When John Nez woke, thinking he heard some small noise at the door, he reached down in his boot and pulled out Tressa's automatic pistol. He'd brought the gun hidden behind and above the glove box in his truck. The harried Mexican Customs Agents, too busy for a thorough search, made only a cursory check of the vehicle, and turned up nothing. John had always been lucky that way. He meant to leave the handgun in Mexico to avoid the more careful scrutiny of the U.S. border agents. For now, though, he was glad he'd kept it. Tressa had not asked about the weapon nor indicated she wanted it back, but he had told her he would return it and he would.

A shadow passed across the front window, then several, and though John was aware there were people still on the street and some of them drunk, this was something else—a feeling born of long experience in dangerous places and one he couldn't shake. There was no lock on the door, only the crude wooden crossbar the old man had been careful to put in place. John Nez, not making a sound, reached to touch Charlie's shoulder. The sleeping figure woke to see his companion with a gun in one hand, and a finger to his lips. John Nez pointed with the pistol and they watched as a slim blade entered at the door's edge and silently lifted the bar to allow the door to start open with little more than a mouse-like squeak.

John eased from the cot and moved in stocking feet toward the front of the room. Charlie Yazzie, still groggy, followed suit. As he passed the table he picked up the near-empty bottle by the neck and was almost to the door when it opened a bit further. A slight figure edged part way in before John made a grab and pulled the person inside. Charlie brandished the bottle, and would have brought it crashing down, had he not heard the female voice.

She raised one arm to shield her head and a small animal sound escaped her. Both men held to the girl as the door swung fully open to reveal several men with automatic weapons already to their shoulders. The lead figure smiled at John's little pistol and slowly shook his head letting John know how futile that might be. The Navajo dropped the gun with a clatter. In his younger days he might have foolishly resisted but had grown more cautious with the years. One of the men flicked on the dim bulb that hung from the ceiling and quickly moved to cover the *Norteñoes* from the side. Another pushed in from the opposite direction, the muzzle of his weapon never leaving its target. The leader came forward and motioned for them to release the girl and for Charlie to put down the bottle, which he did, leaning over to set it gently on the floor. The tall man in charge picked it up and looked at it briefly, before again shaking his head. "I hope you didn't drink much of this, *amigos*, it will rot your guts." He ordered them back with the end of his rifle and motioned they should take a seat at the table. He jerked his head from the girl to the door and she ran.

"Tressa Tarango's cousin," he explained. "Tressa herself, however, seems to have disappeared, at least temporarily."

Charlie nodded, "You must be Chuy Mariano?"

The man grinned. "No, that would be my brother. I'm known as El Gato... Gato Mariano. I am in charge down here...well almost." He said this last with a quizzical glance upward as though hoping for some divine intervention in that respect. "We thank you for bringing little Tressa home, but expected to see Abraham Garza with you. We've been waiting for him. We mean Tressa no harm; there is no need for that. She might know a little something that would be helpful, but she is frightened, and still cautious. I have sent her cousin to reassure her. It is Abraham my uncle wants to talk to. Little Abe is the one we want." The man spoke perfect English and without stopping to think about it.

Gato sat himself across from Charlie and leaned his rifle against one leg. His men kept their eyes, and guns, on the two captives and appeared incapable of blinking.

Gato Mariano was obviously an educated man and one used to being in control. He cocked his head to one side and leaned slightly toward Charlie Yazzie. "You wouldn't happen to have word of my father, in Colorado, would you? My brother tries to find out his condition, but Federal Agents are blocking him…and tracing any calls that inquire about him. I had hoped you might know something?"

Charlie sat back in his chair "Are you going to kill us?" He thought if that were to be the case, he needn't answer at all.

"Kill you?" The Mexican smiled and shook his head, before laughing softly. "Now why would we want to do that? Killing two U.S. citizens, with ties to Drug Enforcement, is the last thing we need right now… or should I say, the last thing my uncle wants. We are businessmen and that would be bad for business. My father's brother is quite old, and more cautious when it comes to raising the hackles of U.S. law enforcement." He shrugged. "Were my father in charge, things might be different, and they will certainly be different, when my turn comes. Right now, I do as my uncle wishes and that's why you're still alive…and might be allowed to remain so, should one of you not do something foolish." Here Gato looked pointedly at John Nez.

Charlie wasn't sure he believed this part but didn't mind telling the Mexican what he'd last heard about his father. "Sancho Mariano," he said, thinking a moment how best to put it, "is...as of two days ago... still alive and fighting for his life. I can assure you he's receiving the best possible care. Some up there are beginning to think he might make it."

Gato, seemed both relieved and a little agitated by this news but nodded and said, "And you might be interested to know the two people from Sinaloa have been taken care of. They won't bother anyone again."

With the approach of dawn, the room grew gradually lighter and Tressa's uncle came from the back room smelling of alcohol and scratching at his underwear. He looked around the room as though not surprised to see armed men guarding his guests. *Buenos dias, Señores. Que pasa?*

El Gato hardly gave him a glance and waved him away. Then, looking out the window at the increasing light, turned back to the two Navajo seated at the table. "From what I hear, Tressa and her husband's family are planning an early procession. If her cousin has found her...and I expect she has...they will be coming past here soon with her husband's remains. The man had a reputation here in this village and I expect it will be something to see—it's said there are many people anxious to make amends with his spirit...now that he's gone." He said this last somewhat dryly but without smiling. "From what Chuy says the woman is quite beautiful...at least my brother thinks she is." Gato said this thoughtfully as though he didn't trust his brother's judgment when it came to women.

John Nez spoke at last, not loudly, but without any sign of fear. "I'm hungry. If you're not going to kill us, then let's have something to eat."

Charlie gave him a sharp glance and nervously pulled at one ear. John's relationship to Thomas Begay was again made clear, like Thomas, John Nez gave undeniable evidence he was capable of getting them both killed.

El Gato frowned and narrowed an eye at the older man...but then broke into a grin as he motioned his men to lower their weapons and whispered to the nearest one to go for *conchas,* the sugary *pan de muertos,* and coffee from the little street-side kitchens.

~~~~~~~~

As the sun rose to warm the rocky peaks to the west, the men stood in front of the house that once belonged to Luca Tarango. The clear air of dawn carried the doleful sound of a church bell, and bystanders, unable to turn away, watched quietly as the Tarango woman came bringing her husband to his final rest. Not everyone thought it right that so notorious a person should be brought back to the village—but none were so foolish as to say so.

Dressed all in black, her face painted in the luminous hues of the *Dia de los Muertos,* there could be no doubt in anyone's mind that Tressa had at last attained some measure of peace. And though his murderous rampage would keep Luca from heaven— Tressa felt she might still have secured him a higher place in hell.

22

Approbation

Charlie Yazzie had been home no more than an hour when he saw Thomas Begay's diesel truck coming. According to Sue the man had been calling since daybreak. She had already told him Charlie and his Uncle John were across the Mexican border and headed for home. She would have her husband call as soon as he made it in, she said.

Thomas stood back from the door as Sue and the kids were on their way out to see the horses; the neighbor's stud had gotten out and jumped the fence the month before and Sue was keeping a close check on her mare to make sure she wasn't getting a belly. The children were excited to think they might have a colt in the spring and grinned up at Thomas.

Sue waved as she herded the children past without stopping. It wasn't hard to see their friend Thomas was a man on a mission.

He confronted Charlie directly, "I guess Sue told you, Harley Ponyboy found Paul up on the Chinle?"

Thomas Begay was never the type to waste time on niceties.

Charlie sat his cup of coffee down on the porch railing and eyed his lanky friend. "Yes, she said Paul was in bad shape—in the hospital in Farmington. No visitors she said. Sue was going to check with Lucy later this morning about us going up there."

"Not yet, but maybe this evening, Lucy thinks. The doc is still running tests. He says they need to get the old man rehydrated and some nourishment back in him before anything else." Thomas stopped and thought back to the other thing the doctor told him. "He did say there are several things that might be causing Paul's mental condition and some of them could be reversible...actually, he said there's about fifty things that could be causing it, and only a few are reversible—and even those are long shots. He's going to talk to a specialist and says he should have a better picture of what's going on in a day or so."

"I'm surprised Harley found old man at all: that's big country up there."

"I guess Harley almost didn't make it in time, and wouldn't have, if not for a Piute sheep herder and his wife. Harley stopped to ask had they seen Paul as they were getting ready to take their sheep down for the winter. The man was in a hurry but said they had seen him and then told Harley, 'That old man seems to know what he's doing.' He hadn't thought it right to meddle in something like that." Thomas nodded to himself. "It was the woman who spoke up and said she knew where he was, and then made her husband go with Harley and show him. She went right along with them and the two of them helped Harley get Paul back down to the truck and started for the hospital. Harley said Paul was pretty much out of it the whole time…didn't even know who he was, probably thought he was dead already."

"Where's Harley now?"

"Up at the hospital…hasn't left since he brought the old man in. Slept right there in the waiting room last night. Lucy was worn out from all the worry these last few days and so were the kids. We finally had to make them go home and get some rest. That was four or five hours ago. I expect they're back up there by now."

Charlie could only shake his head as he ushered Thomas inside and went for another cup and the coffee pot. He'd already eaten but asked Thomas if he could get him something.

"Nah, I had some doughnuts at the hospital. Billy Red Clay brought them when he came by this morning."

"Did everything go all right when you dropped Abe Garza off in Shiprock? Was Bob Freeman there to meet you and all?"

Thomas didn't bother to put anything in his coffee before taking a searing swallow. "That's what I really came to see you about," he said in a quiet voice. "I wanted to be the one to tell you before anyone else had a chance." He couldn't meet

Charlie's gaze and for a moment seemed unable to find the right words to start.

"What happened?"

"About half-way into town we had a flat ...you know I been looking for a good used tire right along... Anyway, all I had was that old worn-out jack that don't work half the time. I was trying to get it under the bumper when a truck pulled up behind us like they were going to offer some help...a better jack maybe; that's what I was hoping. I went on with what I was doing but when I glanced up I saw the Garza kid had a funny look on his face. I turned around and there was this big Mexican guy, and I'm looking into a .45 auto. Well, you know I don't like that Garza kid anyway, and when this other *Chollo* says he's going to take him, I just told him, "Be my guest—he don't mean nothin' to me that boy." Thomas raised both hands palms out. "I didn't see much else I could do...I didn't mean to get shot over that little bastard."

Charlie didn't say a word as he refilled his cup, got up from his chair and took his coffee over to the sink. Looking out the window, to the corrals, he smiled to see his son perched on the top rail, feeding the mare a weed he'd picked along the way. Their toddler, Sasha, was reaching up to her brother; clearly thinking she should be up there too. Charlie sat his cup in the sink and turned back to his friend Thomas. "No, there wasn't anything you could do…I'd of done the same myself I suppose. What did Bob have to say about it?"

"Pretty much the same as you, I guess. He said 'That's just the way the game goes sometimes.' He tried to act like it didn't matter and that they'd catch up to him down at the border…but he didn't sound so sure of that to me."

"Bob's all right, he tried to do the right thing by Little Abe." Charlie had his own doubts about the DEA Agent getting the boy back—now that Chuy Mariano had him. Chuy was tough, smart and connected. He was a man with ways of getting in and out of Mexico that even Bob couldn't imagine.

What might happen to Abe, or even Tressa would now be up to Gato and his uncle in Sonora. It was possible someone might hear what happened eventually, but Charlie somehow doubted even that.

"You probably haven't heard yet, but Captain Beyale won't be coming back to Tribal. My nephew says the man may never be right in his mind again. That's according to the doctors…something about a brain embolism they can't do anything about. Billy's taking it pretty hard, too, like it's his fault."

Charlie hated to hear that. "So who's taking Beyale's place? Do they know yet??"

"Billy says Lieutenant Arviso is in line for the job. If he does get it, Billy might have a shot at *his* job." Thomas didn't really think so. "You know the fuss some of those people put up when Billy made Liaison Officer. Too young, they said."

Charlie nodded. "I'll put in a word for him, again, for whatever that might be worth, but the pushback would be huge even if Arviso is in favor of it."

Thomas agreed, and then hesitated before going on. "The other thing Billy told me was that the autopsy report on Robert Ashki came back indicating no foul play. The NMHP is dropping their investigation. They say they can't find no credible evidence to the contrary."

"Is the FBI going along with the Highway Patrol on that?"

"As far as Billy knows, they probably will. Fred Smith was the one who called, in fact, and let him know about the report." Thomas hesitated... "No one ever mentioned to me there would even be a report...it must have been '*privileged*' information, huh?" Thomas shook his head at this but didn't turn away. "Charlie—John's my uncle. All that time you been gone... you and Uncle Johnny... he never asked you anything about Robert Ashki and that wreck?"

Charlie turned a shade darker. "No, not that I recall. What makes you ask?"

"Oh, nothing really, I guess. Billy mentioned the FBI got the paint analysis back on that off-color sample they took from Ashki's truck."

"Oh, and what did they determine?" Charlie got an empty feeling in the pit of his stomach.

"They thought it likely could have come from any number of older white Chrysler products."

Charlie poured the rest of his coffee down the sink and exhaled with a quiet, "Humph..." He had never mentioned the FBI report to Thomas. Both men were familiar with John Nez's pickup truck, a beat up white Dodge with any number of scrapes and dents. The two friends locked eyes for a moment, neither saying another word—nor was the conversation ever brought up again.

Epilogue

It was over a month later that Charlie received the letter, with no return address, but postmarked Los Angeles, CA.

Mr. Yazzie,
   Just a note so you will know Abraham and me are still alive and doing ok. We got lucky I guess—El Gato's uncle died and his nephew said he had bigger things to worry about. Chuy helped us get out of Mexico and here we are starting over. I think his father may have had a hand in all this. I hear old Sancho's getting better now and has himself a good lawyer. I hope so. He's probably going to need it.
P.S. Don't tell Bob Freeman where we are.

   Tressa

Charlie read the letter over several times and smiling at the postmark, walked over and put the note through his shredder. Bob Freeman called to tell Charlie the fall of the Espinosa family in Sinaloa had pretty much made his current case a non-starter, at least as far as the Federal Prosecutor was concerned. A new cartel had taken power in Sinaloa State, with newer drugs and smarter people. The DEA would have to start all over...which they would. No one ever thought it would be easy.

Addendum

This story hearkens back to a slightly more traditional time on the reservation, and while the places and culture are real, the characters and their names are fictitious. Any resemblance to actual persons living or dead is purely coincidental.

~~~~~~~

Though the book is a work of fiction, a concerted effort was made to maintain the accuracy of the culture and characters. There are many scholarly tomes written by anthropologists, ethnologists, and learned laymen regarding the Navajo culture. On the subject of language and spelling, they often do not agree. When no consensus was apparent we have relied upon "local knowledge."

Many changes have come to the *Dinè*—some of them good, some, not so much. These are the Navajo I remember. I think you may like them.

ABOUT THE AUTHOR

R. Allen Chappell is the author of eight novels and a collection of short stories. Growing up in New Mexico he spent a good portion of his life at the edge of the *Diné Bikeyah*, went to school with the Navajo, and later worked alongside them. He lives in Western Colorado where he continues to pursue a lifelong interest in the prehistory of the Four Corners region and its people and still spends a good bit of his time there.

For the curious, the author's random thoughts on each of his books are listed below in the order of their release.

Navajo Autumn

It was not my original intent to write a series, but this first book was so well received, and with many readers asking for another, I felt compelled to write a sequel—after that there was no turning back. I'm sure I made every mistake a writer can possibly make in a first novel, but I had the advantage of a dedicated little group of detractors, quick to point out its many deficiencies...and I thank them. Without their help, this first book would doubtless have languished, and eventually fallen into the morass—and there would be no series.

I did do one thing right, apparently—the Navajo Nation Mystery series was the first in its category to include a glossary of Navajo words and terms and each book since then has had one.

This book has, over the years, been through many editions and updates. I know, now, how to make it a better book and someday I might. But for now, I will leave it as is. No book is perfect, and this one keeps me grounded.

Boy Made of Dawn

A sequel I very much enjoyed writing and one that drew many new fans to the series. So many, in fact, I quit my day job to pursue writing these stories full-time—not a course I would ordinarily recommend to an author new to the process. In this instance, however, it proved to be the right move. As I learn, I endeavor to make each new book a little better...and to keep their prices low enough that people like me can afford to read them. That's important.

Ancient Blood

The third book in the series and the initial flight into the realm of the Southwestern archaeology I've grown up with. This book introduces Harley Ponyboy: a character who quickly carved out a major niche for himself in the stories that followed. Harley remains the favorite of reservation readers to this day. Also debuting in this novel was Professor George Armstrong Custer, noted archaeologist and Charlie Yazzie's professor at UNM. George, too, has a pivotal role in some of the later books.

Mojado

This book was a departure in cover art, subject matter, and the move to thriller status. A fictional story built around a local tale heard in Mexico years ago. In the first three months following its release, this book sold more copies, and faster, than any of the previous books. It's still a favorite.

Magpie Speaks

A mystery/thriller that goes back to the beginning of the series and exposes the past of several major characters—some of whom play pivotal roles in later books—another favorite of Navajo friends who follow these stories.

Wolves of Winter

As our readership attained a solid position in the genre, I determined to tell the story I had, for many years, envisioned. I am pleased with this book's success on several levels, and in very different genres. I hope one day to revisit this story in one form or another.

The Bible Seller

Yet another cultural departure for the series in which Harley Ponyboy again wrests away the starring role. A story of attraction and deceit told against a backdrop of wanton murder and reservation intrigue. It has fulfilled its promise to become a Canyonlands favorite.

From the Author

Readers may be pleased to know they can preview selected audio book selections for the Navajo Nation Series on our book pages. Our Audio books can be found featured in public libraries, on Audible, and in many retail outlets. There are more to come. Kaipo Schwab, an accomplished actor and storyteller, narrates the first five audio books. I am pleased Kaipo felt these books worthy of his considerable talent. I hope you enjoy these reservation adventures as much as we enjoy bringing them to you.

The author calls Western Colorado home, where he continues to pursue a lifelong interest in the prehistory of the Four Corners region and its people. We remain available to answer questions, and welcome your comments at: rachappell@yahoo.com

If you've enjoyed this book, please consider going to its Amazon book page to leave a short review. It takes only a moment and would be most appreciated.

R. Allen Chappell

Glossary

1. *Adááníí* — undesirable, alcoholic
2. *Acheii* — Grandfather *
3. *Ashki Ana'dlohi* — Laughing boy
4. *A-hah-la'nih* — affectionate greeting*
5. *Billigaana* — white people
6. *Ch'ihónit't* — a spirit path flaw in art.
7. *Chindi* — (or *chinde*) Spirit of the dead *
8. *Diné* — Navajo people
9. *Diné Bikeyah* — Navajo country
10. *Diyin dine'é* —Holy people
11. *Hataalii* — Shaman (Singer)*
12. *Hastiin* — (Hosteen) Man or Mr. *
13. *Hogan* — (Hoogahn) dwelling or house
14. *Hozo* — To walk in beauty *
15. *Ma'iitsoh* — Wolf
16. *Shimásáni* — Grandmother
17. Shizhé'é — Father *
18. *Tsé Bii' Ndzisgaii* — Monument Valley
19. *Yaa' eh t'eeh* — Greeting-Hello
20. *Yeenaaldiooshii* — Skinwalker, witch*
21. *Yóó'a'hááskahh* —One who is lost

*See Notes

Notes

1. *Acheii* — Grandfather. There are several words for Grandfather depending on how formal the intent and the gender of the speaker.

2. *Aa'a'ii* — Long known as a trickster or "thief of little things." It is thought Magpie can speak and sometimes brings messages from the beyond.

4. *A-hah-la'nih* — A greeting: affectionate version of *Yaa' eh t'eeh*, generally only used among family and close friends.

7. *Chindi* — When a person dies inside a *hogan*, it is said that his *chindi* or spirit remains there forever, causing the *hogan* to be abandoned. *Chindi* are not considered benevolent entities. For the traditional Navajo, just speaking a dead person's name may call up his *chindi* and cause harm to the speaker or others.

11. *Hataalii* — Generally known as a "Singer" among the *Diné*, they are considered "Holy Men" and have apprenticed to older practitioners sometimes for many years—to learn the ceremonies. They make the sand paintings that are an integral part of the healing and know the many songs that must be sung in the correct order.

11. *Hastiin* — The literal translation is "man" but is often considered the word for "Mr." as well. "Hosteen" is the usual version Anglos use.

14. *Hozo* — For the Navajo, *"hozo"* (sometimes *hozoji*) is a general state of well-being, both physical and spiritual, that indicates a certain "state of grace," which is referred to as "walking in beauty." Illness or depression is the usual cause of "loss of *hozo*," which may put one out of sync with the people as a whole. There are ceremonies to restore *hozo* and return the ailing person to a oneness with the people.

15. *Ma'iitsoh* — The Navajo Wolf is yet another reference to one of the many forms a witch can take, something like a werewolf in this instance.

18. *Shizhé'é* — (or *Shih-chai)* There are several words for "Father," depending on the degree of formality intended and sometimes even the gender of the speaker.

20. *Yeenaaldiooshii* — These witches, as they are often referred to, are the chief source of evil or fear in traditional Navajo superstitions. They are thought to be capable of many unnatural acts, such as flying or turning themselves into werewolves and other ethereal creatures; hence the term Skinwalkers, referring to their ability to change forms or skins.

R. Allen Chappell